THE FOOTSTEPS
AT THE LOCK

RONALD A. KNOX

DOVER PUBLICATIONS, INC.
NEW YORK

W9-BRB-659

This Dover edition, first published in 1983, is an unabridged republication of the work as originally published by Methuen & Co. Ltd., London, 1928. (The map that originally appeared on the endpapers has been placed after the dedication.)

Manufactured in the United States of America
Dover Publications, Inc., 180 Varick Street, New York, N.Y. 10014

Library of Congress Cataloging in Publication Data

Knox, Ronald Arbuthnott, 1888-1957.
   The footsteps at the lock.

   I. Title.
PR6021.N6F6   1983   823'.912   82-19789
ISBN 0-486-24493-8

TO

DAVID

IN MEMORY OF THE UNCAS

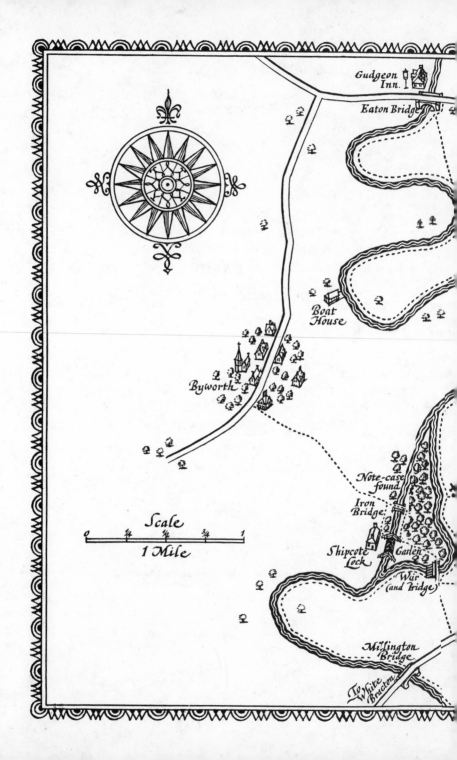

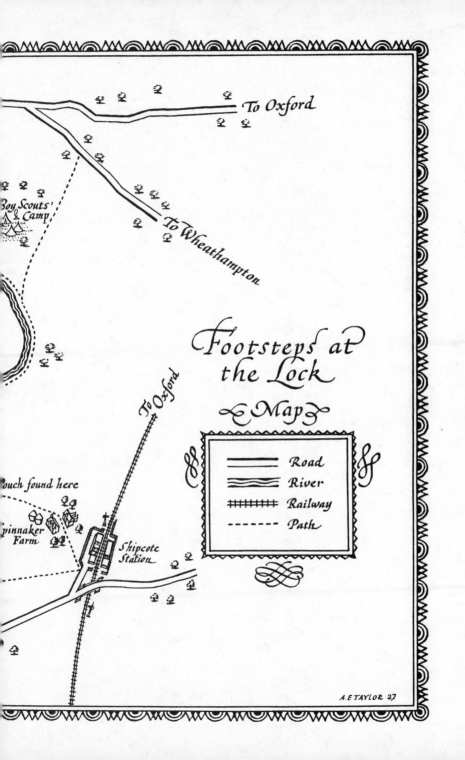

To Oxford

To Wheathampton

Boy Scouts' Camp

Footsteps at
the Lock

Map

To Oxford

pouch found here

Spinnaker
Farm

Shipcote
Station

To Oxford

	Road
	River
	Railway
	Path

A.E TAYLOR 27

CONTENTS

vii

THE FOOTSTEPS AT THE LOCK

CHAPTER I

TWO COUSINS

IT is an undeniable but a mystifying fact of natural ethics that a man has the right to dispose of his own property at death. They can do him no good now, those ancestral acres, those hard-won thousands, nor may any of the trees he planted, save the grim cypress, follow their ephemeral master ; yet, before the partnership of hand and mind is altogether dissolved, a brief flourish at the tail of a will may endow a pauper or disinherit a spendthrift, may be frittered away in the service of a hundred useless or eccentric ends. No good to him—at least, there was once a theory that a man might be happier in the after state for the use of his means here, but we have abolished all that long since ; no good to him, but much to expectant nephews and nieces, much to life-boat funds and cats' homes, much to the Exchequer, wilting for lack of death-duties. Of all this he is the arbiter. Yet we have it on the authority of all the copy-books that money does far more harm in the world than good ; why, then, do we leave the direction of that harm to the one man who, *ex hypothesi*, will be out of the way when it happens ? Why let the testator arrange for the unworthy squandering of his property, when he is to have no tenure in it henceforward except the inalienable grave ?

Such doubts, entirely methodical in character, are suggested by the last will and testament of Sir John Burtell, a barrister of some note in his day, that is, in the latter years of Queen Victoria. A safe man, with no itch for politics or ambition for titles, he retired soon after the death of the Great Queen, leaving the world open to his two sons, John and Charles, then in the flower of their age. He came of a sound stock, and found, besides, some zest in country pursuits ; nor, in the end, was it years that carried him off, but the severe influenza epidemic of 1918. By that time, his two sons had predeceased him. Both took their commissions in 1915 ; both were killed two years later. John's wife had died long since, Charles' widow alienated the old man's sympathies by marrying again and settling in the United States. His will, therefore, on which this story turns, left the bulk of his property, some fifty thousand pounds, to his elder grandson Derek ; in the event of his death it was to revert to Charles' son Nigel.

So far, you might have thought the old gentleman would cheat the lawyers and die intestate. But certain conditions attached to the will made it a document of importance. The testator reflected that one child was an orphan, the other fatherless and as good as motherless ; that they had to grow

to manhood with no parental supervision in times
of great unsettlement. Very wisely, then, he left the
fifty thousand (which was not the whole, but the
bulk of the legacy) in trust, until such time as
Derek (or, failing him, Nigel) should reach the age
of twenty-five. Meanwhile, the boys were rare
visitors to their grandfather's house, and scarcely
welcome ones ; a kind of precocious boredom in
their manner exasperated the old gentleman, none
the less bitterly because it was assumed to be typical
of a period. The avital thunders about politics,
art, morals and religion may be supposed to have
formed the grandsons' character by repulsion.
Derek lived, mostly, with old friends of the family
in the South of France, who let him run wild on the
facile excuse that ' anyhow, the boy will have
money '. Nigel, who never took to his step-
relations, was little better handled ; an exile when
at home, an unappreciated rebel at school, he flung
himself, with a pathetic illusion of originality, into
the career of an aesthete.

The two cousins met little, whether before or
after their grandfather's death ; there was little
in the character of either to make it desirable.
They went to different schools, neither of which
(since schools have a reputation to lose) I intend to
specify. But Oxford, though her critics have been
unkindly of late, has too broad a back to need the
shelter of anonymity ; both matriculated at the
older University, both at Simon Magus College.
Election to colleges is a mystery, as election should
be ; but the two years which Derek had misspent
there might surely have warned the fellows against

risking a second experiment with Nigel. On the other hand, Derek was a normal creature, though morose in disposition, idiotically extravagant, and with a strict periodicity of drunkenness. There was nothing in him, it must be admitted, which gave promise of Nigel's unendurable affectations. Derek was dissolute with a kind of lumpish unimaginativeness which may infect youth in any century. If he gambled to excess, it was because nobody had succeeded in introducing him to any other method by which you could kill time until the age of twenty-five. If he drank, it was with the stupid man's haste to forget and to disguise his own dullness. His dress, his manner, his associates were of the equestrian world ; but his taste was neither for horses nor for horsemanship, only for horsiness. With the Dean he was continually in conflict ; but there was a regularity in his irregu-larities, you knew beforehand just when he would be drunk, and just how drunk he would be ; and there is that in the academic mind which appreciates consistency in whatever direction. He was not clever enough to devise organized mischief ; he was too indolent (it seemed) to bear malice ; he accepted his fines, his gatings, and a couple of rustications with the complacency of the school-boy who (in the language of his terminal report) ' takes punish-ment well '. He made little stir in the University world, and it is probable that during the whole period of his residence he never had an enemy, except his cousin.

Nigel's perceptions were infinitely more acute, his faults infinitely less excusable. He had grown up in the aftermath of war, under the infection of disillusionment. He looked out upon a world of men (school-masters especially) who had fought and bled for the sake of certain simple emotions, with a submerged jealousy which took the form of resentment. These others had had the opportunity which was denied to him, of exploiting the full possibilities of manhood ; he would console himself for the loss by denying that the opportunity was worth having. They had been born to set the world right ; he would retaliate on the cursed spite of his late nativity by doing his best to put the world out of joint again. He would rebel against everything his neighbours bowed down to ; would embrace every form of revolt, however tawdry, however trite ; he would have no aim or ideal except to shock. At school, he had the sense to keep his powder dry, to lock up his splenetic poems, to revenge himself upon his uncongenial surroundings by the secret satisfaction of an undivulged irony. ' Loony Burtell ' they called him ; and he was content, like another Brutus, to bide his time.

Among all her immemorial traditions, Oxford cherishes none staler than that of aestheticism. A small group in each generation lights upon the same old recipe for setting the Isis on fire, and (since undergraduate memory only lives three years) is satisfied that it is a group of lonely pioneers. Nigel had read Wilde at school ; he pillaged epigrams from Saki without appreciating that ironic reservation which is his charm. He offered absinthe to all his visitors, usually explaining that he did not really care for it, but kept it in his rooms in order to put temptation in the way of his scout. He painted his walls a light mauve, and hung them with a few squares of blank cartridge paper on which he was always threatening to do crayon drawings; the beauty of art, he said, lay in its promise—its fulfilment only brought disillusion. He talked in a very slow drawl, with a lisp and a slight stammer which he had cultivated to perfection. He never attended lectures; the dons did not understand, he complained, that undergraduates come up to Oxford in order to teach. He was desperately callow, and quite inordinately conceited.

The older Universities tolerate everything. There are times, and there are Colleges, at which the essential rowdyism of youth clothes itself in a mantle of righteous Philistine indignation, and breaks up the aesthetic group with circumstances of violence. But you can fool some of the people some of the time; and at Simon Magus men cared little what their neighbours did, short of the bagpipes. Nigel found disciples, or at least comrades-in-arms for his movement, in that home of impossible unbeliefs. If you were the kind of person who liked that kind of thing, that was the kind of thing you liked. A round dozen of half-literary, half-histrionic young men from various colleges frequented his rooms, debated on the cut of clothes, and read out their compositions to each other. They spoke of themselves, almost reverently, as 'the men who had made bad'; they declared it their mission to encourage immorality amongst the undergraduates, Bolshevism amongst the scouts, and suicide amongst the dons. It was their favourite creed that England,

and indeed all the English-speaking races, were the spoke in the world's wheel. ' Why should I admire the country I was born in ? ' expostulated Nigel ; and indeed the reason alleged seemed inadequate. His favourite method of denunciation was to say, ' I don't like it ; it's unforeign '.

It will easily be imagined that little sympathy was wasted between the two cousins. Not, indeed, that the desperate poses of the younger could affect the elder with any sense of personal concern. Oxford is a broad stream, in which the varied regatta of life can be managed without jostling. Derek himself was too listless to condemn any form of behaviour ; and his friends, though they agreed among themselves that Nigel was the kind of thing which wasn't done, never dreamed of holding his cousin responsible for him. But the arrival of a namesake in the same college is never welcome ; your letters go astray, well-meaning people mix you up, and send invitations to the wrong man. The two were, moreover, somewhat alike ; the male strain was strong in the Burtell family, and a resemblance had survived closer than is usual between cousins. Each was dark and rather short ; either, in a general way, insipidly good-looking ; each had a pink-and-white complexion. It irritated Derek to be addressed, sometimes, as if he were Nigel's brother ; it irritated him still more when Nigel's casual acquaintances saw him at a distance and saluted him by mistake. He ostentatiously avoided his cousin, and even, as far as he might, the mention of his name.

Nigel, on his part, was not slow to appreciate

this neglect in the attitude of his senior, or to devise
means of retaliation. He identified his cousin as a
centaur, and referred to him sadly as a kind of
family failing. All the forms of abstinence he dis-
played were dictated to him by this repulsion.
'I can't get drunk,' he would say ; 'people would
be certain to mistake me for the Centaur, and I
might be too drunk to explain.' 'No, I don't play
cards ; there is such an intolerable look of Victorian virtue about the Queen of Spades ; it would
be dreadful to sit opposite her night after night.
Besides, the Centaur plays cards.' 'I am really
going to work this term ; then even the Master's
wife will hardly be able to mistake me for the Centaur again.' They say the University is a micro-
cosm, and it is certainly a microphone ; remarks
like these, not always conceived in the best of taste,
came round to Derek, and fanned, from time to time,
the dull embers of his resentment.

After a year of this, Derek went down ; but the
feud did not stop there. Nigel spent his vacations
in London ; and London is even a worse place than
Oxford for avoiding your dislikes. Kind, but imper-
ceptive hostesses threw the two cousins together,
Neither had scaled any particular social heights.
but each straddled on that uneasy ridge which
connects Chelsea with Mayfair. Derek, conscious
of his own conversational limitations, was for ever
being reminded of his cousin's existence. 'Oh yes,
charming fellow ; but have you met Nigel ? '
'Do tell me, Mr. Burtell, what is your brilliant
cousin Nigel doing now ? ' These hollow insipidities
of conversation were whip-lashes to Derek's self-

esteem. But there was worse behind it. In certain subterraneous walks of London society, both cousins were well known ; and in that world, careless of principle and greedy of originality, Nigel shone, a precocious proficient. Without heart, without worth, he dazzled feminine eyes with his reputed accomplishments. There was a woman who committed suicide ; she was a drug-fiend, and nothing was published in the papers ; but there were those, and Derek was among them, who believed that Nigel's callousness had been the cause of the tragedy.

Meanwhile, Nigel was running his course at Oxford : he celebrated his twenty-first birthday by a kind of mock funeral, at which he lay, in ghastly splendour, on a black catafalque, while his friends stood over him and drank absinthe to the memory of his departed youth. Derek was more than two years his senior ; was in measurable distance, therefore, of his promised inheritance ; and others besides the solicitors began to speculate as to the ultimate destination of the fifty thousand pounds. Derek's Oxford bills were still largely unpaid ; meanwhile, he lived recklessly beyond his modest income, secure in the consciousness of the fortune that awaited him. He ran up bills in London ; and, when these new creditors proved more importunate than the old, he applied for financial help to strangers, less Gentile than genteel. More than one promoter of private loans found an excellent business opening in a young man who was no longer a minor, and who had less than two years to wait before he was assured of a substantial capital sum. So things went on, with cordial feelings on both sides, until a faint tremor of apprehension fell upon the creditors' hearts. The loans were being piled up in a reckless way; already the fifty thousand was almost swallowed up; and Derek, as if conscious that the future had no longer any competence to offer him, was ruining his health in a way which suggested that he would not long survive the accession to his forestalled inheritance. His drinking bouts were now almost continual; rumour whispered that he also drugged. Whether he lived beyond the age of twenty-five was a matter of total indifference to society at large. That he should live until he was twenty-five was the earnest prayer of a handful of gentlemen not addicted to the practices of religion. If Derek should die before his twenty-fifth birthday, the fifty thousand would go to Nigel, and the money-lenders would have no assets to satisfy their claims. Panic-stricken, they came together, and met Derek's further appeals for accommodation with a peremptory stipulation that he should insure his life.

With discreet hesitations, a well-known Insurance Company declined to take the risk. Their doctor, with raised eyebrows, protested that he had never seen so young a constitution so seriously undermined. If Mr. Burtell took care of himself, he had no doubt a reasonable chance of achieving his twenty-fifth birthday, but . . . to tell the truth, he was not fully satisfied either of Mr. Burtell's will to do so, or of his power, if he had the will, to break with his bad habits. 'With a chap like Derek,' commented Nigel, to whom the cir-

cumstances were reported, ' the world wants to be
insured against his life rather than his death.'
But there is a way out of every *impasse*, and usually
it is the Indescribable. In case the reader is not
already acquainted with the name and the character
of this vast insurance agency, let him recall the
name of that millionaire who recently flew to Nova
Zèmbla, paying as he did so a shilling per second
by way of insurance money. . . . Yes, that was the
Indescribable. Human ingenuity has still failed to
imagine any form or any degree of danger which the
Indescribable are not prepared (for a consideration)
to underwrite. The fact that Derek Burtell was not
legitimate business made no difference to them.
For a very reasonable premium they backed him to
reach the age of twenty-five, without showing any
curiosity as to his further destiny.

One condition, however, they did make—even
the Indescribable makes conditions. Mr. Burtell
must really put himself under the direction of a
medical adviser. . . . No, unfortunately it would
not be possible for their own doctor to undertake
the task. (It is a matter of honour, and indeed of
income, with the Indescribable's doctor to refuse
every other form of practice.) But if Mr. Burtell
had no objection, they would like to see him put
himself in the hands of Dr. Simmonds, a man in
whom he could have every confidence, a man, indeed,
who had made a life-long study of acrasia. So it
was that, when he was within a month or so of his
all-important twenty-fifth birthday, and when his
cousin was just preparing, without any notable
regrets on either side, to take his degree and go

down from Oxford, Derek found himself closeted
in Dr. Simmonds' consulting-room in Wigpole
Street.

' Open air, that's what you want,' Dr. Simmonds
was saying. ' Open air. Take your mind off the
need for stimulants, and set you up again physically.
See ? '

' I suppose you want me to take a confounded
sea-voyage,' grumbled Derek. ' You fellows always
seem to want to send a man to the ends of the
earth, in the hope that he'll be dead before he comes
back.'

Dr. Simmonds shuddered. He was not exactly
an official of the Indescribable Company, but he
was (how shall we say it ?) in close touch with
them ; and the idea of such a valuable life, with
such a short time to run, being exposed to the
chances of wind and wave did not impress him
favourably.

' Why no, not a sea-voyage. Take a sea-voyage,
and the first thing you know you'll find you're
edging round to the saloon. Don't mind my
speaking frankly, do you ? No, it must be open air
combined with exercise ; not very hard exercise,
you ain't fit for it, but something that'll keep you
occupied, see ? The river, now ; ever go on the
river ? '

' I went to Henley once with some fellows.'

' Well, look here, I'll tell you what. You hire a
boat ; better say a canoe ; don't want to take any
risks with that heart of yours, you know ; you
go down to Oxford and take a friend with you, and
up you go to Lechlade, Cricklade, as far as you can

go without the canoe getting aground. Take it
pretty easy, mind, but keep on the go the whole
time as far as possible. Then you come back to
me, and I'll recommend you some exercises and a
diet, and we'll see what we can make of you.'

It was something of a surprise to Derek's world to
hear that he was indulging in anything so innocuous
as a canoe trip up the river. It was still more of a
surprise to them when they heard the company he
was keeping ; the other place in the canoe was
actually to be occupied by Nigel. And yet there
was sense in the arrangement ; Nigel had to kill
time between his schools and his *viva voce* ; Nigel
was at Oxford, and knew how to manage canoes and
where you hired the beastly things ; besides, there
was a great-aunt in the background, who had
expressed a particular wish to see the two boys
getting on better together, and, though neither
had seen her for a long time, Aunt Alma's circumstances were supposed to be comfortable, and she
had no other legal heir. As for Nigel, he assured
his friends that the prospect of a centaur turned
hippopotamus was altogether too much for him.
It would be interesting to make a tour of rural
England, and satisfy himself that the churches
were really as depopulated as he had been led to
believe. And then, whatever you said against
rivers, at least you had to admit that they set an
example of decadence.

CHAPTER II

SHIPCOTE LOCK

THE morning sun shone on the upper reaches of the Thames with the hazy glow that recalls a night of rain and presages a day of baking heat. It was early July, and the time of day conspired with the season of the year to produce an impression of almost uncanny perfection. The woods that threw out their flanking battalions towards the stream were heavy with consummated leafage; the hay standing in the fields glistened and steamed with the evaporations of yesterday; the larks sang in the unconscious egotism of their perpetual encore; the hedges were still fresh with the year's last revelation, the dog-rose; white wreaths of cloud sailed lazily across the distance, as if assured that they had no speaking part to-day. The cows stood whisking their tails gently, reserving themselves for greater efforts in the coming heat; rabbits sunned themselves among the hillocks, and scuttled away, stricken with imaginary fears; school-children dotted the lanes, their heads together in earnest debate over nothing; the air was full of promise and expectation; a wind blew, steady but with no chill, from the south-west.

And through this world of loveliness the river flowed, a secret world of its own. Lower down, the

Thames mingles with the haunts and the activities
of men ; overgrown towns straggle along its borders,
Maidenhead, Reading, Henley, Wallingford, Abing-
don. But here, in these upper waters, it is divorced
from the companionship of human life ; the villages
stand to one side and let it pass, turning their backs
on it contemptuously at half a mile's distance ; nor
is there any spot between Oxford and Lechlade at
which a cluster of human habitations fringes the
river's banks, and owes its conformation to the
neighbourhood. Unexpectedly it glides at your
feet, in the middle of smiling hayfields or at the
corner of a country lane ; it has a traffic and a life
of its own. Cushioned upon its waters, in punt or
canoe, you see nothing but high banks on each side,
deep in willow-herb and loose-strife, in meadow-
sweet and deadly nightshade ; or a curtain of willows cuts off the landscape from you ; or deep beds
of reeds stand up like forests between you and the
sky-horizon. To meet haymakers in a field, to
pass under one of the rare, purposeless iron bridges,
makes you feel as if you had intersected an altogether different plane of life. Your fellow-citizens
are the fishermen, incorrigible optimists who line
the banks at odd intervals ; the encampments of
boy scouts, mudlarking in the shallows or sunning
themselves naked on the bank ; your stages are the
locks, your landscape the glassy surface and the
tugging eddies of the stream.

And the river, by virtue of its isolation, has its
own sanctuary of wild life. It recks nothing of the
road, a few hundreds of yards distant, where school-
boys throw stones after rabbits and ransack the

hedgerows for nests. Here, in this lucid interval between two continents of human noise and labour, reigns no fear of the intruder Man. Frail and occasional visitors, the river-craft do not interrupt the solitude ; they become, themselves, a part of the landscape, and Nature accepts them, unconcerned. The heron leaves his lonely stance only at a minute's warning ; the kingfisher flies your approach without consternation, as if protected by natural mimicry against its background of blue sky ; fishes plop out of the water almost within reach of your hand, a sudden explosion amidst the silence ; waterhens bob to and fro on the surface, waiting till you are close by before they will show you their hydroplane and submarine tactics ; the voles race you along the bank, or let your prows cut through their wake ; the dragon-flies provide an aerial escort, and flutter temptingly in the van. You are initiated, for once, into the craft of Nature's freemasonry ; the highway you are following is older than the Romans, and you are not reckoned with the profane.

It would be impossible to imagine two human beings less alive to these considerations than the Burtell cousins, as they made their return journey downstream. Neither Derek's cast of mind nor his education had predisposed him to feel or to interpret the impressions made by natural scenery. He lay now extended along the floor of the canoe, a dead-weight amidships, the back of his head just kept erect by the little rest that leaned against the centre thwart, his eyes and face shaded by a brown Homburg hat, tilted extravagantly forward. Nigel, though better placed as a spectator, had equally little appreciation to spare for the scene. In hot weather it was his principle to spend his time in towns, where the sight of your fellow-mortals hard at work, sweating on scaffoldings or huddled together on omnibuses, gave you an agreeable sense of coolness. The effects of summer were always inartistic ; Nature overcrowded the canvas, like a good artist who had struck on a bad period. He had no eyes, then, for his surroundings ; his own appearance, as he sat paddling in the stern, was sufficiently incongruous. As one who must always be acting a part, he had dressed up very carefully as a ' river-man ' ; ' the Jerome K. Jerome touch ', he had explained, ' is what impresses the lock-keepers '. This robust attire was in strange contrast to the delicately-complexioned face that looked out from it, and the long black hair brushed elaborately backwards. A passer-by in a solitary punt, shading his eyes as he watched the pair vanish downstream, might have been pardoned for wondering at the vision.

The blurred roar of a waterfall, and a bifurcation of the stream with a danger-notice on the right-hand branch, heralded the approach of a lock. Shipcote Lock is not a mere precaution against floods ; it is also a short-cut. The channel that flows through it is dead straight for nearly a mile, and only at the end of this is it rejoined, after unnecessary windings, by the weir-stream. Lock and weir are both at the higher end of their respective channels, and behind them, to right of the one and left of the other, stretches a considerable island, the further part of which is woody and uncultivated. A narrow plank bridge, thrown across the weir itself, renders the island accessible from the right ; you can pass over the other branch by way of the lock itself, or (when this is shut up at nights) by a light iron bridge that crosses the lock-stream about a hundred yards below. The lock-keeper's house stands to the left on the mainland ; but of his garden the greater part covers the upper end of the island, jutting out like a wedge and washed by the river on both sides.

If any man has a distaste for the society of his fellows, and loves work out of doors, and running water and the companionship of flowers, who could wish him better than to end his days as a lock-keeper ?   Or rather, to live as a lock-keeper until he can no longer stoop to wind up the winches, or strain to open the reluctant gates. In these upper reaches, only pleasure-boats go by ; and their brief season is limited by the uncertain whims of an English summer. For the rest, when he is not actually plying his trade of outwitting nature, the lock-keeper can give himself wholly, it seems, to gardening, assured from the first that his flowers will grow in ideal surroundings, neighboured by the pleasant wedding of water with stone. Ship-cote Lock is among the most ambitious of these fairy gardens ; its crowded beds of pinks and sweet-william, stocks and nasturtium, snap-dragon and Noah's-nightcap, seem to rise out of the water's edge like a galleon of flowers, with crimson ramblers for its rigging. Man, you would say, has first done violence to nature by dividing the stream, damming up one half and forcing the other into a stone collar ;

and then, adding insult to injury, he has outdared with this profusion of blooms the paler glories of the river bank.

'There' (as Homer says of Calypso's garden) 'even an immortal might gaze and wonder as he approached.' It was not the habit of Nigel Burtell to gaze in wonder at anything. To flowers, especially, he had a strong objection, at least when they grew out of doors. 'They look so painfully natural,' he said, 'like naked savages, you know, all quite simple and unselfconscious. Put them behind the glass of a green-house, and there is something to be said for them; those Alidensian garments lend them a kind of meretricious charm.' It was not, then, any appreciation of the scene in general that made him bring out his camera as the boat drew near the lock. (Photography, he held, was the highest of all the arts, because the camera never tells the truth.) What had riveted his attention was the figure of the lock-keeper himself—a back view of him unexpectedly halved by the fact that he was bending double over some gardening operation. 'Design for an arch,' murmured Nigel to himself, as he pressed the spring. Then he called out 'Lock!' with sudden violence; the reproachful form of the unconscious model straightened itself and turned to meet them. The man's injured expression seemed to imply that he was only a gardener who made a hobby of lock-keeping. But he turned, whistling, to open the gates.

Owing to the recent passage of the gentleman in the punt, the lock was at high level. Nigel paddled in slowly; and the lock-keeper, not anxious to waste time which might be devoted to his darling geraniums, hastened to the lower end of the lock and pulled up the sluices, leaving the collection of the fare till later on.   Some incident of life downstream caught his attention as he stood on the bridge— your solitary liver is ever prodigal of gazing—and it was not till the water had well-nigh flowed out that he went ashore, and took up his familiar stance, buttressing the further end of the wooden lever. By that time, Nigel was standing on the bank, while the canoe, with its remaining occupant, had disappeared from sight below the level of the lock wall.   A desultory conversation was in progress, of which the lock-keeper could only hear one half, like one assisting at a telephone interview; the other side of the discussion remained inaudible.

' How long will it take you to get down to Eaton Bridge ?   A couple of hours ? . . .'

' Well, if you're going to take three hours over it, you may find me there waiting for you.   If the examiners take me early, and don't show an indecent curiosity about the extent of my knowledge, I ought to be clear by eleven.   Then I could take a taxi out and meet you.   What's that . . . ? '

' Oh yes, quite a decent sort of pub, it looked. Wait for me there if you like.   But I expect I'll be there ahead of you.   Left to yourself, you will probably paidle in the burn from morning sun till dine.   Well, so long . . .'

' What ?   Oh, all right, I'll bring it down.   I'd throw it, only you'd never be able to catch it.'

Nigel disappeared for a moment down the steps, and then came up again to settle with the lock-

keeper. ' No,' he said, ' he won't be coming back.
I'm getting off here to join the railway. It's
slightly quicker in these parts, I understand, than
canoeing. By the way, how do I get to the station ? '

If possible, the Englishman always prefaces
direction by correction. ' Want to catch the train,
eh ? Well, you see, what you did ought to have
done was to get off at the bridge. There's a bus
from there goes all the way to the station, to meet
the trains like. Yes, that's what you ought to have
done, get off at the bridge. You'll have to walk
there now, you see.'

' It's not far, is it ? '

' Well, you see, if you was to go by road, you'd
have to go all the way back to the bridge again ;
that would take you better than an hour, that would.
Your best plan, sir, is to take the field path. You
want to cross the bridge, see, over the weir yonder,
and keep straight on across the field, with the hedge
on your left. You'll see Spinnaker's Farm across
on the left, but don't you take no notice of that,
you keep straight on. Maybe a quarter of an hour's
walk it is, across the fields. Yes, that's your best
way now.'

' You don't happen to know the time of the train,
do you ? There's one somewhere about a quarter
past nine.'

' Nine-fourteen, sir, that's the one you want, if
you're going back Oxford way. Oh yes, you'll
have plenty of time to catch that ; it isn't not hardly
five minutes to nine now.'

' Are you sure ? I make it nine o'clock.'

' Well, your watch is fast, sir, that's what it is.

I get the time by wireless every night, you see, so that's how I know. Eight fifty-five, that's all. Your watch is fast, you see, that's what it is.'

'Trains pretty well up to time, I suppose, on a branch line like this?'

'Well, that's what you can't exactly say. Sometimes you wouldn't wish to see a train come in more prompt than what they do; sometimes I won't say but they're a matter of ten minutes or a quarter of an hour late. Depends on how quick they get away from the stations, you see, that's how it is. But if you're going to Oxford, sir, you won't find you're behind time, not but a minute or two; the nine-fourteen wouldn't be later than that, not at this time in the morning she wouldn't. Thank you, sir; very much obliged to you. If you keep straight along that path, you'll be at the station in good time, and it isn't much more than half an hour's run to Oxford from there. Good morning, sir.'

Nigel crossed the lock, threaded his way between the bright nasturtiums and the Canterbury bells, and almost before the gate of the weir bridge was heard swinging to behind him, was out of sight behind the island and the trees. The lock-keeper turned his gaze once more downstream. Derek still lay motionless, with the paddle resting idly on the thwarts; wind and stream were enough to drive the crazy bark at a fair pace through the cutting. 'Well, he ain't in much of a hurry, anyway,' said the lock-keeper, and went back to weed among the geraniums.

CHAPTER III

THE CANOE ADRIFT

I N spite of the computations mentioned in the last chapter, Nigel found himself without a ticket on Oxford platform. He had to accost the collector, to be waved back until the collector had dealt with all the other passengers, and to undergo the indignity of a personally conducted tour to the *guichet*. His digs, however, were in the High ; his education, incomplete in many respects, had at least accustomed him to quick changes, and it was only a minute or two past ten when he presented himself at the door of the Schools, white-tied and respectable.

' What are *you*, sir ? ' asked the porter.

' History.'

' History viva voce examinations don't start till to-morrow. Ten o'clock, sir.'

Nigel turned away, hardly with the air of one disappointed, and retired to his digs. Oxford was full of all the horrors of a Long Vacation ; earnest Americans with guide-books, with sketch-books, with cameras ; charabanc-loads of breezy Mid-landers, losing one another, hailing one another, roaring inaudible jokes across the street ; patient little men who had come up for a summer school of Undertakers, trying to find their way back to

Keble. There seemed to be no more room than during term, whether in the perilous streets or on the thronging pavements; North Oxford went marketing as relentlessly as ever; shop-assistants bicycled past, with lady shop-assistants perched stork-like on their steps; Cowley Fathers stumped along, eyes in the distance and cloak on shoulder; dons met, dons button-holed each other, dons asked each other when each other was going down; only the undergraduate, for once, was a bird of passage. A grim notice of 'Apartments to Let' hung in the window of Nigel's own sitting-room; a pot of ferns stood underneath it—no, this was no place for him. He changed his white tie, hailed a taxi, and within a quarter of an hour had been deposited at Eaton Bridge.

The Gudgeon Inn stands close by Eaton Bridge, with a pleasant though untidy stretch of grass sloping down to the river; at the end is a tiny quay to which a few boats are moored, at the back of it a verandah, where holiday guests can have their tea in wet weather without actually going indoors. On the whole, there are worse places in which to wait for a dilatory cousin. Nigel explained his movements to the young lady at the bar, and, after consulting her as to the hour, ordered a large stone ginger. This, when it was brought out to him on the lawn, he fortified from a handy flask in his pocket, and sat down in its company to wait. It was impossible that Derek should arrive yet; on the other hand, it was pretty clear that he ought to turn up within half an hour or an hour at most; his course lay downstream, and he had a fair wind behind him. There was nothing for it but to sit here and philosophize. Indeed, the slow swirl of the river at his feet invited to philosophy; it chimed in with the mood of a man just coming down from Oxford, and with no very sensational achievements, so far, to be put down to his credit. A large peacock edged suspiciously into view: Nigel picked up some fragments of bread, doped them with gin, and threw them at the bird in the hope that it would become interested. A drunk peacock would surely be an exquisite sight; to see it lose, at last, the shocked staidness of its demeanour. A camping party on the other side of the stream, a little lower down, claimed his attention; two brawny young men appeared to be washing up dishes, and hanging clothes out to dry. Nigel speculated whether it would ever be possible to enjoy the kind of life in which you had to wash up your own dishes and feed on tinned salmon. There seemed to be people who did it for the love of the thing. Probably it was a compensation of some kind; you could explain anything as a compensation nowadays.

Half-past eleven came, and still no sign of the canoe. Nigel wandered up and down restlessly, consulting his watch at intervals; at last he ordered and consumed a solitary luncheon, of which the main features were cold mutton and cherry brandy. At about a quarter to one he decided to wait no longer; he approached the barmaid—he was getting anxious, he explained, about his friend in the canoe. The gentleman had been in poor health recently; it seemed possible that there might have been an accident of some sort. Anyhow, he intended to walk upstream and look for him ; would it be possible for him to have a companion ? He himself was not much of a swimmer, and it might be a good thing to have somebody present who was more of an expert ; was there anybody connected with the inn who could come with him ? It appeared that there was. The odd man would be prepared for any emergency ; he swan like a duck he did. Nigel was introduced to the odd man, who turned out to be a very ordinary man. His engagements seemed to admit a walk of an hour or so spent in a good cause. Together they crossed the bridge, and set out upon the swathe of trodden hay, called by compliment a tow-path, which runs along the eastern bank of the river.

.   .   .   .   .

The Muse of detective fiction—she must surely exist by now—has one disadvantage as compared with her sisters ; she cannot tell a plain unvarnished tale throughout. If she did, there could be no mystery, no situation, no *dénouement* ; the omniscience of the author and the omnipresence of the reader, walking hand in hand, would lay waste the trail ; no clue would be left undiscovered, no detail lack its due emphasis. Needs must, then, that from time to time we should interrupt the thread of dull historical narration ; should see the facts not as they were in themselves but as they presented themselves to those who partook in the events concerned. Let me give you, then, the next stage of my story in the form in which it appeared next morning to a million readers.

PLEASURE TRIP MYSTERY SEQUEL
CANOE OCCUPANT FEARED DROWNED

OXFORD.

Alarm is felt here for the safety of Mr. Derek Burtell (inset), a visitor from London who should have returned yesterday from a canoeing tour to Cricklade. He was last seen at an early hour yesterday morning, leaving Shipcote Lock, which is situated in a somewhat lonely part of the river, about six miles above Eaton Bridge. His cousin, Mr. Nigel Burtell, who had accompanied him up to that point, returned from Shipcote to Oxford by train, it being his intention to rejoin the canoe at Eaton Bridge, to which he motored out from Oxford an hour or two later. After a time the non-arrival of his fellow-traveller gave rise to alarm, and he proceeded upstream by the tow-path in the direction of Shipcote, accompanied by George Lowther, a serving-man at the Gudgeon Inn.

WATER UP TO THE GUNWALE

At about half-past one they sighted the missing gentleman's hat, which was floating in the centre of the stream ; and shortly afterwards the canoe came in view, still afloat but full of water up to the gunwale. No sign was to be seen of its quondam occupant. Lowther immediately stripped and swam out to the canoe, which he brought in to shore without difficulty ; then he pluckily commenced diving near the spot where the canoe had been found, to see if any further signs of the missing gentleman were forthcoming. On righting the canoe and emptying it on the bank, it was discovered that a jagged hole of considerable size had been made in one of the planks of its hull, apparently by some violent collision with the sharp gravel which fringes the bank at various neighbouring points.

HEART FAILURE THEORY

Help was immediately summoned from Shipcote Lock, from Eaton, and from the village of Byworth, close to the scene of the accident. Watermen in punts were at work all yesterday afternoon dragging the bed of the stream, and search parties explored the neighbourhood of the banks, in case Mr. Burtell should have gone ashore and be in need of help. It is feared, however, that he may have succumbed to a heart attack, being prone to weakness of that organ, and fallen overboard through some lurch of the boat, the damage to its hull being inflicted subsequently. The river bed is overgrown with reeds at this point, and the search is necessarily a difficult one. Extensive inquiries have been made locally with a view to establishing the missing gentleman's whereabouts, but up to a late hour last night no success had been reported.

NEVER IN BETTER SPIRITS

A well-known figure in undergraduate Oxford, Mr. Nigel Burtell was yesterday interviewed by our representative. The sudden disappearance of his relative had been, he said, a great shock to him. He had been compelled to leave the boat at Shipcote Ferry, as he believed himself to be due in Oxford for an important examination at ten o'clock yesterday. ' I have never seen my cousin in better spirits,' was his comment. ' The doctor had told him to be careful about his heart, and I can only suppose that he neglected the warning and exposed himself, in my absence, to some fatal strain. We had been touring up to Cricklade, and it was on the return journey that the incident happened. My cousin did not often take exercise, and it is quite possible that the strain was too much for him.'

ACCIDENTS UNAVOIDABLE

Interviewed yesterday, a member of the Thames Conservancy Board explained that river accidents are by no means uncommon ; in his view, however, they were unavoidable. Life-belts were kept at all the locks, and the watermen, to whose splendid services he paid a glowing testimonial, did their best to ensure the public safety. There was, however, no method of patrolling the river in between the locks, and notices were prominently exposed warning the public that persons touring on the river did so at their own risk. Canoes were an unsafe form of boat for those unexperienced in swimming, since a very small alteration of equilibrium was liable to overturn them.

Mr. Derek Burtell is the son of the late Captain John Burtell, killed on active service in France. Educated at Simon Magus College, Oxford, he has recently been living in London, where the mystery of his fate will be felt with keen sympathy by a large circle of friends.

*_** An insurance policy against accident FREE with every copy of this paper.

So far the ephemeral chronicler ; and if anybody thinks it is easy to write that kind of English, he does less than justice to the men who make their living by it. A few details may be added to complete the picture. The spot at which the canoe was found was perhaps some three miles down from Shipcote Lock, close to a disused boat-house on the western bank. The hole in the bottom of the canoe had jagged, splintered edges, as if it had been freshly made—there was no question of an old piece of caulking having come loose. The difficulty, unanimously expressed by a solemn crowd of watermen who inspected it, was how so deep a cut could be made by mere impact against a piece of shingle. It was difficult to imagine how it could be done even if the canoe was being paddled at full speed ; here it was probable that the pace was quite leisurely, even if the boat itself was not drifting at the time of the catastrophe. The owner of the canoe insisted that he had no reason to think it faulty ; and indeed its appearance showed that it was almost new. The two paddles were floating near the hat. Derek's luggage was found waterlogged in the canoe.

Eager bands of amateur detectives searched along either bank, and far back into the woods, to find any trace of the missing man, but with no success. If he had landed on the left bank, he would naturally have made for the village of Byworth, which was only half a mile from the spot ; but none of the villagers, none of the labourers in the fields, had seen any trace of him. The further bank was more lonely (it was too early in the day for fishermen to be out), but there was an encampment of boy scouts a little lower down, and it was unlikely that they would have let a dripping stranger go past unnoticed. Before the end of the day the most optimistic of the bystanders admitted that they were out to find a corpse.

Nigel went back to Oxford by the last train. He had, of course, communicated with the police; there were no parents to communicate with—indeed, it was the melancholy fact, in spite of the journalist's polite reference, that there was not a soul in the world who mourned for Derek dead, or cared whether Derek lived. He had made innumerable acquaintances, but no friends. There was nothing to be done, then, except to wait for news; and from this point of view Oxford was as good a place for Nigel as any; there was his viva, too, on the morrow; and he had in any case to spend a day or two packing up before he left the beautiful city, ' breathing out,' as he said to himself, ' from her gas-works all the disenchantment of middle age '. Reporters, no doubt, would be a nuisance, and even the police might want to ask questions—if Derek's body were found, there would be all the fuss and discomfort of an inquest. He must make up his mind to go through with it. ' It'll be experience for you,' said one of the dons, vaguely enough; but this was poor consolation. Nigel held that nothing distorts one's vision in life like experience.

CHAPTER IV

THE INDESCRIBABLE HAS ITS DOUBTS

WHEN I said that no human soul mourned Derek dead or cared whether Derek lived I spoke too hastily; I should have excepted the Indescribable. To a Company with such vast assets, the sum needed to cover Derek's policy was of course a mere drop in the ocean. But (it has been finely said) business is business; just as a prudent housewife will waste hours tracing a missing sixpence in the accounts sooner than pay in sixpence from her own purse, so the Indescribable would set agencies to work sooner than lose the paltry sum of fifty thousand pounds. It was a matter of principle.

In this illiterate age, it is perhaps too much to expect that my reader is familiar with the name of Miles Bredon. I must, therefore, at the risk of being tedious to the better-informed, remind the public that Miles Bredon was the agency which the Indescribable always set to work on such occasions; he was their very own private detective, paid handsomely to do their work for them, and paid still more handsomely to do nobody else's. The employment, naturally, was an intermittent one, which exactly suited the indolence of the man's taste—his round of golf, an evening spent over his

favourite and unintelligible form of patience, his
country cottage, and the unstaled companionship
of his really admirable wife, this was all Bredon
asked, and this, for some months at a stretch,
would be all that he got. Then there would be a
loss of fashionable jewels, a fire in an East-End
warehouse, and Bredon, greatly protesting, would
be launched out anew upon that career of detection
for which he had so remarkable an instinct, and so
profound a distaste.

He had been summoned up to London for an
emergency interview, and it was with an unpleasant
sense of being ' for it ' that he entered the loathed
portals of Indescribable House. I will not attempt
to give any word-picture of the upstairs room into
which he was shown, for that would be to suggest
that I was familiar with it, whereas neither you,
reader, nor I are ever likely to be shown up beyond
the second floor, even if either of us is lucky enough
to be insured with this admirable Company. Somewhere in the vast labyrinth of the third floor Bredon
disappeared from sight ; we may listen at the key-
hole, if you will, but profane eyes must not peep
through it. I picture gold ash-trays lying about
on the tables, real oak panelling, and one or two
Rubenses on the walls ; but perhaps I exaggerate.
Anyhow, here it was that he was closeted with
Sholto, an important cog in the business and a
personal friend ; with Dr. Tremayne, too, that
eminent practitioner who had been so highly paid
to leave off saving life, and devote his talents to
prophesying the probabilities of death.

Bredon was given something to smoke—I suppose

a two-and-sixpenny cigar. 'It's about this Burtell business,' said Sholto.

'Oh Lord, not that! I read about it in the paper as I came up. I was really delighted to notice how mysterious the circumstances were. I assure you, there is nothing more refreshing to my mind than not solving mysteries. Do you mean to tell me that the Company was involved?'

'It was. It's a matter of fifty thousand.'

'Fifty thousand be hanged! Let 'em sack the under-porter and call it quits. How did this Burtell manage to pay his premiums, anyhow? I know people who know him, and I always understood that he was never supposed to pay for anything.'

'It wasn't he who paid the premiums; it was his creditors. They sent a deputation round here about it; I tell you, it was like the Flight from Egypt. You see, he'd been raising heavy loans, and he couldn't touch his money till he was twenty-five. That's where we came in.'

'And how old is he, or was he?'

'Policy's only got two months to run.'

'Good Lord! Sounds like old Mottram again. What was all this about weak health, doctor? You vetted him, I suppose?'

'Weak health, my dear Bredon, isn't in it. The man was a wreck. I've never seen anybody who'd gone the pace so thoroughly.'

'Punch? Or Judy?—as Father Healy used to say.'

'Oh, anything you like. But this last year or two he'd been drugging. When I saw him, he'd obviously more or less reached the line of perpetual snow. And his heart was all to pieces. I wouldn't have given him two years; but then, we only insured him up to twenty-five. Simmonds said the same. He did his best for him, and tried to pull him round a bit.'

' Was it Simmonds who suggested this canoe-trip ? '

' Yes, it's a fad of his. I think Simmonds must get a commission from the Thames Conservancy; they'd never keep their locks in repair without him.'

' Well, he'd better recommend bath-chairs in future. What does he say about this heart-failure business ? '

' Oh, it's all right; it's perfectly possible. If Burtell had been slacking for a bit, say, and had suddenly tried to put on speed, he might quite easily have had a seizure, fallen over sideways, capsized the boat, and there he is at the bottom, with the Company responsible for fifty thousand.'

' Seems to me my job is to save Simmonds' character. What about hocus-pocus, Sholto—you know, the disappearing trick ? '

' It's possible. I've fished on the Thames before now, and it's possible to go miles, sometimes, without meeting a soul. But how was the fellow going to do it ? You see, the money would go to the cousin ; and it's quite certain that there wasn't any love lost between them. Why should Mr. Derek Burtell obligingly disappear, to let Mr. Nigel Burtell come in for a nice legacy ? '

' What sort of fellow is this Nigel ? He wasn't inset.'

'We've made inquiries, and he seems to be a pretty poisonous sort of worm. Fifty per cent aesthete and the rest devil, I should say. But there are no convictions against him for murder so far, if that's what you mean.'

'Well, we seem to be in with a gaudy crowd. Seems to me the Company ought to engage a parson to inspect people's morals before we insure them. What exactly am I expected to do?'

'Oh, go down to the Upper Thames and look about for cigarette-ends. Not such a bad place either, at this time of year. If they fish out a corpse, it's all up. If they don't we shall have to presume death after a time, unless you can produce the man alive, or evidence that he was alive on September the third. It doesn't do for the Indescribable to keep people waiting. If I were you, I'd go down at once, because the papers have given the thing big head-lines, and there's the hell of a lot of trippers will be coming up the Thames before long. It's good for you, you know; it'll take down your fat. I wish I could be there, to see you diving in the mud on the spot marked with an X. Well, go to it. Them's orders.'

Bredon sent his wife an urgent request to pack and picked her up at the cottage. It was she who drove (while he, as he said, did the thinking) on the motor-infested journey to Oxford. 'I don't like it, Angela,' he said, as he sat beside her. 'I feel as if it was going to be the beast of a complicated business.'

'It may be your idea of a complicated business, it's not mine. All you and I have got to do is to lounge about the Upper River in a canoe until the watermen dig out the body. It's a long time, you know, Miles, since you took me out in a canoe. I shouldn't wonder if my service arm has got a bit flabby. I'm the only person who loses by this, because of course I shall look a fright on the river. Why is it that men always look like heroes when they're boating, and women always look like frumps ? "These little ladies are determined to make the most of the sunshine"—that kind of thing. What's worrying you, anyhow ? '

' Oh, I've no theories about it, but even from what the papers print you can see it isn't a straight-forward case. It's a frame-up of some kind, that's the trouble. It wears all the air of a frame-up, and that means that somebody's been covering his traces, and we've got to find out who, where, and why.'

' But why a frame-up ? '

' Why, don't you see, the whole thing's a little too good to be true. The canoe-trip's all right ; Simmonds is always recommending it. But why should Mr. Derek Burtell take his cousin, whom apparently he loathed, on a tour of that kind ? Nothing puts two people at closer quarters than a week on the river. It doesn't look right, their going together.'

' But they weren't together when the accident happened.'

' I know, and why weren't they ? That's all wrong too. All the week, while they're together, Derek Burtell is at liberty to throw as many fits as he pleases. But he doesn't—he waits till his cousin is out of the way, and then conks out. Meanwhile, the cousin isn't permanently out of the way ; he comes back again just in time to be in at the death.'

' Sure you're not being fanciful ? '

' Woman, I'm never fanciful.   I have no instincts, no premonitions, no unaccountable intuitions.   I just see the logic of the thing, nothing else.   And I say that all this is just a little too good to be coincidence.   Remember, too, that it happens on one of the loneliest parts of the river ; that it happens in the morning, the one time when there wouldn't be any fishermen about.   These young men, you see, had been up the river and were coming down again ; they had had full opportunity to explore the ground beforehand.   No, somehow, somewhere, it's a put-up job.'

' But what kind of a job ?   Suicide ?   I know how fond you are of the suicide theory.'

' Suicide doesn't work.   A canoe's a perfectly sensible kind of boat to go out in if you want to commit suicide, more particularly if you want to let on that it's an accident.   Nobody can say, " How could he have managed to fall out ? " if you're in a canoe.   But, just for that reason, we've no sort of use for a canoe with a hole in the bottom. If you want to drown, the simplest way is to drop into the water and have done with it, not to lie in a scuttled canoe feeling the water gradually come up and soak your bags.   I don't believe there's anybody who could commit suicide in such a cold-blooded way as that.   On the other hand, if he did just jump into the water and drown, leaving

the canoe to mark the spot, why didn't he leave
the canoe afloat properly—or waterlogged if you
like, but at least without a hole in the bottom ?
Assuming that he wants to make the thing look
like accident, that's the very way to advertise the
fact that he did it on purpose.'

' Holmes, I seem to see what you are hinting at.
We're on the tracks of a murder, after all.'

' No, confound it, the murder idea is wrong too.
The Upper River is the last place where you're
likely to meet an old acquaintance with a grievance
and a shot-gun. If it was to be murder, it would
have to be this Nigel who's responsible, and that
doesn't do. For it must have been the other one,
Derek, who proposed the canoe trip. It's asking
too much of coincidence to suppose that the mur-
deree deliberately put himself, for a whole week,
at the disposal of the murderer. Of course, we've
got to take the possibility into account. But I
don't like the possibility.'

' Disappearance, then ? The Mottram touch ?
It might have been worth his while.'

' Yes, but if you want to disappear, you want to
disappear in an orderly and unobtrusive sort of
way ; you want to get clear before anybody notices
a gap in the ranks of Society. You don't want
people scouring round after you ; you don't want
the papers making a stunt of it next morning ; you
don't want to have the bows of your canoe stove
in, so that the police might think you were murdered.
That idea fits in with bits of the story—the deliberate
way, for example, in which the cousin appears to
leave him for two or three hours unaccompanied.

But the bottom of the canoe seems to knock the bottom out of it. No, it's no use worrying, we must have a good look round before we try to go any further. I'm not sure it wouldn't be a good thing to buy half a dozen canoes in Oxford, just to try experiments with.'

'We're not going to stay in Oxford, then? You know, you haven't been very communicative.'

'Not if we can get a room at this inn by Eaton Bridge. The nearer the spot the better. It must be about twenty-four hours now since the thing happened, and I don't want the scent to get cold if I can help it. Besides, I want to get the atmosphere of the place. Oxford's all wrong.'

'I just thought you might be going to interview this cousin person. He must be about in Oxford still.'

'I doubt if the young gentleman shares your admiration for me, Angela. What right have I got to go and interview him? I can't send up a card with " Indescribable Company " marked on it, as if I'd come to see about the electric light. The Company prefers to remain anonymous in these cases. Unless I can scrape an acquaintance with him by accident, the cousin will have to continue in his lamentable ignorance that I exist. No, the Bridge for me, and the lock-keeper ; one can always get conversation out of a lock-keeper.'

'This one may be pretty peevish, though ; he must have been answering a lot of questions these last twenty-four hours.'

'That's where you come in. There are times, you know, when I'm almost glad I married. You'll have to win his heart somehow; let's see, what shall it be? Dogs? They generally keep dogs. No, I know; gardens. They all keep gardens. You will have to take a really intelligent interest in this one.'

'What is the husband of the gardener doing? The husband of the gardener is looking for footprints on the back lawn. All right. If he seems *difficile*, I shall ask for cuttings from his lobelias. But I don't quite see how we're to explain our presence at the lock. The road there doesn't go any further. Do we just say we've been told he's got a pretty garden and——'

'On the contrary, we open the conversation by saying "Lock!" Then you get to work.'

'Oo, are we really going to start boating at once? I say, you'll be pretty tired and pretty late by the time you've paddled me six miles upstream.'

'I had thought of obviating that by taking two paddles. Look out, this is going to be Magdalen Bridge, not Brooklyn Bridge; try to have some regard for the safety of the public.'

CHAPTER V

MR. BURGESS EXPANDS

THE Gudgeon Inn proved to be empty of visitors, its management at once hospitable to strangers and incurious as to their errand. They secured a quite tolerable bedroom, whose windows looked down over the strip of grass on to the river itself. Luncheon was a hasty meal: Bredon was plainly full of impatience to be off, and Angela accommodated herself to his mood. They hired from the inn not only a canoe, but a substantial length of rope, and most of the journey upstream was in the end accomplished by towing—Miles walking on the bank while Angela steered and gave occasional dabs at the water in the stern. Few things travel quicker than a towed canoe. Indeed, the only circumstance which delayed them was the melancholy presence of a few dredgers, whose crews were occupied in dragging the bed of the stream for further traces of the catastrophe. At one point, where the whole stream was barred in this way, they found it necessary to pull over the bank. But this, fortunately, was the spot at which the boy scouts were encamped; and Bredon looked on with benignant interest while no less than fourteen good deeds were registered in their juvenile Treasury of Merit. The scout-master, a man of some age and education, fell into conversation with him while the operation was being conducted.

'Ironical,' said Bredon, 'that so much help should have been so close at hand when the accident took place.'

'Well,' said the stranger, 'I don't know that we should have been very much use. You see, we had only just moved in, and that morning the bigger boys had gone over to Wheathampton with the trek-cart to bring our stores over. Only the little ones were here, cleaning up and so on.'

'Then you were over at Wheathampton yourself ?'

'Why, no; it's true I was in camp. But there are endless little details one has to arrange for, and I wasn't keeping an eye on the stream. Not at all, not at all; the boys enjoy doing it. Good morning to you, sir.'

The plan of campaign had been amended so far as the lock was concerned. If they demanded the opening of the lock, it would be necessary to go further upstream for the look of the thing, and this would be mere waste of time. Bredon hailed the lock-keeper, and asked if they might tie up the boat just underneath while they went over to Shipcote to get some tea. The lock-keeper paused impressively, like one struggling with the fallacy of many questions.

'There isn't nothing against your tying up the boat there, sir, not if you wished to. But you won't get no tea at Shipcote, because Mrs. Barley at the inn don't give teas. No demand for 'em, she says; that's how it is. You'd have got a nice

cup of tea down at the Gudgeon, but you won't get
none not at Shipcote. Of course, if you aren't in a
great hurry, I could ask Mrs. Burgess if she'd put
the pot on for you ; she do sometimes in the season.'

Miles rightly conjectured that Mrs. Burgess was
the lock-keeper's wife. By a trick of human vanity,
we always assume a knowledge of our own surname
in conversation with strangers. This was better
than anything they had dared to hope for ; the
offer was speedily accepted ; their position was
assured ; and Angela's appreciation of the garden
would have been merely perfunctory, if it had not
been genuinely forced from her by the beauty of
what she saw. Within five minutes, she actually
found herself applying to Mr. Burgess for horti-
cultural advice ; she excelled herself in superlatives ;
she called her embarrassed husband to witness that
Mr. Burgess' pinks were a fortnight ahead of their
own. So completely was she absorbed that in the
end it was Mr. Burgess himself, full of importance
over recent events, who called their attention to the
fact that he was, so to speak, the scene of a tragedy.

' Ah, yes, that drowning business,' said Bredon.
' An extraordinary affair—have you ever known the
bottom of a canoe stove in like that by running
aground on a bit of shingle ? '

' No, sir, I haven't, and you can take it from
me that I told you so. For a racing-boat I wouldn't
say, being built for speed and that ; but those
canoes is built very hard, if you see what I mean.
Light, but hard, that's how it is ; it's the quality
of the wood. In a flood, now, I won't say but you
might smash one up, or if you were shooting rapids

with it. But there aren't no rapids here, you
see, not nearer than the Windrush, and if they done
the damage to the boat on the Windrush, how did
they bring her all the way here safe and sound?
That's what I want to know.'

' Looked sound enough, I suppose, when it passed
through the lock? '

' Well, you see, sir, we don't take much stock of
boats as they come through, not in the ordinary
way. Sees too many of 'em, that's what it is.'

' I suppose, if it comes to that, you don't take
much notice of the people who come through, either?
Must be a nuisance when this sort of thing happens,
having to answer a whole pack of questions about
what the gentlemen in the boat looked like, and
what was the exact hour at which they went through,
and all the rest of it.'

' Well, it's curious you should say that, sir,
because it so happened that I knew just when this
boat came through, and was able to give information
according. You see, sir, this young gent gets out,
and he was anxious for to catch the train at Shipcote
Station there. I told him, I did, he ought to have
got off at the bridge higher up ; then you'd have
caught the bus, I says ; the bus runs from the bridge
to Shipcote Station, I says. Oh, he says, very la-di-da
sort of gent he was. Oh, like that he says, I want to
catch the nine-fourteen. Well, I says, you've time
to catch the nine-fourteen by the footpath ; it isn't
hardly not a quarter of an hour's walk, and it's
only five minutes to nine now, I says. The devil
it is, he says, begging your pardon, mum, I make it
nine o'clock if it's a minute, he says. So I told him

I got the time here by wireless, and showed him my watch, same as it might be to you, and that's how it was I come to know what the time was when he went off, you see.'

They had tea, to Angela's delight, in a little arbour overgrown with ramblers and commanding a long vista of the river. She was already losing interest in the purpose of their errand, and accepting the expedition as a holiday. Miles, though he affected an even more conspicuous languour, was addressing strictly business questions to Mr. Burgess, who still hovered about, unskilled to close the flood-gates of his own eloquence.

'But of course that was the gentleman you saw on the bank; he was out of the boat, so you had a good look at him. But you wouldn't have been able to answer for the one who stayed in the canoe —and after all, that's the corpse; you might be called upon to identify him any day.'

'No, sir, that's a fact, you don't see much of a gentleman who just comes through in a boat, especially if he's wearing of a hat, same as what this one done. Same time, I'd know the other one anywhere. Want to catch the nine-fourteen, he says. Oh, says I, you've time to catch the nine-fourteen by the footpath. And so he had, you see.'

'But you'd be ready to swear that there *was* another gentleman who passed through the lock?' asked Bredon. These reminiscences of a dialectical triumph were becoming somewhat wearisome.

'Excuse me, sir, but were you in any way connected with the police?' asked Mr. Burgess, a chill of suspicion creeping into his voice.

' Good God, no,' answered Bredon fervently.

' No offence meant, sir. But you see how it is. If the police comes to me and asks me questions, then I'm prepared to answer 'em, according to what I know, and I can't do more than that, can I ? But it's not for me to go out of my way giving information to the police promiscuous, and putting ideas into their heads. Mind you, I've nothing against the police, but what I say is, if it's their business to find out, they'll ask questions, and then they won't be told no lies. I'm a law-abiding man, I am, and nothing to fear from anybody, you understand ; but I don't hold with getting mixed up with the police, not if you can help it. Supposing you was the police, sir, and you come and ask me, Was there another gentleman come through the lock ? like that, Oh yes, I says. And so there was. But seeing as you're not connected with 'em, sir, I'll tell you more than that. There was one of 'em in the canoe when it come through the lock, but how long did he stay in the canoe ? That's what I say, how long did he stay in the canoe ? '

' Well, if we knew that, we should be able to tell the newspapers something, shouldn't we ? '

' Ah, sir, them as knows isn't always them as tells. Now, look here, sir ; I'm a plain, ordinary man, you know what I mean ; and I don't set up to know more than another man. But I've got eyes, you see. Well, and this is what I'm telling you. When that young gentleman come through the lock in the canoe—same as it might be your canoe, only going down instead of coming up— when that young gentleman come through the lock,

he was all sprawling on his back, same as if he was
asleep; not steering her, sir, if you'd believe me
but just letting her float broadside on and go down
as the wind took her.   Ah, says I to myself, you've
got some game on, you have.   You wouldn't be
shamming asleep like that if you hadn't got some
game on, I says.   Same time, I didn't take any notice
of him; so long as a gentleman pays his fare,
that's all I've got to look to.   But it stuck in my
head like, you know what I mean.   Didn't seem
natural to me, that's how it was.'

'So you didn't do anything about it ? '

'At the time, sir, no, sir.   But a little after,
may have been about half an hour after, or twenty-
five minutes, I went down along the island a bit
to see after some of Mrs. Burgess' hens as had got
loose in the wood like.   Well, sir, you remember
that iron bridge as you come under, just a little
way down the lock stream ?   Kind of iron bridge for
foot passengers, because there's no road leads to it,
nor like to be.'

'Yes, I remember noticing it.   Joins up the
island to the West bank.   What about it ? '

'Maybe you didn't notice that the steps of that
bridge is made of cement, same as the lock here.
Well, I goes past them steps, the ones on the island
bank of it, and what d'you think I see ?   Footmarks, sir ; naked footmarks, for all the world
like Man Friday in the tale.   Seemed to me somebody'd been swimming in the water, or paddling
maybe, and left those marks along of his feet
being wet.   Of course, if you was to go there now
you wouldn't see nothing of 'em ; they'd be all

dried up like by now.   But when I come past, there they were, as plain as for anyone to see, all the way down the steps of the iron bridge.'

'But that's extraordinarily interesting !   Which way would they be pointing ?   I mean, did they go up the steps, or down ?   And were there any footmarks on the other set of stairs, across the bridge ? '

'No, sir, only the one side, same as I'm telling you.   And coming down, sir, toes pointing towards the island.   So that's what makes me say to myself, Did the gentleman stay in the canoe ? '

'Very interesting indeed !   But it beats me to see why he only left marks going down the steps, and none going up.'

'Ah, sir, that's because you don't recollect the bridge properly.   Rises very sudden, sir, with iron bars to support it, coming down close to the water on either side.   And I says to myself, What's to prevent the young gentleman having laid hold of those iron bars, standing up in the canoe, like, and pulled himself up by his arms on to the bridge ? The banks is steep there, you see, and they was muddy after a night of rain ; so if he'd gone ashore he'd have been bound to leave some marks of it. But those prints of his wet feet on the bridge steps, why, if I hadn't have come along within the hour, they'd have faded away altogether, and you and me none the wiser.'

'Then you mean he just got out of the canoe, left it to drift, and went off the nearest way to a road ? '

'Not the road, sir, the railroad.   If he'd have

liked to go down to the end of the island, he'd have
just had to swim the weir stream, and then he'd
be on the field track that goes straight from the
tow-path to the station. Though, mind you, he
might have come right back to the weir, same as the
other gentleman done, and crossed by the weir-
bridge, and there he'd get the short path to the
station, see ?   Of course, I won't say as that would
be easy without me seeing of him ; but you know
how it is, sir, when a man's got his little bit of
garden, he can't be always looking about him, and
I've only one pair of eyes.'

'Funny, though, that nobody else should have
seen him. Because surely they would have mentioned it by now.'

'It would surprise you, sir, to know what a lonely
place this can be, more especially when it's early
morning. Of course, if he'd have taken the longer
path, the one opposite the end of the island, I won't
say but he'd have been seen going through Spinnaker
Farm ; he had to pass through that, you see, to get
to the station. But if he took the shorter path,
from the weir, there wasn't nobody about, not a
living soul. Come to think of it, there was a gentleman went through in a punt just before they came,
because I remember letting of him through. But
he'd be out of sight, you see, before I'd got the
water through the lock again.'

'Angela, we ought to be getting back. We
mustn't take up any more of your time, Mr. Burgess. I'd better see Mrs. Burgess about the tea,
hadn't I ? Good afternoon ; I expect we'll be up
this way again before long.'

Bredon, however, had not yet finished with the neighbourhood. As soon as they reached the junction of the two streams, he piloted the canoe to the right bank, and left Angela to paddle on slowly while he had a word with Spinnaker Farm. Here he was greeted by a vociferous dog, fortunately tied to a barrel, and an old lady with a shrill, kindly voice, who needed little diplomacy in the matter of approach. Indeed, her opening question was, ' Did you come for the tobacco-pouch, sir ? '

' Oh, have you found it ? ' Bredon answered promptly ; he had, fortunately for his success on such occasions, a good reaction-time.

' Yes, we found it sure enough ; my Flossie she see it when she was out in the big field yesterday. Oh, she says, whatever is that ? But she's a good girl, Flossie, she didn't open it ; she brought it straight to me, and of course I kept it in case it was called for. That'll be the one, sir ? '

She produced a voluminous waterproof tobacco-pouch, tightly rolled into a hard cylinder. Bredon knew at the touch that it contained something more interesting than tobacco ; but he saw no reason to mention the point. ' I couldn't be sure where I'd dropped it,' he said. ' Was it along the tow-path ? '

' Yes, sir, on the tow-path, sir ; just where it leaves the river over against the island. I thought at first it might have been dropped by the gentleman who came through yesterday morning early, and I said to myself, " Oh dear, he'll never come back for it ", because he passed in such a hurry you could see he was running for the train.'

Bredon began to regret his *rôle* of pouch-loser;
it would hardly be decent to show too much interest
in the stranger. ' I expect that was the gentleman
I passed myself yesterday morning. About nine
o'clock it would be ; a young, dark-haired gentleman, with no hat on. I'm glad to know he caught
the train, for he looked to me as if he were going to
miss it.'

' That would be the one, sir.' Bredon did not
venture on any closer examination. He hurried
back down the path, unrolling the package as he
went. It proved to be a spool of camera-films—
one that had been used and rolled up by unskilful
hands. ' That ', he said to himself, ' might be much
worse. That might be very much worse.' And he
thrust it away into an inner pocket.

* * * * *

' Well,' he asked, as he executed a kind of back
somersault into the canoe, ' how's that for a day's
outing ? You obviously are the complete river-
girl ; your disguise takes in everybody. I suppose,
after all that, we shall hear at Eaton Bridge that
they've fished up the corpse, and it's no business of
ours how it got there.'

' They'll fish up at least two corpses if you try
to get into the boat like that again. Well, what did
you think of the Burgess theory ? I thought him
rather splendid. Of course, I may have been just
carried away by his eloquence. But it seemed to
me he was the complete detective. I was wondering
whether you and he couldn't swap jobs ; I could
do the gardening part, and I suppose you could
manage to sit backwards on to a lock gate till it

opened. I'm sure the Indescribable would find **Mr. Burgess** a gold-mine.'

' Oh, of course Burgess is all wrong. Anybody could see he's talking through his hat. No, don't ask me why just now ; ask me after dinner. I want to try and work the thing out myself a bit. I wonder if the Gudgeon has such a thing as a dark room ? '

CHAPTER VI

THE ARCHIMEDES TOUCH

THE Gudgeon Inn is the sort of institution that only exists for the sake of people who see life in inverted commas. Externally it is just like a thousand other inns; the creaking sign-board, the modest lintel-announcement of the licence, the perspective of doors and passages that greets you as you enter, show no promise of disillusionment. But once you are really inside, you know the difference. The dining-room has no muslin curtains, there is no bamboo firescreen; the tables are not covered with ash-trays and salt-cellars advertising beer and mineral waters; there is no vast, unwieldy sideboard heaped with unnecessary coffee-pots. The tables are of fumed oak, and the flower-vases on them are of modern crockery in a daring orange; the sideboard is real Elizabethan, and serves no purpose whatever, any more than the three large pewter plates which rest upon it, obviously straight from an old curiosity shop. There are no stuffed animals in glass cases, no sentimental pictures with explicit legends in the manner of the later nineteenth century; no strange sea-shells on the mantelpieces, no horse-hair sofas, no superannuated musical-boxes. The walls are very bare and beautifully whitewashed; a few warming-pans and some mezzotints are all their ornament; there are open fire-places with brightly polished dogs, tiled floors, rush mats, wooden coal-scuttles with archaic mottoes carved on them. In a word, the inn has been recently ' done up '.

' It isn't an inn,' Bredon was complaining to his wife over their evening meal; ' it's an old-world hostelry, and it irritates me. I believe they expected us to dress for dinner; there isn't any commercial room, only a place they call the Ingle Nook; I can't find a dart-board anywhere, or an antimacassar. Their idea of a beer-mug is a thing you stick up on a shelf and look at.'

' It's such a pity you've no taste,' suggested Angela.

' Taste? Who wants taste in a country pub? You can get taste in your own drawing-room. A country pub ought to grow up anyhow; with grandfather clocks that really belonged to grandfathers, and a spotty piano all out of tune, and sham flowers and things. Don't you see that this kind of thing isn't natural? '

' Well, switch off the art-criticism and do a little brain work. Tell me why poor old Burgess is all wrong about the drowning mystery.'

' Oh, that? Well, in the first place, as I said this morning, what's the use of the hole in the canoe? If the man isn't really drowned, but wants us to think he is, why doesn't he pretend the canoe just tipped over on one side and swamped? They often do.'

' It only surprises me that they don't do it oftener. But go on.'

'Here's another improbability—Burtell's got a weak heart. Tremayne's vetted him, and Simmonds has vetted him, and they both know what they're talking about. Now, Burgess wants us to believe that that man pulled himself up by the arms from a canoe on to the top of a bridge, and then, probably, swam the stream. If he did do either of those things, it was suicide all right for a man with a heart like Burtell's. And that brings up a further point —why should he want to leave the boat just there, such a short way down the lock stream? If he'd only held on another half-mile or so, he'd have got past the junction where the weir stream flows in, and then he could land and make tracks for the station without crossing any branch of the river at all. Again, Burgess found the prints of a naked foot. What on earth did Burtell want to go and take off his shoes and socks for? He'd want them when he got ashore. Ninthly, and lastly, if he scuttled the canoe right up there, just below the lock, how did it manage to float down three miles, all water-logged, before it was found at half-past one?'

'Still, you've got to give some account of those footmarks.'

'Oh, I'm not denying there's been some hanky-panky at the bridge. Assuming, of course, that Mr. Burgess is telling the truth, and he doesn't seem to me to have much imagination. I'm only here to establish a death, or if possible the absence of a death. So I'm only concerned with what Mr. Derek Burtell has been up to. But if I were the police, and if I hadn't the singular fondness of the

police for trying to find the body before you do
anything else, I should be beginning to wonder
what Mr. Nigel Burtell has been up to.'

' But his alibi is surely pretty sound.'

' It's too sound, that's the trouble. It looks so
confoundedly like an alibi, if you see what I mean.
He leaves the canoe with just twenty minutes to
catch his train. He engages the lock-keeper in
conversation about the exact time, so that the lock-
keeper can swear not only to him but to the precise
hour at which he left. Then he reappears here
an hour or two later, and starts talking to the
barmaid about the time—I found out that from
her. Then he conceives some anxiety about his
cousin—and why was he so anxious ? Why did
he set out almost expecting to find him drowned ?
—and he marches off up the river, not alone mark
you, but with an independent witness who can
swear to his actions. I dare say it's all right. I
only get the impression that Mr. Nigel Burtell's
behaviour is a little too like an alibi to be true.'

'.Do you always suspect a man if he's got a good
alibi ? '

' No, but hang it all, there's the motive here as
plain as a pikestaff. I gather he wasn't particularly
fond of his cousin in any case. And he was the
residuary legatee ; he walks into the fifty thousand
if his cousin is proved dead. On the other hand, it
was necessary to do something pretty quick ; because by September Derek is due to be twenty-
five, and then the money all goes to the Jews.
On the principle that motive is the first thing to go
for, Mr. Nigel Burtell is the first man to come under

suspicion. And his alibi has got to be pretty good wearing material. Though, as I say, it's no business of mine.'

'What you mean is, you think Nigel Burtell slipped round to the wooded part of the island, waylaid his cousin, and murdered him just at the bridge; then he scuttled the canoe—why? Perhaps he thought it would sink, and so hide the traces. Then he ran back to the station and got there just in time for the train.'

'If so, the young gentleman is probably suffering from a cold. Half an hour's journey in a railway carriage, when you are dripping wet in all your clothes, is trying to the strongest constitution. You seem to forget that he's got to swim the weir stream.'

'But he could take off his clothes to do that.'

'And travel as a third-class faun? No, don't say that men have swum rivers with their clothes balanced on their heads. I don't deny that men have done it, but I'm quite sure Nigel Burtell never did. It's a matter of practice. No, let us amend your proposition by suggesting that he crossed the weir by the bridge, ran up along the further bank of the weir-stream, stripped, swam across, ran through the wood, and so caught and murdered his cousin as he came past. That would explain why the marks on the bridge were the marks of naked feet.'

'That isn't giving him very much time to do it in.'

'Exactly. It isn't the running that is so apt to take up time; it's the killing. A really tidy murder

can seldom be arranged in the fraction of a second.
Besides, what made him want to hop up on to a
bridge ?   The sides are open, so he wasn't hidden.
Of course, if there were a body forthcoming, we
might know more about the cause of death, and
we might be able to see the point of the bridge.   At
present I can't.   But the time !   It meant cutting
the thing beastly close.   It would be all right,
perhaps, either to kill your man or to scuttle your
boat, but could there be time for both ? '

' Miles, I expect you'll think me a most appalling
fool, but I've got an idea.'

' I know what it is.'

' I bet you don't.'

' Tell me.'

' Then you'd say you knew it was that.   *You*
tell *me*.'

' Then you'd say that was your idea.'

' Write it down, then.'

' We both will.'   Miles scribbled a sentence on
the back of an envelope, and Angela on a tiny
memorandum sheet.   Then the documents were
exchanged.

' Yes,' said Miles, ' I don't think you'd better
take to crime.   I can read you like a book, can't I ?
You know, your idea's quite an ingenious one, and I
dare say I didn't think of it more than half an hour
before you did.   But it won't do—you see that,
don't you ? '

Angela seemed a little hurt.   ' You mean, who
pushed off from the lock ? '

' No, that might just be managed.   But the
distance—how is a wind, short of a hurricane,

going to blow a canoe a hundred yards downstream in ten minutes ?   That's where it doesn't work.'

'I suppose not.   Blow, it was rather a clever idea.   Still, you'd got it too.   I suppose you're not going to release any theories, then ?   I know that mulish face of yours when you want to look sphinx-like.'

'I wasn't aware that I had any expression of the kind.'

'Oh, but you have, dearest, it's quite notorious. Only this afternoon, when you were paying for the tea, Mr. Burgess said to me, "Why does he look so sphinx-like, standing among the pinks, like ? " Anyhow, you don't mean to part with your own ideas, do you ? '

'Not till I've got some.   To-morrow, you see, if you're feeling very kind, you are going into Oxford to get that reel of films developed.   If you get them done quick, and stand over the man to see that he does it, I suppose you ought to be able to produce some unfixed prints by the afternoon, oughtn't you ?   Meanwhile, I shall have been conducting a few experiments.'

'What sort of experiments ? '

'Oh, just in drowning myself.'

'Well, don't be too successful about it.   Or if you are, do get found all right ; it would be a great bore not to know whether one was a widow or not.'

'You never know.   I might get carried down into the paper mill, and come out at the other end in folio lengths.   It would be very annoying to have the account of one's own death printed on one, wouldn't it ?   Meanwhile, what do you say to a

little bézique before we retire ourselves ? I wish
you'd let me bring the real cards with me, so that
I could have started a patience.'

. . . . .

It was, as a matter of fact, scarcely luncheon-
time next day when Angela returned, full of mystery. According to a long-standing compact,
they tossed up as to which should make a report
first ; and the lot fell upon Bredon. ' Well,' he
said, ' I've spent my morning in a way very uncommon among English gentlemen. Largely, I
may say, in a bathing suit.'

' Better than nothing,' commented Angela.
' Start from the beginning.'

' I took the canoe down to the lock just below
here, because that's where they've got the Burtell
canoe—it's lying careened on the bank. Of course
I wanted the man to let me take it away with me
and have all sorts of fun with it, but it appeared to
be more than his place was worth. I did, however,
by means of a bet, manage to find out what I wanted
to know—which was, how long it would take the
canoe to fill with a hole that size in its bottom.'

' You mean he let you sink it ? '

' No, but we put it in together and let it sink with
a rope round each thwart to haul it out again
with. I took care to lose my bet, of course. Meanwhile I found out exactly how long it would take to
fill. I also noticed how long it would take to get
one inch of water in, and so on. Then I went
off and did the Archimedes touch.'

' Who's he ? '

' Surely you have not forgotten Archimedes in

the Latin grammar, who was so intent on watching the way his bath was overflowing that he did not even notice his country had been captured? I retired to a position where I could undress with decency, got into the canoe in my gent's University bathing suit, and drifted downstream, baling for dear life. Only I was baling in, not out, if you understand me.'

' But how did you know how much to bale? '

' It was only approximate, of course. But I calculated the time fairly easily by knowing how soon the first inch of water ought to get inside. I don't know if I ever told you that at school they thought me rather a dab at mathematics.'

' You whispered it in my ear, darling, when we sat making love on the promenade at Southend. But what did all this tell you? '

' Why, approximately how far a canoe would drift, with wind and stream in its favour, when it was sinking at a given rate. It didn't get very far. Incidentally, I fell out after a bit, which was what I expected. One's balance is never perfect. However, I swam to shore all right, and dressed. Then I paddled up here, got hold of another canoe, and repeated the same experiment, leaving our canoe to float down empty and baling into it as we went. That showed me how far a canoe would float before it filled when there was no heavy body in it.'

' I still don't see exactly what use it all was. You don't pretend to be able to say exactly how far the Burtells' canoe was paddled down from the lock, and how much it drifted? Or how far it drifted before it got the hole made in it? '

' No, but you can get negative results which are rather important. I tested also, of course, the rate at which a waterlogged canoe floats down-stream, getting no help from the wind. And there-fore I'm in a position to say that the accident, or whatever it was, can't possibly have happened higher up the stream than a certain roughly-calcu-lated point—if it had, the canoe wouldn't have had time to drift down to the place at which it was found. It couldn't conceivably, for example, have drifted all the way down from the bridge over the lock-stream in the time given, with that hole in it. Body or no body.'

' In fact, whatever else happened at the iron bridge, it wasn't there that the boat was scuttled ? I see you're trying to exculpate Mr. Nigel Burtell.'

' I'm not trying to prove anything. But my experiments do seem to suggest that he can't have had a hand in it.'

' That's a tiny bit disappointing. Because, you see, *my* experiments do very much suggest that Mr. Nigel Burtell had a hand in it.'

CHAPTER VII

THE CAMERA CANNOT LIE

ANGELA brought out six prints. She laid them before her husband one by one, tantalizing his curiosity by insisting that he should have a good look at each as it came.

The first print represented a board with the title 'Church Notices'; and underneath this title appeared a lurid poster of a cinema performance, combining a maximum of thrill with a minimum of clothing. It was obvious that the finger of the humorist had been at work; that two photographs had been taken on the same film.

The second was a close-up view of a particularly distressing gargoyle, probably attached to the same Church porch.

The third represented a group of cows, knee-deep in the river, regarding the camera with that patient curiosity which cows register at the sight of any human activity.

The fourth, also taken from the river, showed a thin promontory of land, overgrown with a wealth of garden flowers; in the centre of these stood the figure of a stalwart gardener, from the waist downwards.

The fifth, taken at an irregular angle which played havoc with the perspective, looked down a flight of apparently stone steps, on each of which a footprint was discernible, though only those half-way down were sufficiently in focus to be clearly distinguished. The camera itself had obviously been held on a tilt, as if a very inexpert performer had manipulated it. At the sight of this Bredon whistled sharply.

The sixth was a view of the river, taken from a bridge ; this was sufficiently indicated by the appearance of what looked like an iron girder, much out of focus, at the bottom of the picture. In the centre, fully focussed, floated a canoe, which seemed to be nearly parallel to the bridge, nearly broadside on to the flow of the river. The water was slightly rippled, and a paddle, lying across the centre of the boat, made no clear reflection. The figure of a man lay sprawling at full length on the floor of the canoe, the knees just under the front thwart ; the head was turned sideways, and was propped up by a rest and a cushion. The whole attitude suggested a complete abandonment of repose ; something about the bend of the neck, something about the way in which the left arm lay crushed under the body, suggested that it was not the attitude in which a man would naturally have fallen asleep. A hat shaded most of the face, but revealed a clean-shaven chin. The back seat of the boat was empty ; the other paddle leaned carelessly against it.

' Is he d-dead ? ' asked Angela, her hand on her husband's shoulder.

' Dead, or dead drunk, or drugged, perhaps. I think the person who took this picture meant us to think he was dead, anyhow. He's not a very pretty sight, you see, in any case. On the face of it, I must say it looks as if somebody had—well, had finished him off and then taken a photograph of him.'

'But that's rather horrible. It seems so disgustingly cold-blooded.'

'It needn't have been the murderer, of course. It might have been somebody who found him lying dead—apparently dead—and thought it important to have a snapshot of him looking like that. Anyhow, the man who took that photograph is the man we want to get hold of. He must be able to give us news of Derek Burtell which is later than the lock-keeper's.'

'You're certain it was taken at the lock-stream bridge ? Oh yes, of course, the footprint-photograph shows that.'

'Even if it didn't, there could hardly be any doubt. You haven't looked attentively enough at Number Four, or you'd have recognized an old friend.'

'Oo, is that Mr. Burgess ? '

'There's no doubt about the lock and the island. There can't be two locks arranged like that. Now, you say this throws suspicion on Nigel Burtell. Let's hear how you'd work it out.'

'Dash it all, it makes him out such a perfect brute. But you say he is one. Let's assume that his alibi is all wrong ; that he didn't really take the train to Oxford at all, but went there by a fast motor—if he ever did go to Oxford. No, that won't do ; he couldn't get to the motor soon enough.

Let's say that he didn't go to Oxford at all, for the sake of argument. That gives him all the time there is. He waits till Mr. Burgess' back is turned, which doesn't seem to be a very difficult thing to do ; then he slinks down along the island, through the woods, and lies in wait for the canoe. Let's say that his cousin is under the influence of a drug ; that seems probable enough. He leaves his camera on the bridge, then goes down a little lower, takes off his clothes, and puts them there all ready. He comes up above the bridge again, swims out to the canoe as it floats by, and—then I suppose he does something horrible, stabs his cousin with a hat-pin or something. He swims to the bridge, ahead of the canoe, climbs up the framework of the bridge, and takes his photograph from there. Then he runs down the steps, all wet, and swims out to the canoe again ; brings it in to the bank, and puts on his clothes. Then he sits down in the stern of the canoe, as if nothing had happened, and paddles it down a good long distance. He ties a weight to the body, digs a hole in the bottom of the canoe, gets out and makes tracks for the high road, or perhaps for Wheathampton Station. It doesn't seem to work out awfully well.'

'What an imagination you've got ! But there's one point, don't you see, where you must be wrong. He took a photograph of the footprints *before* he took a photograph of the body in the canoe. Therefore the footprints were made before he climbed up on to the bridge, not after he went down.'

'Blow, I'd forgotten that. But then how do

you account for the footsteps going down, not coming up ? '

' He walked up the stairs backwards. You can see that, if you look at the photograph carefully. The marks are the marks of heels. You don't walk downstairs on your heels, you walk on your toes and the flat part of the soles. These marks show that he walked up backwards.'

' But why backwards ? '

' Possibly just to create confusion. More probably because the prints of his toes might, in the millionth chance, have given him away. If he'd a hammer toe, for example, that would show up quite clearly. I dare say Messrs. Wickstead would be able to provide us with a very nice sketch of Mr. Nigel Burtell's foot. But heels are so much alike, you can't put in any Bertillon-work on them.'

' Yes, I suppose that's true.'

' But there's another thing. Nigel, if it was Nigel, hadn't been in the water when he climbed that bridge.'

' I don't see how you make that out.'

' Why, if one's been in the water one drips. A few drops would have been bound to fall on the steps, and then they would have been reproduced in the photograph. Since there are no marks except the footprints, it's clear that the prints were made by somebody who had nothing on, or anyhow nothing on his feet, who had not yet been into the water.'

' Why were his feet wet, then ? '

' Because he'd been walking in the long grass, which was still wet from the night's rain. I imagine it had been raining in the night.'

'Why should it have been?'

'Because, if you will look carefully at Exhibit Four, you will see a puddle.'

'Golly, what a man!'

'I suppose, then, that Nigel, if it was Nigel, did leave his clothes a little below the bridge. He walked through the wet grass, and, realizing that his wet feet would leave prints, which might conceivably be examined by some passer-by, went up the steps backwards.'

'But I still don't see what he wanted to photograph the footprints for.'

'I've no reason to think that he did *want* to. All we know is that he did. I don't know if you often go upstairs backwards, but if you have the habit, you will realize that it's apt to make your stance a little uncertain. And if you are carrying a camera at the time, it is quite possible for some slight lurch to make you pull the trigger by mistake. Then, realizing that you've pulled the trigger, or fearing that you have, you pass on from Number Five to Number Six. Number Five doesn't look to me like a photograph taken on purpose. It's all skew-eyed, you see.

'I see. Then he photographed his man first, and murdered him afterwards?'

'I don't know that he murdered him at all, in the way you mean. I think, after he'd taken the photograph, he let himself down by the framework of the bridge, put the camera on board, and pushed the canoe gently in to the bank, where his clothes were. Then he dressed again, sat down in the stern, and paddled on. I don't think he dug a hole in the

canoe and left the man in it to drown.   I think he
drowned his man first, tying a weight on him, I
suppose, or getting him under a bank somewhere,
and *then* scuttled the canoe.   If you look carefully,
you can see that the hole in the canoe was made
from the outside, not from the inside.   It's bigger
on the outside, on the inside it's quite small, not
the size of a threepenny bit.   He must have hauled
the bows of the canoe out of water to do that, and
it would be easier to do it when the canoe was empty.
Besides, I take it he didn't want to run any risks
of a rescue.   He saw to it, while he was about it,
that his man drowned all right.'

　　' And you do really think it was Nigel Burtell ? '
　　' I do and I don't.   He's got a perfect alibi, as
far as we know.   Yet he stood to gain by the whole
thing, because the money was coming to him.   I
love my Nigel with an N, because he was needy.   I
hate him with an N, because he was nowhere near.
I don't see what to make of it.   The old lady at
Spinnaker Farm told me that a gentleman came
through that morning in a tearing hurry, wanting to
catch a train.   I suppose that must have been the
nine-fourteen.   I supposed therefore that the gentleman must have been Nigel.   What was he doing at
Spinnaker Farm, if he had really come from the
weir bridge ?   On the other hand, how on earth
had he the time to do all the things we want him
to have done ?   All this is very perplexing, and
I think I am going to have an interview with
Nigel.'

　　' I thought you said that was impossible.'
　　' Not now, because I've got an introduction.   I

am going to take back his films, which I found
lying about in the fields by the river.'

'And ask him for an explanation of Numbers
Five and Six ?   Miles, dear, that's much more direct
than your methods generally are.'

'Why, no.   On the spool I shall give him, Numbers Five and Six will have got fogged somehow.
Sort of thing that's always happening.'

'But they aren't fogged.'

'Never mind ; what man has done man can do.
Or woman, anyhow.   Your camera takes the same
size of film as those, doesn't it ?   Very well then,
you and I are going to take the car over to Lechlade.   Or possibly Cricklade.'

The porch at Lechlade was clearly the porch they
wanted ; it was a matter of more research to find the
identical cinema poster, but fortunately it remained
unchanged.   'We needn't worry to fake the thing
too carefully,' observed Bredon, 'it will be easy to
make him believe that he made a mistake.'   The
whole expedition only occupied some forty minutes ;
before the hour was up, they were on the river
again, looking out for the sight, not uncommon
on such a hot afternoon, of cows standing about in
shallow water.   For the sake of appearances, they
paddled up a little beyond Shipcote Lock, returning
there for tea.   It was hardly to be expected that
Mr. Burgess would be posing again for his portrait,
and it was necessary for Bredon to understudy
the part.   Numbers Five and Six on the new film
were exposed with the camera tilted up in the air,
and the fake reel was complete.   Angela had made
some photographic purchases in Lechlade, and the

films were developed, successfully enough, the same evening.

'They've all come out splendidly,' she announced, as she returned, wiping her hands, from the impro-vised dark-room. 'There's one thing, though. If it wasn't Nigel who took those photographs, won't he be a bit surprised at your assuming that it was? And if it was Nigel who took them, won't you rather put him on his guard by letting on where it was you found them?'

'I don't think we need worry very much over that. You see, I shall explain that I found them by accident, and had to develop them in order to get any sort of idea who they belonged to. Nigel may deny all knowledge of them, but he must admit that it was a reasonable guess of mine to suppose they were his, since he was known to have been up the river as far as Lechlade. And of course I shall have to practise a certain economy of truth in explaining where I found them. I shall have to say that I found them lying in a hedge somewhere near Shipcote Station. That won't tell him which path they were found on; and if I put on a suffi-ciently stupid air, he won't suspect that I suspect anything. But I ought to be able to get a little out of him, I think. Archimedes to-day, Machia-velli to-morrow.'

CHAPTER VIII

A COMMON-ROOM DINNER

BY the next afternoon the prints were dry
and ready for inspection. Bredon, however,
delayed his visit to Oxford until after tea-
time, to be more certain of finding his man in. He
was punished for his delay; a prolonged block
detained him at Carfax, and during its inch-by-inch
progress he was briskly hailed from the pavement
by Uncle Robert. All families keep an uncle or an
aunt in Oxford; most families slink about Oxford
with guilty consciences when they pay it a visit,
because the Uncle or Aunt has not been informed.
Uncle Robert's ' What on earth brought *you* down
here?' was distinctly tactless; Bredon had no
desire to advertise his mission. In the end, he only
got away by promising to dine with Uncle Robert
in Salisbury Common-room that evening, after a
warning telegram to Angela.

Nigel's digs were in that state of chaos which
can only be achieved when rooms are being dis-
mantled and re-furnished simultaneously. All Oxford lodging-house-keepers cling to the illusion
that they can let their rooms to undergraduates
' furnished '; generations of undergraduates come
in, and tactfully extrude the unwelcome ornaments.
It need hardly be said that Nigel had made a

particularly clean sweep of all the ' things ' which his landlady had expected him to harbour. Now, Nigel's darling monstrosities had been swept from the walls, Nigel's French novels lay in piles about the floor, Nigel's mauve curtains were folded, never again to look out from those windows ; meanwhile the tide of redecoration was already beginning to flow in ; ' The Soul's Awakening ' and ' The Monarch of the Glen ' stood ready to resume their immemorial places, and in that wilderness the aspidistra prepared to flourish anew. The outgoing tenant had a slight air of Marius sitting on the ruins of Carthage, and Bredon hastened to apologize for the untimeliness of his interruption.

' Not at all,' was the answer. ' Life would be unlivable but for the interruptions. You'll have some absinthe, of course ? '

' No, really, thanks. It's very kind of you. I only looked in about a reel of films which I found the day before yesterday, near the river. I'd no idea, of course, who they belonged to, so I had them developed. It was easy to see the photographs had been taken by somebody who had just been up the river ; and of course . . . the papers . . . one knew you had been up that way, and I thought perhaps it might have been you who'd dropped them. I was coming in to Oxford anyhow, so I thought I'd look in on the chance.'

There was a perceptible hesitation in the other's manner, but nothing of fear, it seemed—hardly even of embarrassment. ' Most awfully good of you. It's a bore losing one's films, isn't it ? They're one's children, in a way—or rather, of course, they're

Apollo's really. So irrevocable. They record moments, and moments are always irrevocable.'

Miles repressed a strong tendency to scream.
But he did not want to hasten over the interview;
he must, if possible, get a good look at this young
man, but the light was bad, and it was difficult to
make sure of his face. 'I suppose it was a bit of a
liberty,' he said, 'developing them; but what
else was I to do? I'm afraid the last two haven't
come out very well.'

The other still hesitated for a moment; but it was
difficult to know whether he was wondering how
much the other knew, or merely collecting himself
for fresh epigrams. 'I can't remember what they
were,' he said at last. 'Did they convey anything to
you—some wraith of meaning?'

'I'm afraid they were hopelessly fogged.'

'Ah, yes; Apollo turned infanticide once more.
The God of light, but he strikes with blindness. I
do hope the cows came out? I meant to enlarge
that one, and give it to my landlady, if possible with
a quotation from Wordsworth underneath.'

Bredon had by now taken the parcel from his
pocket and unwrapped it. 'Yes, yes,' went on
Nigel, 'the church at Lechlade! A fantasy, you
know; an idea of poor Derek's—he was fond of
faked photographs. And that gargoyle—I took
that because it's the precise image of our Dean.
I only wished it had been a rainy day. The cows,
as I say, were for the landlady; they are in my
simpler manner. But the lock—that is my *chef
d'oeuvre*! A lock-keeper really keeping his lock,
really defending it; "You shall come through,"

he seems to say, " only by playing leapfrog over my
living body ". It's a souvenir, too, because it was
at that lock I had to take leave of my cousin. Did
you ever notice how annoying it is to have to talk
regretfully about a person you quite particularly
disliked ? '

' Those last two are very badly fogged, you know,'
said Bredon, refusing the invitation to digress.
' It looks to me as if there was something wrong
with your shutter. You wouldn't like me to
have a look at it, I suppose ? I know something
about cameras.'

For the first time in the interview, Nigel seemed
really taken off his guard. ' What ? . . . The
camera ? . . . Oh, well, it's packed. In fact, I
believe it's sent off. It's extremely kind of you—
but of course, you are a sort of foster-father to these
picture-children of mine. You must really keep the
copies you have taken ; I can have some others
printed. I wish you would have had some absinthe.
By the way,' he continued abruptly, ' where was it
exactly that you picked up the film ? In a hedge,
you said ? '

' You remind me, I must apologize for forgetting
something ; I found it wrapped in a waterproof
tobacco-pouch, which presumably belongs to you
too. Here it is. Yes, I was joining my wife, you
know, on a river trip, and she had gone on ahead
—she was to pick me up at Shipcote Lock. So
I went to Shipcote Station, and took the field path
to the weir. You may remember, perhaps, that
there is a point at which two paths join, one leading
to the weir and the other to a farm. It was just

at the junction I found the thing, lying half hidden in the grass. I had read in the papers, of course, that you took the train at Shipcote Station after you had left your cousin. So naturally it occurred to me that the films might be yours.'

' That would be it, to be sure. I was a little hurried, you know, at the end of my walk to the station. The train was there, standing in the station, and one always assumes that a train like that is just about to move—why, I don't know, for it is contrary to all one's experience of country trains. Anyhow, I ran, and the films must have been jolted out of my pocket. It is pathetic to think of them in the hedgerow, stretching out their orphaned hands to an unnatural father. And with all those undeveloped possibilities about them ! It affects me deeply.'

' Funny the way things do disappear and don't. It's more than two days now, isn't it, since you first missed your cousin, and nothing's been heard of him alive or dead. You'll excuse a stranger's impertinence, I hope, but I should be tremendously interested to know if you yourself have any guess what has happened. One's always hearing the thing talked of, don't you know, and it seems so silly to be able to say I've met you, without being able to say what you thought about it all.'

' Oh, personally I think he committed suicide. There wasn't much else to do, you know ; he was a hopeless crock, and he couldn't get on without the dope.'

' But the hole in the bottom of the boat . . .'

' Ah, there I'm afraid you trespass on family

history. I don't think he wanted it to be known
that he'd committed suicide, because there's some
property I should fall heir to if he died. He hadn't
much imagination, Derek, but he hated me with a
hatred that was almost artistic. He wanted everybody to think that he had just disappeared. And
in his vague, stupid way he thought the canoe had
better disappear too. So he dug a hole in the bottom
of it, expecting that it would sink.'

'That's a very interesting idea. Very interesting.
But I really oughtn't to be keeping you from your
packing any longer. I suppose you'll be off to-
morrow ? '

'Unless they find anything, and there's an inquest. My last term, you know. Poor Oxford ! '

'May I have the envelope back with the prints ?
I've nothing else to take them in. It's very kind
of you to let me keep them as a memento of my
little rencontre. No, please don't come down. I
shall find my way out all right. Good evening.'
And, as the door closed behind him, Bredon added,
' If Providence ever turned out such another ghastly
little worm as you, I should begin to doubt whether
there was a Providence '. However, he had the
picture of Nigel's appearance, and the imprint, if he
wanted it, of Nigel's thumb, so that the afternoon's
work had not been wasted. His evening, too, for all
the hasty anathemas he pronounced against Uncle
Robert, was destined to be not entirely uneventful.

A Common-room dinner is an experience which
strikes a chill into the heart of the bravest, when it
comes to him for the first time. True, it has not
all the horrors of High Table ; he has not to endure

the fancied scrutiny of an undergraduate perspective. But in Common-room the academic atmosphere is all the more pervasive for being concentrated at such close quarters. Who is this man next to you, to whom you have not been introduced ? Is he a mere guest like yourself, or is he a Fellow ? In the latter case, presumably, there is some subject on which he is a European authority, if only you could find out what it was. Are the frigid advances occasionally made to you an attempt at welcome ? And if so, can you gauge from their frequency or heartiness the local popularity of your host ? Uncle Robert was a supernumerary member of the Common-room, and a bore at that. His guests were usually men of his own kidney, and there was a general tendency to glare at them without speaking. Bredon felt, in an expressive modern phrase, like something the cat had brought in.

The conversation turned, at first, on greyhound-racing, a subject which the company treated with a broad-mindedness that sprang from inexperience. One very old gentleman had to be convinced, with great difficulty, that it was the hare, not the hounds, which worked by electricity ; he was positive of the contrary—it was notorious. The shaded lights cast a decorous radiance ; portraits of old Fellows looked down quizzically from their frames, as if enjoying a joke at the expense of their successors ; scouts whispered at your elbow in accents which suggested the attempt to achieve efficiency without servility. Exquisite pieces of silver reflected your neighbour's face at a hundred ridiculous angles. The wine saved the situation ; the wine was good.

'Did it ever strike you,' an old gentleman was saying just opposite, in a loud, well-modulated voice that sounded as if it had been designed to control traffic,—'did it ever strike you, Filmore, what a very singular thing it is that dogs should bark when they are in pursuit of their prey? Very much as if Nature intended that they should be given warning of their enemy's approach. Doesn't work, you know, from the evolution point of view; in a Darwinian world the dog which barks lowest ought to catch the most rabbits, and so the bark ought to disappear, don't you see? There was a man reading a very interesting paper about that at one of these congresses the other day; and he said, you know, he thought the bark of the dog was intended to drown the squealing of the rabbit, so that the other rabbits shouldn't know anything disastrous was happening. A most singular idea.'

'Is he a scientist?' asked Bredon in a low voice.

'No. Ancient history,' returned his Uncle. 'Man called Carmichael. Always full of odd ideas. Never stops talking.'

The man next Bredon on the other side was now heard to say, in answer to some question, 'Yes, Magus men, both of them. The younger one only just going down. Good riddance'. Bredon had the instinct we all sometimes have, that the subject of the conversation would interest him. He stole a look at his neighbour, and suddenly realized why there had been something reminiscent about his appearance. There was only a touch of the Lechlade gargoyle about his face, but it was perfectly unmistakable. This, then, must be the

Dean of Simon Magus, and his topic, obviously, the Burtell cousins.

' Suicide, I suppose ? ' asked a voice from beyond him.

' I don't think so. Burtell hadn't enough instinct of tidiness to finish up in that way. No, I think it was a genuine accident, but of course there are any amount of possibilities. Loss of memory, for example—they say he drugged, and I should think it's possible to bring on loss of memory in that way. He may be anywhere by now ; and I don't think it's for the College to put on detectives to find him.'

' Talking of detectives,' broke in Mr. Carmichael from the other side of the table, ' I had a very curious experience myself once in connexion with a murder case.' (As this story has already been told at greater length, even, than Mr. Carmichael used in telling it, I will not even give an abstract of it here.) ' Which just shows ', he concluded, ' how one's judgments are apt to go astray. If it wasn't for that warning, I should be inclined to say that there is no difficulty in solving this Burtell business, no difficulty at all.'

' Oh, good, Carmichael,' chuckled a junior fellow. ' This is in your best form. Tell us all about it.'

' I was wrong. I should have said, it is very easy to see why the Thames watermen have failed to recover the body. Whether the young man is the victim of accident, murder, suicide, or disappearance I don't know at all. But it's quite easy to see why the body hasn't been found. They are looking in the wrong place for it.'

' Oh, come on ; where ought they to be looking ? '

'Above Shipcote Lock, not below it. They must have found the body by now, if there was a body to find. Yet, if the young fellow had been wandering about between Shipcote and Eaton Bridge, somebody must have come across him. I say, then, his disappearance, whatever its cause, must have taken place above, not below the lock.'

Bredon broke in in spite of himself. 'But the elder Burtell was in the canoe when it left the lock. The lock-keeper saw him.'

'I saw the lock-keeper. I make a hobby of these things, you know. I asked the lock-keeper, "Could you take your oath in a court of law that the gentleman in the canoe *moved*?" And of course he couldn't. All he saw was the figure of a man, with the hat well drawn down over the face. Very well, then, the figure in the boat was a dummy. Consider, the hole in the canoe shows that the boat was intended to sink, or at least to overbalance, and discharge its load. Why? If there was a dead body in the boat, why not let it be dragged up? Unless of course it was the wrong body, but I dismiss that suggestion as too fantastic. The face, the hands, would no doubt be made of soap. What the clothes were made of I don't know. But it must have been a dummy. Otherwise there was no motive for letting it sink.'

Bredon excused himself early on the ground that the lights of his car were deficient. 'No,' he said to himself as he settled down at the wheel, 'Mr. Carmichael has still something to learn about the possibilities of life. But I like his negative criticism. Why did they want the boat to sink, after all?'

CHAPTER IX

NIGEL GOES DOWN

ANGELA came down to breakfast to find her husband bending over a map, on which he seemed to be underlining in pencil various inns or villages along the river, and measuring the distances between them with a halfpenny.

'It's a good game,' she said, 'but rather early in the morning for it.'

'What game?'

'Thought you might be playing shove-halfpenny. What are you at, anyhow?'

'It may be news to you that a halfpenny is an inch in diameter.'

'Thank you. Don't tell me how many thruppenny bits will go on a half-crown, or I shall scream. Yes, I knew you were measuring distances. Some womanly intuition told me so. But what's the idea, particularly?'

'I thought we'd take the motor out to-day, and try some of these places along the river to see where it was the Burtell cousins stopped on their trip. We might be able to collect some reminiscences of them—whether, for example, there was a third person with them at any stage of their journey. You know, I'm beginning to want a third person badly.'

'Are you going to have beer at all these pubs ? It looks to me as if I should have to drive home.'

'Heaven help the woman, she talks as if you could go into a pub and order beer at any hour of the day you like. No, we've got to think up some reason for visiting these places and asking questions. What shall it be ? '

'Give your name as Carmichael, and say you want to look in the bath-room to see if any of the soap's missing.'

'Don't rag. This is the sort of lie you are generally rather good at thinking up.'

'Don't flatter, and don't put the corner of the map in the marmalade. You could, of course, arm yourself with a set of cheap railway-guides or something of that sort, and pretend to be travelling them—ask them to put one in the commercial room. But you wouldn't get much out of them that way. No, I think you'll have to tell a little of the truth, Miles dear. I think we must pretend that the Burtells left something behind—say a camera ; we know they had a camera with them. In decency they'll have to let us go up into the bedroom and look round for it. Or in the coffee-room, at places where they stopped for luncheon. You'll have to be just a friend of Nigel Burtell's, and you happen to be motoring in this part of the country. You're not *quite* certain which pubs they stopped at, because Nigel Burtell couldn't remember all the names himself. Wouldn't something like that do ? Of course you can have a drink as well, when it isn't closing-time.'

This, eventually, was the plan of campaign

adopted. It would be tedious to record their
researches in detail. Bredon had argued out their
probable stages with some accuracy, assuming, with
justice, that on the morning of Derek's disappearance
they had come from the nearest inn above Shipcote, that at Millington Bridge. Everywhere the
impressions left behind them were those of an
ordinary pleasure tour ; nothing remarkable was
recorded about their behaviour. The only excep-
tion was at Millington Bridge itself, at which they
had arrived late after a long day on the river,
about ten o'clock, and had not wanted an evening
meal.

'Very late they was, and it was your speaking
of the camera put me in mind of it ; because the
first gentleman came up and he said have you got
two rooms, and I said yes, but you're late, you
know, we don't ordinarily take in people so late ;
where's the other gentleman. Oh, he says, he
left his camera behind in the canoe, and he's gone
back to fetch it, in case it should rain in the night.
And rain it did, too, regular downpour. I'll go up
to my room, he says, for I'm dog-tired, and the
other gentleman won't be more than ten minutes
or so. It wasn't hardly that, not hardly five
minutes, before I heard the second knock, and as
soon as I saw some one with a camera standing
outside, Oh, I says, you're the other gentleman ;
you'll be in Number Three. So Lizzy showed him
the way upstairs, and that's the room the camera
should have been in if it had been left behind.
Let's see, that was the gentleman that had his
breakfast in bed ; left it on a tray on the mat,

I did. Number Two came down to breakfast, and it was him as paid the bill ; I see him go off myself, but whether he had the camera with him or no I couldn't really say. The other gentleman must have gone on earlier, for I never saw him go off, and of course it would be more likely he took the camera with him. I did both the rooms myself, after they'd gone, and it isn't likely I should have failed to overlook anything, is it ? '

Bredon, who was alert for any indication, suggested afterwards that it sounded as if the two cousins might have quarrelled, since they neither reached nor left the inn together ; but he agreed with Angela that this was very little result to derive from their morning's inquiries. ' It's all very well,' he said, ' but we must do something. If the fellow's still alive, he's stealing a march on us all the time, and may be God knows where by now. Besides, one of the papers has been suggesting to its readers that they should all take their holiday on the Thames, and lend a hand with searching ; they'll be all over the place by to-morrow.'

It was at about six that evening, when they were sitting out on the lawn by the river, that a visitor was announced for Bredon. He had scarcely had time to rise from his chair when the visitor followed in person.

' Leyland ! ' cried Bredon. ' Are the police beginning to take the thing seriously, then ? '

' Yes, too late, as usual. How are you, Mrs. Bredon ? And, as usual the county police didn't call in Scotland Yard until they had made an utter mess of the thing themselves. Let your man get away, give him four hours start, and then call in the Yard—that's the way it's done.'

' Let what man get away ? '

' Why, this Burtell.'

' Which Burtell ?   Nigel ? '

' That's the one.'

' Nigel Burtell ?   But I saw him yesterday.'

' It would have been a good deal more interesting to me if you'd seen him to-day.   Did he say any-thing yesterday about leaving Oxford ? '

' He said he'd probably be going down.   But that's all right, he'd been packing up for some time. I suppose he'd got a home address where you could get at him ? '

' Lost Luggage Office, Paddington, that's all the address he's got.   At least, that's where his trunks have gone to.   But where *he* is, God knows ;   he may be in Weymouth by now, or Bath, or Bristol, or Newport, or Cardiff, or Swansea ;   he's gone, anyhow.'

' Disappeared too, by Gad,' said Bredon.

' These things do run in families,' suggested Angela helpfully.   ' In *our* family, we're always appearing when we're not wanted to, witness Uncle Robert.   What makes you so certain, Mr. Leyland, that the young man is seeing his own country first ? '

' We can stop him if he tries the mail-boat to Rosslare.   But I don't suppose he has.   South Wales is a wonderful place for disappearing—a network of towns, and all the trains crowded, and the local police spending their whole time looking out for labour troubles.   Anyhow, it's too late now to do anything but go back on his tracks a bit.'

'You seem to have hunted *us* down pretty successfully,' said Angela. 'Who told you we were
here ?   I thought we were most frightfully incognito.
Unless Uncle Robert gave us away, of course.'

'Well, you see, I'd been studying up this case
a bit beforehand.   I knew it would come to us in
the long run.   And in hunting out the *dossier* of
the Burtell family, it didn't take long before I came
across the Indescribable.   So I knew Bredon would
be on the case, and would have got two or three
days' start of me—these lucky devils of amateurs
always do.   So I thought I'd come straight here
and find out if he'd any tips for an old comrade-
in-arms.'

'As a matter of fact,' said Bredon, 'you're
welcome to any information I've got.   I suppose
I know as much about this job as anybody.   But
the curse of the thing is, I know too much ; I know
enough to make it a sight more complicated than
it looks.   You want to get on the trail of Nigel
Burtell.   Well, all I can tell you is that as far as
I can see Nigel Burtell had no hand in his cousin's
disappearance.   He wasn't there ; he simply wasn't
on the map.'

'How do you make that out ? '

'Why, somebody paddled the canoe downstream,
or towed it, or got it downstream somehow, over
a mile before it was scuttled.   If somebody hadn't,
the canoe could never have got down as far as it
did—even assuming that it would drift straight,
which most canoes don't ; they nose into the bank
and out again.   Getting the canoe that far downstream would take at least a quarter of an hour.

And by a quarter of an hour after the canoe left the lock, Nigel Burtell was at Shipcote Station, or close to it. Therefore it was not Nigel who brought the canoe downstream. If it wasn't Nigel, it must either have been his cousin—and in that case Nigel was not a murderer; or else it was some third person; and if so, that third person, not Nigel, is responsible, somehow, for Derek Burtell's disappearance. Do you get me?'

'I get you. But that depends on the alibi being good. Have you found out whether the train was up to time? And whether Nigel Burtell really caught it? He's a bit slippy, you know, with trains. That's how he got off to-day.'

'Yes, by the way, how was that?'

'Well, of course, the county police had just enough sense to keep him under observation. When he went to the station, one of their men followed him. He took a ticket to London, had his luggage labelled Paddington, all but a hand-bag he carried, and got into a coach on the fast train, twelve fifty-two. He put his bag down on the seat, and stood waiting about on the platform. The man who was watching him took a carriage just behind him —same corridor. Just as they were beginning to shut the doors, Burtell bought a paper and strolled into his compartment, as cool as you please. He must have walked straight up the corridor, forward, dodged out at the other end, and tucked himself away somewhere just as the train was starting. When the train had gone, he strolled through the barrier, bought a ticket to Swindon, picked up a second hand-bag which he'd left lying about, and

took the one five—Swindon and Weymouth train.
All that, of course, we only found out afterwards.
The man next door didn't notice his absence for a bit,
then had to search the whole train for him, finally
got off at Reading. By that time it was too late
to do anything. It wasn't a very bright trick, but
it was well carried out—played his part to the life.
Mayn't he have done something clever over that
journey from Shipcote ? '

'Well, you can test the alibi for yourself. I
couldn't go round interviewing porters and people.
It's a pretty one-horse sort of station, Shipcote, and
I dare say they'll remember as far back as Monday.
But it's dead certain he arrived here in a taxi that
morning before eleven o'clock. Where did he get
that taxi, if not at Oxford ? And how did he get
from Shipcote to Oxford, if not by train—the
nine-fourteen train ? I believe you'll be barking
up the wrong tree there.'

'But hang it all, look at the motive—a cool fifty
thousand ! And look at this sudden disappearance !
You can't *not* suspect Nigel Burtell.'

'I've been doing nothing else for the last week.
You don't know all the facts yet.' And Bredon
proceeded to outline the lock-keeper's disclosures,
while Angela went upstairs and fetched the photographs. 'Now,' he concluded, 'you'll see that I
had some ground for suspecting young Nigel. It
wasn't mere Scotland Yard officiousness. Who
could possibly be interested in having a photograph
of Derek Burtell's corpse, except the man who stood
to win a legacy by his death, *if that death could be
proved ?* '

' Yes, that sounds all right. . . . And, if you come to think of it, how could he be such a fool as to drop those films out of his pocket ? He must have valued them a good deal. Looks much more as if he'd planted them out in that hedge on purpose.'

' Yes, I thought of that too,' said Bredon. ' And so nicely packed away in a watertight cover. You mean, I suppose, he wanted some stranger to find those films by accident, and hand them over to the police, so that the police should have evidence of the death ? '

' That would have to be it. Though, mind you, it's pretty poor evidence of the death. And quite unnecessary evidence, if only the body had been found. Did Nigel Burtell not *expect* the body to be found ? Did he spirit it away somewhere ? And if so, why on earth should he ? '

' Yes, but we're going ahead too fast. We're speculating about Nigel's motives when, as far as we can see, it can't have been Nigel.'

' What about his alibi at the other end ? He arrived here at eleven, or thereabouts ; why shouldn't he have gone up river, brought off the murder, come back again, and sat down on this very lawn with his watch in his hand, wondering when dear Derek was going to turn up ? '

' I know, I know. But it would be pretty risky. Anybody *might* have come out on to the lawn, and noticed his absence. There were some men camping on the opposite bank, who might see him going away and remember seeing it. If he went along the tow-path, he had to pass a whole encampment

of boy scouts. Finally, I may remark that he
hadn't paid for his ginger-beer. I got that fact out
of the barmaid. And somehow, if you order your
drinks and don't pay for them, all inns have a
curious way of noticing it when you leave the
premises.'

' Still, it's worth looking into. Even if Nigel
Burtell had no motive, who else could it be ?   Who
else was there about, to come under suspicion ? '

' There were lots of other people about. The
folk at Spinnaker Farm, for example, and the lock-
keeper, Mr. Burgess, though he is not one of your
strong, silent men. He is a man of words rather
than action.'

' Yes, but what conceivable reason could casual
strangers like that have had for murdering one of
the Burtells ? '

' If you knew Nigel Burtell better, you'd know
that any stranger might easily be impelled to kill
him at sight. Still, the other one need not have
been so revolting. I admit the difficulty. But,
you know, it seems to me there is evidence that a
third party somehow comes into the case.'

' What evidence ? '

' Why, the old lady at Spinnaker Farm was
positive that she'd seen somebody hurrying through
that morning to catch the train. Now, that somebody wasn't Derek Burtell.'

' Why shouldn't it have been Derek Burtell,
disappearing ? '

' Because he hadn't time to get there. He hadn't
had time to paddle a mile downstream ; and I
don't believe in his coming across country, because

his heart was so rotten he wouldn't have dared to swim the weir stream.'

' He might have crossed at the weir bridge.'

' Exactly, but then, being in a hurry, he would have taken the direct path to the station, the same path Nigel took. There would be no earthly object in wandering round by way of Spinnaker Farm. And there's the same difficulty in supposing that it was Nigel Burtell who passed through Spinnaker Farm. He had just time to do it, but what motive had he ? It was bang out of his way.'

' Couldn't he have gone out of his way deliberately, so as to plant out those films on a spot where he was supposed not to have been ? '

' Yes, but why just there ? Why go the whole way round, at the risk of missing his train, when he could have cut through the hedge at any point, and finished up *via* Spinnaker Farm, dropping the films just outside it, and so making sure that they would be found first thing ? It doesn't really work, you know, as a motive. But look here, you'd better try Spinnaker Farm ; I couldn't question the old lady, you see, because I'd no *locus standi.*'

' I'm going to try Spinnaker Farm, and a whole lot of other places besides. No, thanks, I mustn't stop to dine. I'm making my headquarters at Oxford, because I want to be able to dash away in any direction at short notice. But I'll look in to-morrow some time. By Gad, Bredon, I wish I could always pick your brains like this.'

CHAPTER X

DISCORDANT NOTES

THE Burtell sensation was still making good copy in the newspapers. It was part of Leyland's technique, perhaps a fault in it, that he never put a suspected man on his guard; consequently, although the police and the harbour authorities were warned of Nigel's disappearance, nothing revealed the fact in print. On the other hand, descriptions of Derek were widely circulated, and it was understood to be the ' official theory ' that the unfortunate young gentleman, who was known to be in weak nervous health, must in all probability be wandering about somewhere, suffering from a loss of memory. Nothing stimulates the public imagination so powerfully as the existence of an official theory; its merits and demerits were hotly debated in clubs and railway-carriages; bets were freely exchanged, hairdressers became intolerable on the subject, and even dentists would gag you and then let you have the benefit of their opinions on it. The forebodings Bredon had expressed were amply justified. To the intense irritation of the local fishermen, the banks of the river were lined all Saturday afternoon by amateur detectives who had bicycled over to try their hand at the game; the locks were almost congested with inquisitive punts and pleasure-boats ; a couple of charabancs ran from Oxford, and their enterprise did not prove a disappointment.

It was not only on the Upper River, or in the neighbourhood of Oxford, that the search went on. Photography has made it possible for us all, wherever we are, to join in the criminal-hunt ; and that peculiarly blurred impression which reproduction in a daily paper superinduces on a photograph has added zest to the sport—there is scarcely any stranger whom you cannot, by a stretch of imagination, identify with the wanted man. So far as Nigel was concerned, the police were in a difficulty. Nigel, though he affected the camera himself, could never be induced to sit for it. No portrait of him was forthcoming except a photograph taken when he was seven, and a Futurist sketch by a friend in Chelsea which might equally well have represented any other man, woman, or ant-heap. But Derek's portrait was forthcoming, and was printed in thousands of papers, with the most encouraging results. Imaginary Dereks were held up at Aberdeen, at Enniskillen, and at Bucharest ; all three had to be released with profuse apologies. A well-known medium published the fact that Derek was dead ; but happy, very happy. Unfortunately, on the same day a rival medium announced that Derek was alive and well, but had lost his memory. Which put revelations, for the moment, at a discount.

But this world-wide publicity hardly affected the persons genuinely concerned. What was more serious was that one or two gentlemen of leisure had apparently set their hearts on solving the

mystery ; and these showed every sign of infesting
the district permanently. One of them, a Mr.
Erasmus Quirk, took rooms at the Gudgeon itself
on the Thursday, a short time before Leyland's
arrival, and it looked as if the Bredons would have
to live at close quarters with him. That Mr.
Erasmus Quirk was an American, his pronunciation
of our common speech gave ample evidence. His
personal aspect hardly lived up to his speech, apart
from the ritual horn spectacles. One's impression
of our male visitors from the United States is that
they are all very fine and large, with square shoulders
and a certain attitude of domination. Mr. Quirk
seemed to be a little weed of a man, who stooped so
that you almost put him down for a hunchback ;
his face was very pale, and disfigured by a yellow
blotch on the left cheek ; his hair closely cropped,
so that it revealed to the full a little tonsure of
apparently premature baldness. Every movement
of his was unobtrusive ; his hands were glued in his
coat pockets ; and—a rare gift among his com-
patriots—he seemed altogether disinclined for
company.

He was not allowed, however, to indulge whatever
disinclination he may have felt. Angela had an
inexhaustible capacity for acquaintance with strangers ; it did not matter if they were boring strangers
—she collected bores. She had that useful habit
of enjoying an interview in retrospect which makes
it possible to sit through hours of conversational
tedium. Mr. Quirk had got to be brought out of
his shell, and he came out obediently after dinner.
Angela sat knitting, with that air of pleased atten-

tion which only knitting can give, in the intolerably chaste drawing-room of the Gudgeon, while Mr. Quirk poured out his artless confidences. He was, it seemed, a member of the Detective Club of America ; and it was his duty to write up a detective mystery of some kind before the fall, as a condition of his membership. He had been vegetating at Burford, not far off, when the newspapers put him wise to the Burtell mystification ; and it was a matter of little difficulty to pack his traps and proceed to the scene of action. He invited Angela to say whether it wasn't just an extraordinary piece of luck. It was his conjecture that he might have gone round Europe on all fours with a magnifying glass without managing to strike oil like this. In the States they had a very great admiration for the methods of detection used over here ; he could assure Mrs. Bredon that every development in the Burtell case was being followed with the very greatest interest by every paper on the other side. He didn't suppose Mrs. Bredon quite understood the way he felt about it ; but it seemed to him just extraordinary the way the police in England allowed every fool of an amateur to get busy over a case like this ; why, in Chicago it was to be surmised that the civilian population would be being held up with revolvers at a barrier. It was just another instance of the remarkable hospitality you always got from the British nation.

To all this monologue Angela paid a demure attention, and it was not until Mr. Quirk began speculating whether he owed the presence of such delightful companions as Mr. and Mrs. Bredon to

the tragedy recently reported in the locality that
she was suddenly faced with the necessity of disclosures on her own part. It would be absurd to
deny that Miles was interested in the case ; his
daily proceedings would have given a ready lie to
the statement. She fell back, therefore—I am
afraid it was her custom—on a misleading series
of half-truths ; her husband had been remotely
acquainted with the young man who had disappeared, and certain business friends had urged
him, since he was at leisure, to apply what diligence
he could to the solution of the mystery. His was
not in any sense an official errand. And so the
difficulty was tided over, with a minimum of
prevarication and a minimum of enlightenment.

Mr. Quirk assured her that he would be the last
person to jump another man's claim in any way,
but he would esteem it a very great privilege if
Mrs. Bredon could inform him, without any breach
of confidence, what was generally thought to have
been the exact scene of the tragedy. It would be
a bit discouraging to have to go over six miles of
river with a fine-tooth comb ; and if Mr. Bredon's
deductions had led him to any conclusion about
the precise locality that was concerned, why, Mr.
Quirk would be extraordinarily obliged if Mrs.
Bredon could put him wise to them.

' Oh, there's no secret about that,' said Angela.
' You'll find the spot marked, not with a cross,
but with a troop of about sixteen boy scouts with
no clothes on, diving into the river all day in the
hopes of fishing something up. Or, if for any
reason their operations should be suspended, you'll

know the place because it's just opposite a disused boat-house, the only one of its kind. The boat-house would be on the right-hand side as you go up, but it's easier to get at the river from the other side, because of the tow-path.'

Leyland called round the next morning soon before luncheon. They sat and talked on the lawn, while Mr. Quirk, who had returned from a morning ramble, watched them, with Angela, from the drawing-room window. Leyland and Bredon were examining what looked like photographs. ' How lucky ', observed Mr. Quirk, ' that your husband should be a photographic expert.'

' Why, how on earth did you know ? ' asked Angela, genuinely surprised.

' I don't pride myself very much on my observation, Mrs. Bredon, but I think I can recognize the stains on a man's hands when he has been developing films recently.'

Leyland had a long tour of examination to report, which for the most part had produced painfully negative results. They remembered, at Shipcote Station, a gentleman catching the nine-fourteen to Oxford at the last moment. The ticket-collector at Oxford remembered a gentleman travelling by that train who had no ticket, and had to buy one at the *guichet*. The porter at the schools remembered a gentleman presenting himself for his viva a day too soon. All these agreed roughly in their description of Nigel ; and the fact that it was really Nigel who went back on that train seemed established beyond all possibility of doubt by the testimony of his landlady, who had met him at the

door when he came to his digs. With some difficulty, Leyland even found the taxi-driver who took
up a fare close to Carfax and put him down at the
Gudgeon ' round about eleven o'clock '.

' That alibi seems all right, don't it ? ' suggested
Leyland.

' Yes, only (as I say) it's just a bit too perfect.
The young man seems to have been at such elaborate
pains to leave memories of himself wherever he
went.   There's not a link missing in the chain, you
see ; it looks as if he'd definitely meant to establish
his whereabouts at every moment of the day.   But
perhaps I'm fanciful.   What about the other end ?
Did you get any evidence about his staying here
all the time between eleven and one o'clock that
morning ? '

The evidence here seemed less satisfactory. The
barmaid could remember Nigel's arrival ; she had
told him that it was not possible to serve him with
cherry brandy at that hour ; she had served him,
however, with ginger-beer. She had not watched
him at all as he sat on the lawn, though she had
passed by once with a message, and had seen him
sitting there—she was not quite sure what the time
would be. The people camping on the opposite
bank had been conscious of his presence ; they had
noticed his attempts to feed the peacock ; but they,
too, could only say that it would be some time
between eleven and twelve. His further movements were not definitely dated, except by the fact
that he ordered luncheon at a quarter, or it might
be, half-past twelve. ' Granted that he was feeding
the peacock about a quarter-past eleven,' said

Leyland, ' that gives him an hour to hurry along the tow-path, do what he came to do, and get back.'

' Yes, but you don't believe that. You don't believe he would take the risk. This is what I should consider a real alibi—a natural one. He made no efforts to advertise his presence—didn't rush into the bar for a cherry brandy, for example, exactly at twelve o'clock. No, my feeling is, that up to eleven, Master Nigel was very careful to be where somebody could see him ; after that, he doesn't appear to have minded. I wonder why ? Dash it all, I suppose it ought to suggest something.'

Leyland shook his head. ' All too confoundedly theoretical. I tried Spinnaker Farm, too ; but there they could give me nothing in the way of a description. The old lady had only seen the stranger from an upstairs window as he hurried through the yard ; she had guessed that he was running for the train, and had looked out to see the smoke of the train later on, from anxiety to know whether he had caught it or not.'

' Did the stranger see *her* ? ' asked Bredon.

' Yes, oddly enough he must have ; because he took off his hat to her. Rather an unusual exercise of politeness, for a man catching a train.'

' Precisely. But, you see, once more he makes absolutely certain of his alibi.'

' Then I tried the lock-keeper. He was absolutely positive that he saw nobody else about so early in the morning, except the boy who brings the milk, and the man who went up in a punt just before the Burtells passed. He never saw the man in the punt again. Had the man in the punt come back yet ? (I asked). He wasn't certain, didn't think he had, but hadn't paid much attention to him. As for the canoe, he described Nigel quite unmistakably ; he was sure that there was another gentleman in the punt, but had not seen him move ; nor had he heard him speak, because he was below the level of the lock, mostly. I asked, Mustn't he have moved so as to push the boat out of the lock ? Mr. Burgess, who sticks (I fancy) to his old mumpsimus, thought that the other gentleman might have given the canoe a shove to get it clear of the lock— he was down at the bottom of the steps, it seems, at the time. So that was all Mr. Burgess could tell me, except about his discovery this morning.'

' A discovery this morning ? You never told me about that.'

' I was saving it up. Yes, Mr. Burgess, it seems, is neglecting his garden nowadays, and spends his odd time poking about in the lock-stream with one of those long hayfork things (you must have seen them) which watermen always have. Well, this morning he was prodding about off the island, just below the bridge, and, more by accident than by design, his hayfork came up with something that looked like a pouch on the end of it. It fell in again, but Burgess fished round and got it out again. Here it is.'

Leyland took out a green leather wallet, much faded and disfigured by water, which was clearly meant to contain Treasury notes. From its inner pocket he produced two five-pound notes—it was these that Mr. Quirk mistook for photographs. There was nothing else in the wallet.

'You know, that's confoundedly interesting,' said Bredon. 'I must say it looks as if that wallet had dropped off a genuine corpse. Imagine that there was no corpse—that Derek was simply doing the disappearing trick ; it would surely have been possible to find a less expensive souvenir to leave lying about—a shoe, for example. And even if he had to jettison a purse, one note would have been quite enough to leave in it. Whereas wallets do fall out of pockets. But of course, we've no evidence that it was Derek's at all.'

'Excuse me, we have. I telegraphed to his bank for the numbers of any notes he'd drawn out in the last three weeks, and these numbers were among them.'

'Come, that's better. . . . The actual notes—and two of them. It certainly looks like an involuntary jettison. And that would presumably mean, either that he met somebody just below the bridge, and the wallet fell out, perhaps in the course of a struggle ; or else that that was the exact spot at which the canoe toppled over and the body fell out. I can't see any other way to it, unless it were sheer insane accident.'

'That's about my own feeling. It's not far, mark you, from the place where the tobacco-pouch was found, with the films in it.'

'There's a little lad to see you, sir,' announced the landlady without warning.

Bredon had not been slow to cultivate the acquaintance of the boy scouts, and he had little doubt that it was one of these unofficial allies who was looking for him. It must surely mean a discovery.

Excusing himself to Leyland, he hurried to the front door, and found his expectations justified. The matted hair proclaimed that his visitor had not been long out of the water; and the disorder of his clothes seemed to suggest that their resumption was only a reluctant sacrifice to the *convenances*. On his face was a broad smile, and in his hand a small, dark object.

'Found the gentleman's money-purse, sir,' he said.

CHAPTER XI

MR. ERASMUS QUIRK

'IT'S no good,' said Leyland; 'it doesn't make the least little bit of sense. Don't say that the second wallet didn't really belong to Derek Burtell; that his card was put inside it for a ruse. That note is numbered continuously with the ones we found in the other wallet; all three were among the notes he took out of his bank about a fortnight ago. Two purses, one opposite the end of the island, one opposite the disused boat-house; two notes in one, Derek Burtell's notes, one note in the other, Derek Burtell's note, and a card, Derek Burtell's card—what on earth has he or anybody else been up to?'

'No, you can search me. I've known men wear two handkerchiefs, or two watches, or two pipes; but never two purses. Besides, even if he did, what's the good? Unless, indeed, one fell out in the course of a struggle or in some moment of excitement, while he was alive, and the other slipped from his pocket as his body rolled over into the river. That's the nearest I can get, but it seems pretty fantastic.'

'Well, it's better than nothing,' admitted Leyland. 'Fantastic, but not impossible.'

'Yes, but you don't realize the worst of it,'

Bredon pointed out. ' The place at which Burgess found the first wallet, just below the bridge of the island, wasn't the place at which the canoe was scuttled.'

' How do you make that out ? '

' Don't I keep on telling you that a canoe with a hole that size in it could only float a few hundred yards before it got water-logged ?   And that, once it's water-logged, it makes practically no headway at all, because it's only got the stream to drift it, not the wind ?   The stream couldn't possibly have floated the canoe down all that distance between (say) half-past nine and half-past one.   So that you have to make two separate episodes in this mad canoe journey—one at the bridge, where the pouch was dropped, one lower down, where the boat was scuttled.   It's all too dashed untidy for words.'

' I'll tell you what ; I'm coming to feel that the only thing is to get on to Nigel Burtell's tracks. Derek Burtell may be alive or dead ; to go chasing round for him is possibly to make fools of ourselves. But Nigel Burtell is presumably alive ; he's done a clear bolt, which shows he's got a guilty conscience —he must be able to tell us something.   I believe we ought to devote ourselves to tracing him.'

' That's all very well for you ; but it's not what I'm paid to do.   If there's been a murder, the Indescribable doesn't care a tinker's curse who did it ; my job is to find Derek.   But incidentally, there is surely one other person to track down.'

' Who ? '

' The man in the punt.   He wasn't far off when

the thing happened. He had only to cut across
by land, and he could overtake a canoe that was
being slackly paddled, or wasn't being paddled at
all. He could get back to his punt, and go on
upstream, looking as innocent as you please. I
say, then, that (though there's nothing to implicate
him directly) he's a possible suspect. And meanwhile his movements ought to be traceable. He
must have hired the punt somewhere to start with ;
he must have left it somewhere, or else be still
in it, probably somewhere upstream. It's surely
worth finding out who he is.'

It was at this point that their conversation was
interrupted by Mr. Quirk. How long he might
have been listening to them was not apparent ;
he moved softly over the grass, and seemed to be
interested in the view as he walked. But it was
plainly with a purpose that he approached them ;
and, with the candour which makes for the American
people most of its friends and all its enemies, he
plunged at once into business.

' See here, gentlemen,' he said, ' you don't need
to tell *me* that you're both on the Burtell stunt.
Now, I'm very much interested in the Burtell stunt
myself. And I've none of your advantages ; I only
know what I read in the newspapers, and I guess
what's printed in the newspapers is just about
what you want known. But, see here, I've a proposition to make to you which I'd like you to
consider. I may not be up to all your dodges this
side, but I hold my A1 Sleuth certificate from the
Detective Society of America, and I do try very
humbly to follow in the footsteps of your great

Holmes. And my proposition is this : if I can lay
my finger on a point in this case which you gentlemen, with all your wonderful advantages, haven't
yet noticed—an important point, mark you, that
may put you on the right track—then you gentlemen
will let me work in with you to find this Burtell.
It would give me very great pleasure to be associated
with you in your researches, and of course, if this
gentleman here is connected with the police, I don't
want him to spill any secrets to me that the Force
might not want spilled. That's only reasonable.
All I want is to get a pointer from you now and
again, so that we can have a common policy, and
our researches shan't overlap. Now, I don't know
what you're going to say ; I dare say you're wanting
to kick me downstairs for my confounded impertinence ; but if you've got any use for me, here
I am.'

'I'm on, so far as I'm concerned,' replied Bredon.
'But then, thank God, I'm a free agent. What
do you say, Leyland ? '

'Well, I'm not a free agent. But I don't mind
giving Mr. Quirk pointers, as he calls them, when
I think he's on a wrong track, if he really has got
something to contribute to the clearing up of all
this business, and is prepared to prove it now. It's
not a case for bargaining, Mr. Quirk. If you can
really put us on the track of something, here and
now, then I shall believe that you're a man worth
having on my side, and I shall be prepared to keep
you there.'

'Well, I guess I'll have to be content with that.
Mind you, I'm not saying that this fact is an impor-

tant fact ; I can't just relate it to the other facts of the case ; and there, you see, you have the pull on me, knowing more of them. But let me put it to you just like this : What proof have you that Derek Burtell slept at Millington Bridge last Sunday night, the night before he kind of disappeared ? '

' But why on earth not ? ' expostulated Bredon.

' That's what I can't say, why not ; I only ask whether he did.'

' But I mean, what earthly reason is there for doubting that he did ? '

' Well, I hope Mrs. Bredon hasn't been indiscreet, but she was telling me these Burtell cousins didn't seem to have been any too fond of each other. And she said the landlady at Millington Bridge told her that they didn't come to the inn together, those two, and didn't breakfast together, and didn't leave together. Now, in the States we pay a good deal of attention to the problem of human testimony ; and some of our greatest speculators in that line have pointed out that an uneducated person will always pass inference for fact. Now, supposing that the same man came up to the hotel twice in the same night, pretending to be a different man the second time, isn't it likely she would say two strangers came to her inn to spend the night ? What we don't know is that she ever saw the two strangers together.'

' Bredon,' said Leyland, ' I believe it's worth looking into this. Couldn't we go over and examine that landlady again ? '

' Rather. Let's have some luncheon first, though. I'm hanged if I see what it all means, if this turns out to be true, but it's certainly worth trying.'

The landlady was thoroughly flustered by the appearance of a police inspector, and became more garrulous than ever. Leyland began by demanding the production of the hotel register, which put the poor old lady in the wrong from the first, because, like most country inn-keepers, she had failed to keep any register since the War.   Yes, it would have been about ten o'clock the first gentleman came, and it was quite dark there at the door, so she didn't take much notice of what he looked like; she thought he was a nice-looking young gentleman, held himself very straight, and talked in a slow voice, very drawling and easy.

'That's Nigel all right,' said Bredon.   'And he had no camera with him?'

The landlady hadn't thought to look.   He carried a pack over his shoulders, same as if it might have been his luggage. 'I'll go up to my room,' he had said, 'for I'm dog-tired; no, no supper, thanking you all the same.'   She had then showed him Number Two, a low room on the first floor, facing the back-yard, and Number Three, just opposite, which was a more comfortable room in every way, with a nice view over the front of the hotel, so she thought he'd take that one; but no, nothing would serve him but he must have Number Two.

'Instructive,' said Leyland. 'If Mr. Quirk is right, our friend probably wanted to climb out of the window. May we go round and see it? He couldn't climb out of the front room without risking being seen.'

The window of Number Two certainly seemed
to bear out the theory. It was large, and low in
the wall; and an outhouse roof made it a very
simple climb down. Proceeding, the landlady
explained that the second gentleman arrived about
five or ten minutes later, and she knew who he was
by the camera slung across his back. She couldn't
hardly say whether he was like the other gentleman,
but she thought yes; and as for his voice, why,
the second gentleman didn't hardly so much as open
his mouth, except to say Thank you. Had the
second gentleman a pack on his shoulders too?
Why no, she thought not, but she didn't feel surprised over that, seeing as the pack the first gentleman had was plenty for two; very big pack it was.
Was the first gentleman still moving in his bedroom
when the second gentleman came upstairs? Ah,
she'd have to ask the girl that, it was Lizzy took
the second gentleman upstairs. Lizzy was then
summoned, and said No, she had not heard the
other gentleman move, not to remember it.

' Were his boots outside the door? ' asked
Leyland.

No, it appeared that neither gentleman had put
his boots out to be cleaned. Recalled, and asked
whether this behaviour was usual among travellers,
the landlady deposed that she couldn't hardly say;
some did, some didn't. But these river folk would
as like as not be wearing sandshoes or something
of that; and if so, why then their boots wouldn't
want no cleaning. Were both beds slept in?
Lizzy had to be recalled. Yes, both beds had been
slept in, very much tumbled about they was, and

both basins used. The first gentleman gave no orders about calling; the second asked to have a tray left outside on the mat, with a pot of tea and a couple of nice poached eggs. That was at half-past seven, and the other gentleman, that was the gentleman from Number Two, he came down about a quarter before eight. Did he have breakfast? Oh yes, a pot of tea and a couple of nice poached eggs.

'Good God,' said Bredon, 'did the man get through four poached eggs in a morning?'

'Might have shied the bedroom eggs into those bushes,' suggested Leyland. 'The birds would have got them by now.'

Number Two, it appeared, had not taken long over his breakfast, but had paid his bill and set out for the river about a quarter-past eight. As for Number Three, there wasn't nobody could speak to having seen *him* go out. But the bill was paid for both.

'Has anybody been staying here since,' asked Leyland, 'or would the rooms be more or less as they were left?'

No, there had been no later visitors; it wasn't hardly the season, not so early in the month. But Lizzy, of course, she had done the rooms after the gentleman left. Still, they were welcome to go up and see. They inspected both rooms, Leyland and Bredon addressing particular attention to the window-frame of Number Two, in the hope that they might find some traces of a hurried exit. But no scratches were apparent; and it looked as if they would have to return home with the unsatisfactory experience of a theory formed, tested, and corroborated, but not proved. They were already on their way downstairs when the American spoke almost for the first time :

' It's with considerable diffidence that I make any suggestions to such competent investigators, but isn't it possible that we might still find some thumb-marks ? Our experts in the United States have laid it down that, if there was any grease on the hand, a finger or thumb-mark, even when invisible to the naked eye, may persist for a considerable number of days. And I've noticed myself in your country that the hotel servants aren't always just very particular in the way they do the rooms. Now, I would suggest, that if you've got any powder in your kit, you might just try the carafes in those rooms for finger-prints.'

It seemed a desperate remedy ; but in default of a better suggestion it was tried. The impossible resulted ; on either decanter appeared at least one thumb-print, in tolerably definite outline. There was a tense silence as Leyland carried them to the window, and held them up side by side. There could be no reasonable doubt of the fact—the thumb-marks were exactly similar. Both decanters were carefully wrapped up, and carried off as spoils of the victory.

' Mr. Quirk,' said Leyland, ' I'm hanged if I know what to make of your discovery. But you've proved your idea up to the hilt, and I must say I hope you'll keep on working at the case. I'm always ready to give you any " pointers ", as you call them, within reason. You're staying at the Gudgeon, I think ? '

' You'll find me right there until this business is cleared up, Inspector.   I don't know what it is, but a real detective puzzle kind of gets hold of a man the way he can't drop it if he wanted to.   And I have to be on this side for nearly two months yet, so that the Gudgeon Hotel is a good enough address for me.   Without mentioning the company.'

' Bredon,' said Leyland, ' you're being very silent. I believe you've got one of your ideas—you're on the track of a solution.'

' Not within miles of one,' admitted Bredon cheerfully.   ' But I enjoy fresh complications, as long as they're not off the point.   And I don't think this complication *is* off the point.'

CHAPTER XII

THE SECRET OF THE ISLAND

BREDON did not expand until he and Leyland were alone together. ' I'm going to leave it to you ,' he said, ' how much you take Mr. Quirk into your confidence. Meanwhile, I must tell you that I've got Nigel Burtell's finger-prints ; and I'm confoundedly glad that I did. When I called on him to show him those photographs, I took good care that he should finger the envelope in which the photographs were, and that he should return it to me. As soon as I'd left him I took a photo of the prints, and here it is. Unless my memory is at fault, I think it's the duplicate of the marks on those decanters.'

His forecast was fully justified. ' Well,' said Leyland, ' we've got the facts clear, anyhow. Until Sunday night, according to what you tell me, the Burtell cousins travelled together. On Sunday night Nigel Burtell was the only one who slept at Millington Bridge ; and he took particularly good care to let it be supposed that Derek was there too. He must have been at pains, for example, to tumble the bedclothes in Number Three.'

' Yes, and don't make any mistake about it—you can't tumble the bedclothes in ten minutes. People

do in books, but in real life you can't make a bed
look as if it had been lain on unless you actually
lie on it for an hour or more.   Nigel Burtell, I take
it, must have divided his night between the two
bedrooms and the two beds.   That night, of course,
he climbed out of the window and came back again
to the inn door posing as the gentleman with the
camera.   He had the reputation, you know, of being
quite a decent actor as amateurs go.   The next
morning found him in Number Three—he had locked
the door of Number Two when he changed beds
in the night.   He made a feint of eating the breakfast, washed in that room and then in Number Two,
packed, came down and ate his second breakfast,
and went off, paying the bill.   Not a bad night's
work.   But whatever for ? '

'I may be a fool,' said Leyland meditatively,
' but I believe I'm getting nearer the solution of
the whole thing.   Look here, let me just rough it
out, and see what you think of it.   I'm taking it
as a fixed certainty—almost the only fixed certainty
we've lighted on so far—that Nigel Burtell deliberately pretended to be two people on the Sunday
night, although his cousin was certainly with him
when they paddled down the river next morning.
The only strong motive I can see for Nigel's fantastic behaviour is a fantastic motive.   He acted
as he acted because he wanted it to be thought that
Derek Burtell was alive, wheras in reality he was
dead.   That means he had already murdered his
cousin, on the Sunday.'

' It would be an ingenious idea, certainly.   You
mean that he left the body in the canoe, and tethered

the canoe somewhere where it was not likely to be found ? '

' Possibly. Or possibly he sank the body, somewhere where he could get at it again easily. Meanwhile, since there had been two gentlemen staying in all the inns they had visited hitherto, he must create the impression that two gentlemen had slept at Millington Bridge. He did that, as we know. But his precautions went further ; he was determined to play the old Cid trick with his brother's body, pretending he was still alive, I mean ; and to do that right under the nose of the lock-keeper. He arranged the body in the attitude of a man lying asleep—or possibly drugged—on the floor of the canoe, and then solemnly paddled down to Shipcote Lock. By a piece of luck for him, the water in the lock was at high level. If it had been at low level, the lock-keeper would have come out on to the nearer bridge to turn the winches, and would have been staring right down into the canoe. As it was, the lock-keeper had only to open the gates at that end ; and he did so, after the manner of lock-keepers, with his back turned to the audience.'

' Yes, Nigel was taking a risk. But, as you say, the luck was with him.'

' From the further, lower end of the lock there was not much danger. In turning the winches, the lock-keeper still had his back to the canoe ; and in a short time, as the water got lower, the canoe itself faded out of sight. Then it was that Nigel stood on the edge of the lock, and began a one-sided conversation with the lifeless figure in the canoe. No answers were audible, but that would not create

any surprise in the lock-keeper ; between the depth
of the walls and the rushing of the water he wouldn't
be likely to hear the other side of the conversation.
Only one difficulty remained—how to get the canoe
clear of the lock, when the man inside it was dead.
This difficulty Nigel solved, rather ingeniously, by
pretending that he had remembered something at
the last moment—the camera, or something like
that—and running down the steps to the canoe.
Here, still out of sight, he gave the canoe one good,
straight shove, enough to carry it out into the
stream, where the wind would catch it and help
it along. Then he proceeded to establish his
alibi.'

'And meanwhile ? '

'Meanwhile—why, I'm coming round to your
idea of a third person, only I believe that third
person to have been an accomplice. The accomplice's job was to dispose, somehow, of the body,
and then paddle on downstream, to a point remote
from Shipcote, where he would scuttle the canoe
and make off.'

'You're suggesting that this accomplice disposed
of the body first, and then paddled downstream
without it ? '

'Yes. You see, as a matter of fact both the
river and its banks appear to have been entirely
deserted at that hour in the morning. But they
couldn't bet on their being deserted. Now, if they
were seen, it was essential that there should be
only one human figure in the canoe. If there were
only one, the casual passer-by would be prepared
to swear afterwards that it was Derek. Casual

passers-by will always swear anything.   The accomplice, therefore, went on by himself; it didn't
matter how many people saw him, except at the
precise moment when he was engaged in scuttling
the boat.   It meant, you see, that he must leave
the body somewhere, and somewhere where it
wouldn't be found.'

'Yes, I see that.   I suppose, by the way, you're
taking it for granted that they meant to spirit
the body away somewhere, not to let it be found
in the river?'

'I'm working on that supposition.   After all,
though it is possible for a body to sink and never
be recovered, the chances are very much against
it.   So that if the dragging hasn't brought a body
to light, that means there probably isn't a body
there.   And if so, that's because Nigel and his
accomplice—to call them that for the sake of
argument—didn't want the body to be found.'

'Excellent.   And, of course, that means in its
turn——'

'That the body itself wouldn't bear inspection;
there were marks of violence, or some other marks
on it, which wouldn't look well at a coroner's
inquest.   The body, then, must be left lying about
for a time.   The accomplice couldn't take it in his
canoe, Nigel couldn't take it in his railway carriage.
It would have been possible, but laborious, to sink
it somewhere and recover it afterwards.   It would
be a simpler plan to hide it somewhere on land till
they could fetch it away.'

'They hadn't very long, you know.   The search
began about four hours afterwards.'

'Exactly. All the better reason for choosing a place where people wouldn't look. And, for that reason, I'm inclined to think that they hid the body on the island. That other end of the island, you remember, away from the lock, is all deep in woods, and there's plenty of bracken and undergrowth. Searchers would go up the river all the way to the lock, and would scour either bank for miles round. But the island would by just the place where they wouldn't look. They would assume that if Derek had lost his memory, or if he had done a bolt for it, he would be miles away by that time. Did anybody search the island, as a matter of fact ? '

'I don't think they did. But there's one point to consider—leaving the body on the island would make it precious difficult to cart it away again. They could hardly reach it, either by land or on water, without being seen.'

'I know. And yet, would it be so very difficult for them to take advantage of the searching operations ? Nigel, at all events, seems to have been up till all hours on the Monday night looking for the corpse—what if he knew where it was, and found it ? And having found it, proceeded to dispose of it ? '

'Well, there's still time to have a look round. Or do you want specially to get back to Oxford ? If you're a strong man with the paddle, it wouldn't take us long to go up there in the canoe, and that makes it easier to hunt round.'

'Just the two of us ? '

'I'm not going three in a canoe for anybody. Angela has insisted on spending two nights at home ;

she has some absurd idea that her children like her
to be about. And I don't think Mr. Quirk is on
in this act. Let it be just the two of us.'

The river lay infinitely beautiful, windless under
a cloudless sky. The tiniest fidgeting motion of
your body pencilled fresh ripples on the cool surface
of the stream. The red earth of the banks, and
the green fringe that surmounted them, showed in
mellow contrast under the equable light of evening.
The reeds stood straight and motionless as sentinels,
just fringed with a distant horizon of tree-tops.
The splashing of cows in the shallows, the churning
of far-off reaping-machines, the cries of children,
punctuated the stillness with companionship. Mint
and meadow-sweet and lying hay blended their
scents with intolerable sweetness in that most
delicate of all mediums, the smell of clean river-
water. The stream, now dazzling in the sunlight,
now mysterious and dark under the tree-shadows,
seemed to conspire with the easy strokes of the
paddle. Nature had determined, it appeared, to
forget the tragedy and go on as if nothing had
happened. Only the occasional dredgers reminded
them of the past and their grim errand.

The island confronted them at last, a haunted
spot, you would say, with its laced interplay of
sun and shadow. There must be a complex in the
blood of us island-born people that makes us feel,
in the presence of an island, something of mystery
and charm ; it came out in us when we dug sand
castles on the beach, it comes out in us still wherever
the water isolates the land. But above all in lakes
or in rivers ; for here the strip of sundering tide is

so narrow, the unattainable shore so near. Who has ever seen a Thames island that has not peopled it, in his imagination, with merry, lurking outlaws, or with the shy forms of some forgotten race of men ? As you approached Shipcote Island, experience might remind you that at its higher end it was yoked with bridges and tamed with the laborious effort of human cultivation. But the illusion persisted in fancy ; it seemed a spot remote, holy, uncontaminated by the daily instance of the surrounding world.

'Just here, I think,' said Leyland. 'It was immediately off this part of the island that Burgess found the note-case. By his description it must originally have been lying quite close in to the shore—as if somebody or something had disembarked just here. There's no sign of any disturbance on the bank, though, is there ? '

But this impression proved only skin-deep. They had scarcely landed, when they found an unmistakable path through the bracken ; a path, as they noticed with excitement, such as would be made by the dragging of a weight through the tangled fronds, not the mere casual wake left by a foot-passenger. For a few yards it diverged only a little from the line of the shore, then, behind a screen of overhanging bushes, it climbed up the slope towards the centre of the island, through the thickest of the fern. Here and there was a bare patch of clayey soil, and always the clay was seamed as if by the jutting extremities of some heavy weight dragged over it. Yet the direction was uncertain, as if the man who had made this path had been doubtful of his objective; it had purposeless (or were they purposeful?) windings. It came to a standstill, you might say, close to the summit of the island, where the trees grew thickly, but there was an interval in the carpet of the fern; a bare patch of clay, still wet under the protecting shadow of the branches. And here, it seemed, the burden must have been laid down, for there was a firm though indistinct impress on the clay. Bredon and Leyland drew nearer, scanning the surface for any trace of a more definite outline. 'Look!' said Leyland suddenly. About half-way down the area of the disturbance was a tiny depression which only one object could have caused. It was the imprint of a button; to judge by its size, a coat-button.

'M'm!' said Bredon; 'those are hardly the tracks of a living man.'

'He'd be a fool, wouldn't he, if he wanted to rest or sleep, to rest or sleep on a rheumaticky spot like this? He had plenty of bracken to make his bed if he wanted to. No, the body that lay there was dead, or at least drugged.'

'Not much difference, either, if Derek Burtell was in question. He hadn't the sort of constitution that would stand a clay bath.'

'And what happened *then*?' asked Leyland. 'Did they take it back the same way or—no, the track goes on further. But it wasn't dragged any further; it must have been carried. Though I'm bound to say there's no clear mark of two men here: they must have been careful to keep the same track. Let's see the thing through.'

This time, the path made no divagations except where they were imposed on it by the steepness of the ground.   It led straight down to the water of the weir stream, and came out on to a patch of open grass by the water side.   The bank itself was of hardish clay, and here, just opposite the end of their track, they found the unmistakable indentation that is made by the sharp bows of a boat run suddenly in to land.

'And then ? ' asked Leyland.

'No need to ask what they did then.   They didn't take the body downstream again, to be found by the first fool who searched for it.   They didn't put it ashore on the other side and give themselves the trouble of lugging it across country. They took it up to the weir, dragged the canoe and the body across the bank, then paddled upstream a bit, and lowered the body, weighted, of course, into the stream.   They left it exactly where no living man was ever likely to look for it—in the wrong stretch of the river, on the wrong side of a Thames Conservancy lock.'

'By Gad, yes, that was the thing to do.   What about looking for traces by the side of the weir ? '

'No good ;   it's hard ground and smooth grass ; you wouldn't get any traces.   Besides, anybody drags his boat over there if he wants to avoid the lock fee.   I've done it once myself, I'm sorry to say, in the course of the last week.   But that's what they did ;   that's what they did, unless they were fools.   The question is, can we start dragging the river *above* Shipcote Lock without looking like madmen ? '

CHAPTER XIII

PURSUED

LEYLAND had determined to devote the next day to making inquiries about the man in the punt. Bredon, who had decided to take things easily, contented himself with looking through Leyland's notes of his preliminary information about the case ; some of which may as well be here transcribed for the reader's benefit.

'Relations living.—(1) Mrs. Charles Burtell, now Haverford ; has m. Julius Haverford, 513, 24th Street West, Idaho, an American lawyer. Has lived in U.S. ever since her marriage ; Nigel B. used to go over there during summer holidays and vacations. Is now travelling on the Continent of Europe, address not known.

'(2) Mrs. Coolman, sister of John Burtell (grandfather), widow of James Coolman, Lancashire business man who left her v. well off. Address, Brimley House, Wallingford. No will known to exist ; she was childless, so that D. and N. Burtell are nearest relatives. Has not seen them since infancy, but takes an interest in them. Unfortunately is now v. ill, and Dr. will not hear of her being interviewed.

'No other surviving relatives of any importance.

. . . . .

'Motives of disappearance.—(1) By death of D.,

125

N. stands to gain £50,000 free of encumbrance,+ expectations from " Aunt Alma ", i.e. Mrs. Coolman.

' (2) D. might evade creditors by successful dis-appearance ; but this only possible by secret arrangement with N., who would be treated as heir. This v. improbable, since D. notoriously on bad terms with N.

' (3) Origin of this bad feeling not exactly trace-able, but certainly increased by discreditable love affair eighteen months ago. The two cousin rivals ; N. apparently successful, but woman committed suicide (drugs). Consult records of inquest.

' (4) Possibly D. merely wished to slip out of society (heavy drug taker). But circs. seem un-necessarily elaborate.

.   .   .   .   .

' Personal characteristics.—D. is reputed slow, lazy, and unimaginative ; fond of low friends. Talks French well. Bets and gambles cons`derably. N. gives himself out Bolshevist etc. ; some brains, talent for acting ; Bohemian pose (?) ; friends say not to be taken seriously.

.   .   .   .   .

' Next destinations.—D. apparently expected to return to London flat, where letters were to await arrival. N's. letters were to be forwarded to same address. Did N. mean to stay in London with D. ? No other address given to Oxford lodgings ; luggage only marked (railway label) " Paddington ".

.   .   .   .   .

' Possibility of murder by persons unknown.—It does not appear D. had any violent or bitter enemies. No one had any motive for killing him except N.

Add, however, the possibility of some one interested in Mrs. Coolman's money. Mrs. C. has a protégé, E(dward ?) Farris, orphaned son of friends, who has been brought up by and lived with her. Some chance that she may have left property to him by will ; perhaps contingently ; if so, he might have motive for disposing of (one or both) Burtell cousins. (N.B. Letter from Mrs. C. to D., found among his papers in London, expresses strong desire for D. and N. to be reconciled, since they were reported to her as having quarrelled. Perhaps significant.)'

Leyland had, of course, jotted down other notes, but these, for the most part, would be no news to the reader. Bredon, as he read, admired both the thoroughness of his method and the directness of his mind ; you could see Leyland's suspicions leaping up (he said to himself) like the little numbers on an automatic cash register. Then his thoughts turned to Mr. Quirk, his solitary companion at the inn. What did Mr. Quirk suspect, what did he wish it to be thought he suspected ? It would be interesting, if it were in any way possible, to sound Mr. Quirk on the subject, without giving away (in Leyland's absence) their discoveries on the island, and the doubts which those discoveries had corroborated or suggested. Perhaps, after all, an appeal to the man's vanity was simplest. Anyhow, it would be no harm trying. He went down into the ' Ingle-nook Room ', shuddering as he passed under that inscription. Mr. Quirk was not there, but a smoking cigarette-end, and a novel carelessly laid aside page-downwards, proved that he had only just left it. Bredon picked up the novel, wondering what volume in the limited and old-fashioned library of the Gudgeon would have appealed to the American's tastes. It was Warren's *Ten Thousand a Year*. 'Yes,' said Bredon to himself, 'that clinches it.'

Mr. Quirk himself entered a moment or two later. 'Ah, Mr. Quirk,' said Bredon, 'I was just running through some notes of the case which Leyland made, and I'm sure he wouldn't mind my mentioning one fact which might help us to solve our little difficulty of yesterday. Did you know that the Burtell brothers had a great-aunt who was very much concerned about their rumoured dislike of each other ? And that only a little over a week ago she was urging them to a reconciliation ? '

'Why,' said Mr. Quirk, 'that's a very interesting fact ; but as far as my observation goes, what we do in life is one thing and what our great-aunts want us to do is another.'

'I agree. But this great-aunt was in some ways out of the common. She was very rich, and she had nobody else to leave her money to—nobody in the family, at any rate. Further, since her name was Alma, I think it's a safe guess that the year of her birth was not much later than 1854.'

'You mean that her testamentary dispositions were on the way to becoming a practical problem. Why, that's so. And you think these young men kind of faked their river trip so as to give auntie the idea they were old school chums.'

'Well, it's at least possible. Now, suppose that they have a quarrel. From all that one hears of them, nothing is more likely. Supposing, on the

last day of their trip, that the elder, Derek, said
he couldn't bear it any longer—got off the canoe
before their night stage was reached, and went off
to an inn by himself. The younger would have no
impluse to call him back; he goes on to their
arranged destination; and then, on his way up to
the hotel, he has a sudden doubt. What if Aunt
Alma—she lives not very far from Oxford—should
make inquiries about their trip, and find that after
all they finished up in two separate hotels? Is it
worth running the risk, when a comparatively little
ingenuity will create the impression that *two* travellers spent the night there?'

'I should be the first to compliment you, Mr.
Bredon, on your very remarkable piece of analysis.
But if you ask me, I think it would need some
more powerful motive than that to account for the
young man's behaviour. I've studied the records
of crime a good deal; and it's my conviction that
people don't resort to desperate shifts unless they're
in desperate situations. Now, when you find this
kind of juggling going on on the very eve of a great
fatality, doesn't it suggest itself to you, as it suggests
itself to me, that that fatality was foreseen, and
that the juggling was practised in an effort to
avoid it?'

'Yes; that's sound; that's quite sound. Don't
invoke coincidence if you can help it. You think
Derek Burtell knew he had enemies on his track?
As far as I know, we've no record of any such
enemies existing.'

'That young man seems to have lived in the
Bohemian world a deal more than was good for

him. It isn't likely that the police have got a full
record of all the embroglios he may have been
involved in. And it's to be remembered he was a
very rich man besides that.'

' Only in prospect. To murder him before he
was twenty-five would be killing the goose that lays
the golden eggs.'

' That's so. And yet it's not at all impossible
that some gang of crooks were after him, with the
idea of murdering or kidnapping him and then
personating him to get the money. You may not
be aware, Mr. Bredon, that in our country kidnapping is almost a recognized means of getting
your living. But I can't say ; it may have been
that, it may have been a private vendetta. But
it seems to me when a man pretends to sleep in
a particular place, and then sends another man
there to personate him, it means that man's going
in peril of his life, and he's anxious to sleep anywhere
else except just there.'

' It's a very interesting idea of yours. But suppose
it's true, why should his cousin consent to put himself in such a position of danger ? Surely the odds
were that the murderer would do *him* in by mistake.'

' I've thought of that, and I'll tell you how it
seems to me—he didn't know just how close these
people were on his track. He didn't think they
were near enough to do him any harm that night ;
but he wanted to leave a false trail behind him.
He wanted them to go on tracking that canoe down
the river, when he himself had left it and skipped
off to London or wherever he reckoned he'd be safe.'

' But he *did* rejoin the canoe next day—at least,

unless all our evidence is incorrect.' Bredon thought for a moment of Mr. Carmichael, and his theory of the soap dummy.

'That's just what complicates the thing; but I've two ways of explaining that. Either he changed his mind—heard some news which made that precaution seem unnecessary; or, more probably than that, he was playing a game of double bluff, if you understand what I mean. These are pretty cute fellows (he'd say to himself) and it's not likely they'd be taken in by an old dodge like this. If they come here and make inquiries, they'll tumble to it soon enough that I didn't really sleep here; they'll think I've tried to give them the slip and gone off to London. Meanwhile, the old canoe is good enough for me. So he joined the canoe again next morning.'

'Crooks seem to have very complicated processes of thought by your account of them. But I dare say you're right. And you think that in reality the pursuit was far closer than poor Burtell thought? So that the very next day they caught him up and did for him?'

'That would be my idea. They must have been extraordinarily close on his tracks, shadowing him all the time—they didn't show up, you see, until his cousin had left the canoe.'

'But there's another thing—granted that Nigel Burtell ran no danger from his cousin's pursuers, wasn't there a worse danger still, the danger of his being mistaken for their accomplice?'

'Their accomplice? I don't just see how there'd be any great danger of that.'

' Why, juries are only human.   Here is this young man, his cousin's only companion—the moment he leaves the boat, the cousin gets murdered.   When his cousin fails to turn up at the rendezvous, he shows a suspicious anxiety as to what may have become of him.   He himself, it is to be observed, has been careful to cover his tracks by an alibi. All that business at Millington Bridge shows that he was aware of the danger which hung over his cousin's head ; and what steps has he taken to avert it ?   On the contrary, he has quietly walked out of the way, so as to let the murderers have their chance.   If it is murder, he is the sole bene- ficiary of the murder ; if it is kidnapping, the kid- nappers can get no further with their plan unless they manage to square him.   Doesn't all that build up rather a heavy case against young Nigel ? '

' Why, yes, in the abstract.   But, the way justice works, you can't incriminate a man as an accomplice unless you catch the principals.   You'll have to catch them first, and then confront him with them. And here's this besides, he may have a trump card up his sleeve which we know nothing about.   We shan't hear of that until we find him ; and where is he ?   You'll excuse my giving the impression of kind of criticizing your excellent police, but don't they attach any significance to his disappearance ? A man who's got an alibi like his doesn't want to arouse suspicion by making tracks for South America.'

' You mean that the murderers——'

' I say nothing about murder.   I only say that these two cousins have disappeared, one after the other, and old man Burtell's legacy is going to God knows who. Isn't it natural to calculate that if we can catch the men who've mislaid one, we might catch the men who've mislaid both ? '

' I doubt if Leyland's thought of that. I should mention it to him certainly, if I were you. But Nigel's disappearance had the air of being a deliberate performance. He took his ticket for one train and then hopped on to another.'

' Say, you don't know much about crooks if you think they can't hustle a man on a platform the way he'll think he's getting into the right train when he's getting into the wrong one. Why, I've read of a case where they changed the labels on a coach merely to get hold of one man. But then, you seem to be making a dead set to fix the blame on this unfortunate Nigel. If he slips into a wrong train, you make out that he's trying to dodge the police. If he's got murderers on his track, and knows it, why shouldn't he be just trying to dodge them ? '

' Yes, you do make it all hang together. Mind you, I think you're arguing too much from your experience on the other side. It seems to me that English criminals haven't usually the cleverness, or the powers of combination, to bring off a coup of this kind.'

' Who said they were English ? Haven't I read that this Derek Burtell was brought up in the South of France ? Mind you, it's with the greatest possible deference that I make all these suggestions ; I'm only a humble amateur.'

CHAPTER XIV

THE MAN IN THE PUNT

LEYLAND did not come back till early on Monday morning; and when he came out to the Gudgeon he found Angela already returned. He was plainly despondent.

'There's simply nothing right about this case,' he explained. 'Nothing ever seems to work out according to schedule. What could be easier, in an ordinary way, than to trace the movements of a man who's gone up river in a punt? He must pass through the locks; he must go up the main stream—you couldn't take a punt up the Windrush, for example; he can't leave it about anywhere, at this time of the year, without its being noticed. And yet I've lost all trace of him.'

'Poor Mr. Leyland,' said Angela. 'Did you start from Oxford, or where?'

'Yes, naturally I went round the boat places on the Upper River; that didn't take long. I found the man who'd hired the punt to him—the same man, as a matter of fact, from whom the Burtells got their canoe. It was a big punt, with awnings for sleeping out, and the man seems to have come on board with a great crowd of tins and things as if he meant to do his own cooking. He paid a deposit, and hired the punt for a fortnight—gave

his name as Luke Wallace, and an address somewhere
in Cricklewood. I got through to Cricklewood at
once—there are advantages about being a police-
man—and   the   station   there,   after   making
inquiries, found that no such name was known anywhere in the neighbourhood.   A false address sounds
promising, thought I ; we aren't on the track of
some common holiday-maker.   I found out the date
when the man hired the punt : it seems that he
had already spent two nights on the river when he
reached Shipcote.   That's natural enough ;   he
wasn't hurrying.   I tried the locks between this
and Oxford, to see if they could give me any information about the man ;   they only seemed to
remember the circumstance of his passing ; one
of them showed me, with great pride, the counter-
foil of his lock ticket, F.N.2—as if that did any
good.'
    ' Better than nothing,' suggested Bredon.   ' By
an outside chance you might find it lying about
somewhere.'
    ' Yes, but who bothers about a lock ticket ?   He
wasn't coming back.   Probably just pitched it into
the water then and there.   However, I got the
number.   And of course we know his number at
Shipcote, because it was the one just before the
Burtells '.   At the inns, so far, they'd seen nothing
of him.'
    ' Poor man, he must have been using condensed
milk,' said Angela with a shudder.
    ' Well, above Shipcote Lock he seems to have
changed his method entirely.   At Millington Bridge,
for example—I can't think why the landlady didn't

tell us about it—he went in and had an early
luncheon. How early ? (I asked). Oh, about half-
past eleven it would be. Now, notice—this man
was clear of Shipcote Lock before nine. The distance he did before lunch was only the distance the
Burtells had covered between their breakfast and
nine o'clock. Of course, there's the difference
between a canoe going downstream and a punt
going upstream. I suppose the distance will be
about two miles—rather less, if anything. There's
no reason why our friend in the punt should have
been feeling energetic on a hot morning ; but it
naturally occurs to the mind that he *may* have been
hanging about Shipcote Lock at the very time when
the murder was committed. Which makes me all
the more anxious to meet him.'

'Did he show any interest in the movements of
the Burtells ? ' asked Bredon.

'That's the extraordinary thing. Hitherto he
hadn't touched at a hotel, or asked a single question
at the locks. But from now onwards he seems to
have blazed his trail like a—like an elephant on a
lawn-tennis court. At Millington Bridge, for example,
he asked all sorts of questions about the Burtells
—how long they stayed and whether they saw much
of each other and so on. It was the maid he asked,
not the landlady ; I suppose otherwise she'd have
been certain to mention it. He even asked whether
they'd been seen about together much. All this,
of course, was before any news of Burtell's disappearance had come through. Then he went off,
upstream.'

'Are you sure he went upstream ? ' objected

Bredon. 'That pub at Millington Bridge stands well away from the river ; they can't have seen him from there.'

' No, but there's a boat place at the bridge, and the man in charge there saw him going upstream. He remembered it afterwards, of course, because the Burtell news came through, and everybody on the river began to remember everything that had happened that day, and a good many things which hadn't. I asked him why on earth he didn't mention the man in the punt before—why he never told the police about him. He said it never occured to him, because the accident had happened so far down that it was impossible for a man punting upstream to have been anywhere near the scene of the accident, and yet reach Millington Bridge by half-past eleven. That was true, of course ; he had no reason, you see, to suppose that there'd been anything fishy happening at the lock. Anyhow, he was positive of the fact because he remembered discussing the matter with old Mr. So-and-so, and I could ask old Mr. So-and-so if I didn't believe him. I didn't worry ; the information seemed good enough. I walked up by the river to the next lock ; on the way I passed a rather derelict sort of inn, and made inquiries there just for luck. The Blue Cow, I think, it was called.'

' I remember it,' said Bredon. ' That was where the Burtells had dinner, the same evening on which they reached Millington Bridge. You remember it, don't you, Angela ? '

' Yes ; we speculated, if you remember, what they could possibly have got to eat there, at such an hour.'

'Did the man in the punt call there?' asked Bredon.

'He did, and he actually called for letters. There were no letters here, only a telegram, which he read. It was addressed to somebody of the name of Wallace—that was the same name he'd given to the people who hired him the punt at Oxford. An alias, I imagine. As soon as he had read the telegram, he asked for a railway guide and a 'bus time-table. He had tea, and during tea he started asking the same set of questions about the Burtells —did they dine together? Did they go off together? and so on. After tea he got into the punt and started off downstream.'

'So you came down again?'

'No, I went up to the next lock to make sure. The man there was quite positive that no punt had come up at the time mentioned. The news of Burtell's disappearance had been telegraphed through by that time, and he came downstream himself to help in the search. His wife, who looked after the lock in his absence, never had to open it all the time he was away. And, what's more, he didn't pass any punt of the type described on his way down to Shipcote. Burgess is equally clear that the punt never came back through Shipcote; that is easy to determine; for, if it had, the man would have shown his ticket. So, you see, the man in the punt seems to have vanished between Shipcote and the next lock above it, and taken his punt with him.'

'Folds his punt like the Arabs, and silently fades away,' suggested Angela. 'But you looked for it, I suppose?'

' Very much so. I hired a boat and a waterman, and we rowed all the way down to Shipcote. We looked under the trees where they overhung the river ; we went through all the craft at Millington Bridge ; we did everything to find the beastly punt except dive for it. One thing's quite certain—I'm going to have that upper reach dragged, even if I lose the last shred of my reputation for sanity.'

' What about the man's looks ? ' suggested Bredon. ' Did anybody give you a decent description of him ? '

' They were pretty clear about that. All agreed that he looked a very muscular man ; that he was clean-shaven, and had rather shiny hair, black ; that he was rather above the average height— nothing much that was positive (there never is) but enough to rule out plenty of candidates. Naturally, I also made a point of finding out for certain whether he was alone—did he travel, for example, with the awnings of the punt up, so that there might have been a second person concealed in it ? All my authorities seemed to agree, as far as they remem- bered the circumstances, that he was alone ; Burgess, indeed, is quite positive about that.'

' Well, for heaven's sake let's try to get the crazy thing reconstructed. Angela, we've been making some advances in our business since you left, so you mustn't interrupt us.'

' I will be as silent as a mouse. By the way, when you've finished, remind me to tell you what John said about the perambulator ; it was really rather smart. But for the present, have it your own silly way.'

'Well, then,' said Leyland, 'we'd better start by assuming that Nigel and the unknown—let's call him Wallace, as it's the name he seems to travel by—that Nigel and Wallace were in collusion. On Monday morning, after occupying two rooms and paying his bill as if he were two people, Nigel leaves the inn at Millington Bridge. Somewhere he picks up his cousin, who is by that time probably dead, or at least drugged. He paddles down to Shipcote Lock, and just above the lock he passes, no doubt without pretending to recognize, his accomplice.'

'Steady one moment,' said Bredon. 'Had they arranged to meet just there, or was it accidental?'

'I think it must have been by arrangement. Nigel obviously had the nine-fourteen train in view, so there's no reason why they should not have arranged a definite time of meeting. And, from what followed, it seems as if they knew their ground all right. Nigel, as we know, left the lock for the station, probably giving the canoe a shove before he left, so as to push it out into the fairway. Here, for the time being, his job ended. Wallace, meanwhile, had tied his punt up somewhere, just above the lock, and came down along the bank to intercept the drifting canoe. Now, which bank did he take? The western bank, surely, on the side away from the weir. That would save him swimming the weir stream. Not much danger in passing Burgess' house, while Burgess was busy working the lock.'

'Yes, but if he did that, why were the footprints at the island side of the bridge? Why not on the mainland side? That's where he'd want to climb up, if your account is right.'

' You forget—he had to have his base on the island, so as to dispose of the body. He came down the western bank, crossed the iron bridge, and then behaved precisely as we made Nigel behave. He took off his clothes, climbed the bridge with his feet wet from the grass, took a photograph (Number Five) of his own footprints by mistake ; took another photograph, Number Six, of Derek's body floating in the canoe—on purpose. Then he climbed down, put the camera on board, pushed the canoe into the island bank, and got back into his clothes again. He lifted the body out of the canoe, well on to the bank ; then he dragged it through the bracken up to the top of the island, and left it dumped on that clay surface. He's made no mistakes, has he, so far ? '

' Yes, one, and a very bad one. In lifting the body out of the canoe, he allowed that purse to slip out of the pocket. That—with the photograph of the footprints on the bridge—put us on to the idea that there had been dirty work at the island. They meant us to think that the whole business had happened much lower down.'

' That's true enough. And yet they dropped the films just opposite the middle of the island. Surely that must have been done on purpose ? '

' Yes, but did they mean those films to mark the spot ? I think they were meant to look as if they'd been dropped accidentally just anywhere, by a man making his way along the tow-path.'

' Yes, that's better. Wallace, then, joins the canoe, paddles it down, scuttles it, and makes off. He must have walked pretty hard to get back to his punt. Then he fools about asking questions till the hue and cry starts. That is his signal: late at night, when the hue and cry makes the river full of traffic to cover his movements, he gets a second canoe, paddles up to the island, on the weir-stream side of it, embarks the body, with or without Nigel, on the canoe, ferries it up to the weir, drags over the weir, and finally deposits the body somewhere above Shipcote. Two points remain obscure —what did he do with his punt? And where or how did he get hold of the second canoe? The answer to Number One may be found by searching the river bed. The answer to Number Two isn't really difficult—there are lots of canoes here, and most of them were out that night, when the body was missing. It would be easy for Nigel to get one of them, and hand it over to his accomplice. That's one of the things which makes me pretty certain that Nigel was in it all.'

'I should go steady over that, though. Old Quirk has got a quite different story about it.' And Bredon detailed the American's speculations of the previous morning. 'We haven't yet found anything that makes it quite certain Nigel was in it. We can't prove that Derek Burtell was already helpless when he passed through Shipcote Lock, though it looks very much as if he was. We can't prove that there was a pre-arranged rendezvous with Wallace at the lock; he might, as Quirk suggests, have seen Nigel get off at that point, and seen that it would be an excellent opportunity for carrying off his design. We still don't know why he took the photograph; it's difficult to see what

Wallace, or any stranger, could have gained by its existence. But we haven't got the noose round Nigel yet, even if we succeed in finding him. Meanwhile, at the risk of being wearisome, I must insist that there are two things we haven't accounted for.'

' I know one, sir,' broke in Angela, waving her hand over her head after the manner of an impetuous school-boy in class. ' The second note-case—how did it come to exist, and how did it come to fall into the river just there ? '

' Second part doesn't matter,' replied her husband. ' If he had a second note-case, it might have been lying in the canoe, and fallen out when the canoe swamped. Or it might have been thrown in there as a blind. But we still don't know why he had two.'

' And the other difficulty ? ' asked Leyland.

' We still don't know who passed through Spinnaker Farm a little before a quarter-past nine that morning. Not Nigel, for it was out of his way. Not Derek, for he was dead. Not Wallace, for he couldn't have got there in the time. That still worries me a good deal.'

' You'd better ask Mr. Quirk about it,' suggested Angela.

CHAPTER XV

A NEW LEGACY

ON the Saturday before the interview recorded in the last chapter, Mrs. Coolman, sister of the late Sir John Burtell, died quietly in her sleep.

I am sorry that so many characters in this story should appear only to disappear ; but in this case, at least, no mystery hung over the circumstances. Mrs. Coolman was seventy-two years of age ; she had been, for some time, in failing health ; she died, unquestionably, of heart failure, and the medical certificate was signed accordingly. Her acquaintance with her great-nephews had been, as I have already indicated, of the slightest. Her atmosphere, her world, were not theirs ; she had grown up, she had been wooed and won, in the great days of English respectability ; her marriage with a Lancashire manufacturer had precipitated that respectability in an acute form ; and if her brother, Sir John, irritated his grandsons by his *fin de siècle* point of view, it must be supposed that the sister's attitude towards life would have been even less congenial. Derek and Nigel, therefore, never visited her after they reached the age of protest ; and it might easily have been anticipated that they would pass out of her life altogether, in view of the company they kept and the uniform dissoluteness of their character.

Moreover, though a widow and childless, Mrs. Coolman was a mother by adoption. Her young *protegé*, Edward Farris, had been orphaned in infancy ; it was she who had given him a home and provided for his education ; she who had secured him an excellent commercial post ; she who, soon afterwards, had insisted upon his resigning that post in order to live at Brimley House as her secretary and dance attendance upon her declining years. It was assumed as a matter of course by her friends, and perhaps by Farris himself, that her adopted son would also be her adopted heir. But old age brings with it, often enough, a return to earlier loyalties and a fond memory of younger days. She had been singularly attached to her only brother ; that attachment extended itself to his sons, particularly to his elder son, John ; and, when all these ties were lost to her, something of that earlier affection seemed to reincarnate itself in a wistful solicitude about the career of her grand-nephew Derek, whose picture survived in her heart painted in all the false colours of nursery innocence. She made inquiries about him, and those inquiries were answered, by his tutors and friends, with that charitable evasiveness which was to be expected. You do not shock the refined ears of a lady who dates from the Crimea by describing too faithfully the habits of a young ne'er-do-weel. Derek was being rather wild—so much she gathered ; the euphemism awoke in her a touch of maternal pity, and she loved the imaginary Derek all the more for being in need of 'something to steady him.'

Edward Farris was human; and it is to be supposed that he cannot have seconded with a very good grace the overtures made towards Derek by his great-aunt. Yet it does honour to his altruism, or perhaps to his prudence, that the old lady did not learn from him any fact which was injurious to Derek's reputation except the fact, too notorious to be concealed, that Derek and Nigel were scarcely on speaking terms. It was, as we have seen, one of the latest wishes she expressed that the uncongenial pair should find more in common; it was chiefly as the result of this wish that the canoe expedition was undertaken; and we may regard it as certain that Derek had not neglected to inform her of his compliance. When Derek disappeared, his great-aunt had already been overtaken by her last illness; the doctor would not hear of the grim news finding its way into her sick-room, and the papers were carefully kept from her. She died, then, in full knowledge that John Burtell's grandsons had effected a reconciliation, in ignorance of the tragic sequel which the reconciliation produced.

It was in this stage of half-enlightenment that she drew up her last will and testament. For the adopted son, whose prospects she had made and marred, she secured a decent provision. The whole of her remaining property, she declared,—it meant nearly a hundred thousand—was to pass absolutely to her elder grandnephew, the son of her beloved nephew John. The lawyer's diplomacy was taxed to the uttermost. He knew, as he sat by her

bedside, that half England was hallooing after
Derek as a fugitive, the other half pronouncing
obituaries on him as a corpse. He knew that any
reference to the fact might precipitate his client's
death. Yet the will, as she had outlined it to him,
would mean, in all probability, that she would die
intestate. The lawyer hummed and hawed; he
excelled himself in the iteration of those complicated rigmaroles by which the laity are hoodwinked.
It would never do, he said, to leave the will like
that; it would be a severe breach of legal custom
if no residuary legatee were named. Perhaps Mr.
Nigel Burtell might be mentioned? To his surprise, Mrs. Coolman was adamant. A few months
before, her family fondness had inspired her to
buy a book of poems which Nigel had produced,
in the hope of paying his Oxford bills with the
proceeds. *Mens hominum praesaga parum!* The
book reached Aunt Alma's breakfast-table; Aunt
Alma read it. Neither the sentiments it expressed
nor its manner of expressing them were adapted to
the taste of the seventies. With a certain tightening
of the lips, the dying Victorian consented to name
Edward Farris her heir, as Derek's alternative.

The firm of solicitors which drew up the will was
the firm which also represented Derek's own inter-
ests. Leyland had consulted them long and earn-
estly as to the financial situation; they knew,
therefore, that Leyland was in charge of the police
investigations. Throwing etiquette to the winds,
they wrote an 'Urgent' letter to Leyland at his
Oxford address, detailing the circumstances in full
and asking what action the police would like to

see taken—were the provisions of the will to be made public ? This letter was immediately carried over to Eaton Bridge by a man on a motor-bicycle, and Leyland was still closeted with the Bredons when he took it and opened it.

'We must talk to Mr. Quirk about that,' was Bredon's rather unexpected comment, when the situation was outlined to him.

'Mr. Quirk ? What's he got to do with it ? '

'Well, you see, it goes to support his theory. He was insisting, only yesterday, that we had no evidence to incriminate Nigel Burtell ; in his view, both cousins were being pursued by a man, or a gang of men, who stood to gain by Derek's death. I pointed out that, as far as I could see, Nigel was the only person who stood to gain by Derek's death ; it left him heir to the fifty thousand. But this new development alters the whole look of the thing— assuming, of course, that the old lady's intentions were known. There was a much bigger sum, twice the amount, to which Derek was heir, in which Nigel is not interested.'

'You mean that if Derek Burtell is alive—or rather, if he was alive on Saturday, the hundred thousand is his, and Nigel is the heir to it ? Whereas if Derek Burtell died before last Saturday, the whole thing goes to Farris, and Nigel has no more claim on it than you or I have ? '

'That's the situation, I take it. This will, mark you, was only signed last Wednesday. But assuming that Nigel knew, or had a good guess, how his great-aunt was going to cut up, he had less reason than anybody in the world to murder his

cousin. There I'm with Quirk entirely. Only—
did Nigel know ? '

' Meanwhile, Leyland, there's another man for
you to watch. If there was a man who had a
motive for murdering Derek Burtell, last week and
not later, his name was Edward Farris.'

Here the door opened, and Mr. Quirk himself
looked round it. He was about to withdraw, seeing
that a conclave was in process, but Angela quickly
recalled him. ' Cuckoo, Mr. Quirk ! ' she said
frivolously. ' You can come in now. There's been
another triumph for Transatlantic methods.'

' Is that so ? ' said Mr. Quirk, unruffled. ' I
should be particularly glad to think that any little
ratiocinations of mine had contributed to the
solution of a Class One mystery. But I'll remember
my bargain, Mr. Leyland ; I won't ask you for
anything more than pointers, if you can help me
to keep on the straight track.'

' Why, Mr. Quirk,' answered Leyland, ' I don't
think there's any need to keep you in the dark about
our latest piece of information ; it will be common
property soon. Bredon, I gather, didn't care for
your interpretation of the story yesterday, because
you hadn't allowed for Nigel Burtell being either
the murderer or the murderer's accomplice. He
thought, then, that nobody except Nigel had any
motive for getting rid of Derek. It proves now
that a will was drawn up in Derek Burtell's favour
last Wednesday, which makes him a rich man, if
he's alive.'

' And if he's dead ? ' asked the American, polishing
his glasses.

'If he's dead, the person who stands to gain is not his cousin, but a stranger to him—a man called Farris, who was very much in the testator's confidence. An old great-aunt of the two cousins it was. This Farris, you can see for yourself, had abundant motive for disposing of Derek Burtell if he could.'

'Then this Nigel wouldn't be concerned any way in the new will?'

'Only if his cousin was still alive at the time when the old lady died, last Saturday. Then he might be.'

'It's not an uncommon thing in the States', said Mr. Quirk meditatively, 'for crimes of violence to be attempted in connexion with large legacies of money. In our country, it's considered to be one of the leading incentives. But, see here, did young Burtell know that this legacy was coming to him? Because if he didn't know that, it's not likely he knew that there were murderers on his trail. And if he didn't know there were murderers on his trail, why, it's not just easy to account for his very peculiar movements at Millington Bridge.'

'And there's this, too,' suggested Bredon. 'If he knew it was his money they were after, and if they could only touch the money by murdering him before Aunt Alma died, why didn't he take better precautions—put himself under police protection, for example? To go off on a canoe tour with only one companion, and that companion unfriendly, was surely asking for trouble.'

'I can't say that I go all the way with you there,' replied Mr. Quirk. 'Some people, if they hear that

gunmen are out after them, seem to take a regular
pride in trying to dodge the pursuit by their own
cleverness—it's a kind of sporting instinct, I reckon.
And, mind you, a river trip isn't such a bad way of
leaving your pursuers behind, unless they're prepared to shoot. They can't follow you in a boat
without hiring a boat, and making themselves
conspicuous that way. They can't follow you along
the bank without giving you the chance to get
away by landing on the wrong bank. No, I see
more difficulty myself in finding out just how Derek
Burtell caught on that his life was worth taking.
If this will was only drawn up last Wednesday, it
doesn't seem as if auntie had been very clear in
her own mind about her testamentary dispositions.
And yet it was before she made up her mind that
the murder seems to have happened.'

'That's true, you know, Bredon,' said Leyland.
'Put yourself in this young Farris' place, even
supposing that he's a practised criminal—is he going
to risk committing a murder when it may prove,
after all, quite unnecessary?'

'It was now or never' objected Bredon. 'She
was in bad health; if her health got worse, it would
scarcely be decent for Farris to leave her, and if
once she died, no amount of murder would secure
the dibs.'

'That would have to mean', said Leyland, 'that
Farris both knew Derek Burtell was the heir, and
knew that he himself was the runner-up. Could
he be sure of that? Could he be sure, for example,
that Nigel Burtell wouldn't be the next candidate?'

'You seem resolved to acquit Nigel now,' replied

Bredon. 'But it still seems to me a possible theory, in spite of Mr. Quirk's suggestion, that Nigel was in it all.'

'What's that?' asked Mr. Quirk sharply. 'Wasn't it Nigel who consented to impersonate Derek Burtell at Millington Bridge, the way he'd get a lead on his pursuers?'

'Yes,' returned Bredon dryly, 'but did that do Nigel any harm, if at the same time he let Farris know that it was only bluff? Isn't it possible that it was a put-up job from the start between Farris and Nigel Burtell—that Nigel was really leading his cousin on into danger, while he pretended to be shielding him? That he and Farris agreed to go shares, Nigel getting his fifty thousand in any case from the original legacy, and either he or Farris collecting Aunt Alma's?'

'Well,' observed Mr. Quirk, 'you still haven't found your Nigel. It seems to me a very pertinent fact that it was on Saturday Mrs. Coolman died, and it was on Thursday Nigel Burtell disappeared. Say, doesn't that look like foul play? As if Farris had been determined to take no risks, and had put both cousins out of the way before the old lady's will took effect?'

'It's a nice point,' said Angela. 'Meanwhile, I'm getting horribly hungry for luncheon.'

CHAPTER XVI

BREDON PLAYS PATIENCE

LEYLAND hurried back after luncheon to catch the three-twelve. It was essential for him, he said, to see the solicitors; possible that he would have to break his journey at Wallingford on the way back. Mr. Quirk unexpectedly asked him for a lift into Oxford; it was his idea that something might be done towards tracing the movements of the man in the punt before he reached the river at all. His purchases, probably made at Oxford, of provisions for a river tour might yet be remembered by the shop people. Leyland agreed that such investigations would be best carried out by private effort; he was not anxious to start false alarms, still less true alarms, as to the suspicions entertained by the Force. Bredon also applauded the expedition; he himself had a commission for Mr. Quirk to execute in Oxford; as to its precise nature, Angela was pertinaciously inquisitive, her husband obstinately dumb.

Once they were left to themselves, he insisted that they must take a holiday. He was bored, he said, with the very name of Burtell; he had long since ceased to feel the smallest interest as to the whereabouts of either cousin, in this or in a future existence; they would forget their solicitudes, and spend an afternoon mudlarking on the Windrush. Angela had the gift, rare in her sex, of falling in with masculine moods without affectation ; and their day was all the more pleasant for being totally unworthy of record. If Thames banishes care by his easefulness, the tributary Windrush is an even more certain remedy ; that tempestuous rush over the shallows, those sudden windings, those perils of overhanging trees, demand entire concentration if you are to make headway against the unruly stream. An afternoon spent on the Thames is spent with an old, tried, mature companion, who refreshes you even by his silence ; an afternoon on the Windrush is like an afternoon spent with a restless, inquisitive child ; you find in perpetual distraction the source of repose. Both Miles and Angela had been stung with nettles, scratched with brambles, tormented by thistles underfoot, lashed with willow-branches, wetted by sudden inundations, tired out by ceaseless paddling, punting, and towing, before they returned to the Gudgeon ; the Burtell mystery seemed, by that time, a remote memory of the past, so much of mimic struggle and of miniature history had been fought through in the interval.

Mr. Quirk met them on their return, at about a quarter-past six, cool, polite, and inexhaustibly loquacious. His success with the shops had been only partial ; at one large store there had been distinct memories, fortified by ' the books ', of a stranger who had made considerable purchases with a view to camping on the river ; the date tallied, but unfortunately no mental picture survived of ' Mr. Wallace ', still less any legend as to his previous

movements. At the same time, in answer to a
raised eyebrow, Mr. Quirk was happy to assure Mr.
Bredon that his commission had been carried out.
Nor was Angela left long in suspense. Dinner was
no sooner over than four packs of cards appeared
from nowhere, and her husband sat down to his
interminable and intolerable game of patience.

' Miles,' she said reprovingly, ' you know you
aren't allowed to play patience when you're on a
job ! Does this mean you've given it up altogether ? '

' No, it means that I want to smooth out the
creases in my mind. Too much accumulation of
evidence always means tangle and brain-fag. I
must take my mind off the thing if I'm to see it
at arm's length, and that may mean seeing it from
a new angle. Remember Mottram, remember the
Load of Mischief, and try not to edge those cards off
the table by leaning against it. I shall retire to bed
punctually at eleven ; have no fears. But meanwhile,
leave me to my paste-board. Go and tell Quirk what
a handsome fellow I was when you first knew me.'

The Ingle-room was still a welter of unintelligibly
disposed cards, Miles was still wandering to and fro,
ruffling his hair as he controlled their destinies,
when Leyland looked in next morning. His errand
was an urgent one. Ever since Nigel Burtell's
disappearance, the police had naturally intercepted
all the correspondence which reached his Oxford
lodgings, but hitherto their curiosity had gone
unrewarded. There was a healthy crop of bills, but
never anything in the nature of a private missive.
By that morning's post—it was Tuesday morning
—a single post card had arrived, the address printed

in block capitals, the post-mark Paddington, the back covered with a series of apparently unrelated figures, which clearly indicated a cipher. 'I don't deny that I had a try at it myself,' confessed Leyland, 'though I never was much use at ciphers. It beats me, anyhow, and I thought your husband might make a better job of it. Of course, if he's taken to Patience——'

'I'll take it in to him,' said Angela. 'He can't do worse than kick me out. You've got a copy, I suppose? Very well, I'll give him the original, and you and I and Mr. Quirk will put out heads together over the copy.'

Bredon hardly looked up when she came into the room. 'What? A cipher? Oh Lord! Never mind, prop it up against that inkstand on the table there ; I'll look at it from time to time when I want a rest. Better give me a pencil and a clean sheet of paper, in case it happens to arouse my interest. But it's probably one of these insoluble ones. Good. And don't forget to shut the door gently.'

'We mustn't hope for much from him,' admitted Angela as she returned to the parlour—'the refectory' Bredon always called it. 'Do they use ciphers much in the States, Mr. Quirk? Now, let's have a look at it.'

The cipher, in case the reader cares to try his hand at it, was not at first sight very illuminating. It consisted of a row of figures, with no other mark, no spacing even, to guide in their interpretation. They ran thus :

'9123468537332006448121021817841607954824I0 37I255944I029I529I7904.'

'Sixty-four in all,' commented Leyland. ' It's obviously impossible that one cipher should stand for one letter, because that means your alphabet is reduced to ten letters. They must be groups of figures, then, that represent letters ; and they can't be groups of three, five, six, or seven, supposing the groups to be uniform, because that wouldn't divide out right. I take it, then, that they are groups of two, four, or eight. The trouble is, you see, there are no repetitions. That's to say, if you make the groups eights or fours there are no repetitions at all, and, even if you make the groups twos, the only repetitions you get are 91 and 37, each with a single repetition.'

'And that's nonsense, isn't it ? ' agreed Angela. ' Because it would have to mean that the message used all the letters of the alphabet and four non-existent letters, and only repeated itself twice.'

'I recollect ', said Mr. Quirk, ' one of leading cryptographers in the States telling me that letter-ciphers had been practically abandoned nowadays, and word-ciphers were used instead. Say, isn't it likely a message of sixteen words, instead of sixteen letters ? '

'And if it is, we can take our boots off and go to bed,' replied Leyland. ' You can't solve a word-cipher on a single message, unless you've got the key beforehand. Stands to reason they wouldn't be using any of the recognized codes. Well, here's for it.'

Their brows were knitted over it three-quarters of an hour later, when Bredon suddenly shouted from the door of the Ingle-room :

'The groups are threes.'

'Go back and count again,' retorted Angela

indignantly. ' You can't have even looked at the thing. Three won't go into 64.'

' You *will* go the wrong way about these things. You sit over the cipher and try to worry it out, and of course it won't come out. But if you do as I do, keep taking a look at it and then going away and forgetting about it, you come to it fresh every time. And then, with luck, you see the arrangement of groups which makes the whole thing look natural. It's the eye does it, not the brain.'

' Well, how do you work out the threes, anyhow ? '

' Don't count up to nine ; count up to twelve. You can count tens, elevens, or twelves as if they were single units.'

' Have you read it yet ? '

' No, but you ought to be able to do it now. I'm busy.'

They rewrote the cipher accordingly, and it certainly did look more promising. ' 912/346/853/733/200/644/812/1021/817/841/607/954/824/1037/1255/944/1029/152/917/904.'

Bredon came down to luncheon rubbing his hands, with the intimation that he had ' got it out '.

' The cipher ? '

' No, the patience. It was a long sight more difficult. Leyland gone back to Oxford ? '

' No, he's scouring round the country investigating another of Mr. Quirk's great ideas. You do give us all plenty of exercise, I must say. Come on, Mr. Quirk, spill it.'

With some hesitation, Mr. Quirk unfolded his great idea. He argued, in the first place, that it must be a book-cipher of some description ; that

was the only possible method for a couple of amateur
cryptographers.   If it was a book, it must be a book
which was in the possession of both parties.   'Now,
we know Nigel Burtell was one of the two parties ;
who's the other ?   I put it to you—Derek Burtell ! '
   ' Derek !   But you've spent a week trying to
convince us that they're both in a watery grave.'
   ' I must admit that I have been led to revise
my conclusions very considerably.   One of our
greatest American thinkers has said that it's only
a fool who doesn't acknowledge his mistakes.   Now,
according to my latest view both those two cousins
are alive, and what's more, they're in correspondence
with one another.'
   ' This all opens up very wide possibilities.   But
let us have the great idea.'
   Stripped of some circumlocution, the great idea
was as follows.   The cipher must have been pre-
arranged between the two cousins, possibly just
before they parted, but more probably in the course
of their tour.   It appeared that, for whatever
reason, they had separated on the Sunday night,
Nigel sleeping at Millington Bridge, as we have
seen, and Derek presumably finding a bed somewhere else.   It looked, therefore, as if the cousins
had meant to part for good on the Sunday night,
keeping the cipher as a means of correspondence.
Each, then, had already access to the book from
which the cipher was taken ; Nigel at Millington
Bridge, and Derek—where ?   Derek could not have
been far off ; they had been on the river till late,
and there were no last trains to be caught.   Derek,
therefore, was somewhere close at hand ; Mr. Quirk

had been looking at the map, and he suggested White Bracton, a village inland, it was true, but only a mile and a half by road from the bridge. Assuming that Derek spent the night there, the book which gave the clue to the cipher had been, and probably still was, at the White Bracton Inn.

'Isn't it a brain-wave ? ' said Angela. ' Wasn't it a very remarkable idea ? '

' It was ', Bredon admitted, ' a very remarkable idea. But it's rough luck on Leyland to be sent scouting across to White Bracton for the book, when of course, equally, it's here.'

' What's that ? ' asked Mr. Quirk.

' Of course it's here. Any country hotel keeps a railway time-table. Most country hotels don't keep Bradshaw, which fortunately narrows the area of our search.'

' Oh, oh, oh, how perfectly beastly of you ! ' moaned Angela. ' You mean the groups were the names of trains ? '

' Of course they were. That's the advantage of playing patience. You come fresh to the puzzle every time ; and about the sixteenth time those figures suddenly stand out in your mind as train times—8.24, 10.37, 12.55, and so on. Of course the extra noughts in 200 and 607 are only to make the cipher look uniform. Once you've got the idea, you see that it must be so. The cipher runs up to 12 because the clock runs up to twelve. There are a lot of eights and nines about, because most morning trains start at eight something or nine something. Oh, it's as clear as daylight.'

' Except what the thing means,' Angela pointed out.

'Well, obviously the time of a train can only suggest a word or a letter if you connect it with the name of the station it starts from. I assume you have to take a page of the time-table, and find a station from which the first train or the last train—the first train, I suppose, from the nature of the figures—starts at nine-twelve, then one from which the first train starts at three-forty-six, and so on. It must be Great Western, because it's the only railway in these parts. It must be a main line, or you wouldn't get a train starting as early as three forty-six. Oh, have you got a time-table there, Mr. Quirk?'

Mr. Quirk had produced a local guide from somewhere, and was scanning its pages. 'Here, you'd better do this,' he said. 'I never was much good with Bradshaw.'

'Well, we'll try, anyhow. Take down, please, Mrs. Bredon. London, Reading, Chippenham, Weymouth and Taunton; that sounds good enough. Dash, it's not so easy after all. . . . Hullo, here's a three forty-six in the morning starting from Oxford. Nine-twelve—that would be rather a one-horse sort of place; here you are, Hungerford. And Woodborough, wherever that is, leads off with an eight fifty-three.'

'Hungerford Oxford Woodborough. What a jolly message to get!' said Angela.

'Oh, why did they never teach you acrostics when you were young? Look at the initials— "HOW"; what's wrong with that?'

'Miles, you are a pet sometimes. This is fearfully inciting. Now for the seven thirty-three.'

'Moderately important, but not very important. I think we read straight down the page as far as possible. Seven thirty-three; that's Devizes. An arrival, really, but he wouldn't notice that. And two o'clock must be some terrific big junction . . . no, it isn't. . . . Good God, think of arriving at Ilfracombe at two in the morning!'

'DI, then the next one will be another D,' suggested Angela. 'Try Didcot.'

'Didcot it is; and DID it is. Now, eight-twelve is a more local sort of time; Aldermaston will do. What happens, I wonder, when there aren't enough stations to go round? Oh, I suppose you take the second earliest train.'

'Miles, this is too exciting; I can't stand it. Let's just take down the names, and read the initials afterwards.'

'All right. Here goes.' And it went, until the last group was registered, and Angela, who had been keeping her hand over the page, revealed the following names in column formation:

'Hungerford Oxford Woodborough Devizes Ilfracombe Didcot Aldermaston Lavington Midgham Athelney Chippenham Upwey Thatcham Upwey Paddington Dorchester Edington Reading Evershot Kintbury.'

'Yes,' said Bredon. 'Not a bad stunt. He missed out Theale, which ought to come before Thatcham, otherwise he seems to have made no mistakes.'

'Miles, don't be so provoking! Don't you see that this message is most frightfully important?'

'Oh,' said Bredon. 'You think it is?'

CHAPTER XVII

MR. QUIRK DISAPPEARS

THERE are few more humiliating sensations than that of the man who comes into a room bursting with stale news. When Leyland returned he was plainly full of important secrets. He did not even hesitate at seeing Mr. Quirk in the room. ' Derek Burtell's alive ! ' he announced. ' I must have a pint of bitter.'

' Alive ? ' queried Bredon.

' Well, he's putting his signature to cipher messages, anyhow.' Something in Angela's face checked him ; he was conscious of a repression. ' Good Lord ! ' he said, ' don't say you've been and read the cipher, Bredon ! '

' I'm afraid he has,' Angela apologized. ' If he wasn't so loathsomely idle he'd have read it three hours ago, and saved you that long, silly journey to White Bracton.'

' Oh, I shouldn't have wanted to be saved that,' said Leyland. ' That was all right—I found out more than the meaning of the cipher, you know.'

' This is very interesting,' put in Mr. Quirk. ' You mean, I guess, that we've all got something to learn not only from the cipher itself, but from the way you found it ? '

' Oh, this morning's been full of adventures.

163

For one thing, I called at the lock above Millington Bridge, and was told that the punt had been found. Nothing desperately mysterious about it, either. It was tucked away in a curious, purposeless kind of stone quay there is, hidden behind rushes, at the opposite side of the river just close to the Blue Cow.   Of course, it's pretty evident that there was something fishy about Mr. Wallace, or he wouldn't have hidden the punt away like that.   I suppose he made for the railway—it's not far from the river there.'

'Not so very fishy either, if you come to think of it,' said Bredon. 'If he was making for the railway, he had to cross the river, and there's no regular ferry at the Blue Cow ; besides, he wanted to go downstream a bit.   Naturally he took his punt with him ; naturally, if he wanted to go over-land, he stowed it away in a place where the casual passer-by wouldn't find it.   You can explain his movements by haste, without suspecting secrecy.'

'Anyhow, there the punt is, with some remains of the man's stores in it, but no clue to his identity or his destination.   However, that isn't all.'

'You were going to tell us,' Mr. Quirk pointed out, 'what it was you found at White Bracton.'

'Yes, I was.   There are several pubs at White Bracton, but only one that looks as if it wanted you to stay at it.   The White Hart, its name is. But when I went in I found it was the sort of place where nobody pays any attention to you ; you rap on the floor with your stick, and nothing happens, except that a dog barks somewhere in the distance ; you could run off with the stuffed trout, and no one the wiser. Just opposite me was one of those letter-racks they have at all these inns; and on the rack there was a single letter.

'For several reasons that letter interested me. In the first place, it was addressed by somebody who was writing with his left hand; it isn't difficult to see when that's happened. In the second place, although the name was written in full, " Mr. H. Anderton," the address wasn't in full; it was simply " The Inn, White Bracton ". In the third place, the letter had been there a week, to judge by the post-mark, and nobody had claimed it.

'Those derelict letters always interest me; it comes, I suppose, Bredon, of being a professional spy. And this one, lying about in a place which I'd gone to on purpose in the hope of picking up information, intrigued me particularly. The post-mark said " Oxford ", but there was nothing enlightening in that. I dallied with the temptation for a moment, then slipped the letter into my pocket, and left the White Hart without asking any questions at all. When I was round the corner, I opened the letter, and found that it was exactly the thing I had come for. It was from somebody who signed himself Nigel to somebody whom he addressed as Derek; and it explained in words of one syllable the whole system of the Bradshaw cipher which you solved this morning.'

'Have you got the letter here?' asked Bredon. 'I'd rather like to see the post-mark. Yes, the post-mark's all right; it was posted late on the day of Derek's disappearance. And the envelope was untouched, I suppose, when you found it?

But of course, you'd have been bound to notice
if it had been tampered with. Yes, that letter's
genuine enough, and, as Mr. Quirk says, it's all very
interesting. I suppose you've got specimens of
Nigel Burtell's handwriting to compare it with ? '

' Trust me for that. The whole thing's genuine.
And it looks rather as if we'd got to revise our
whole view of the business, don't it ? '

' As how ? '

' Why, on the face of it it looks as if the two
cousins were both alive, and in active correspondence
with one another. And if that's so, all the other
clues we've been following up, the photographs,
and the two sovereign-purses, and you-know-what
on the island, must all have been simply a blind
of some sort. And the hole in the canoe must
be either a blind or an accident. And I don't quite
see that we want to find the man in the punt any
more. We certainly don't want to drag the river
above Shipcote.'

' Yes, but you're going much too fast. You say,
on the face of it both cousins are alive. But is
that a necessary conclusion ? '

' No, not necessary, of course. But it proves,
surely, that one or other of them's alive ? It's not
very likely that a third person would be in the
secret of the cipher.'

' Yes, I think it's reasonable to assume that at least
one of them is alive. But then, you go on to say
that they're in active correspondence. There I don't
agree with you at all ; it seems to me much the most
interesting feature of the case that the correspondence between them is so extraordinarily passive.'

' How passive ? '

' Why, my dear chump, don't you see that neither
of them knows where the other is, or what's happening to him ?   A week ago, Nigel wrote a very
intimate letter to his cousin, addressing it to the
inn at White Bracton.   He had reason to believe
that his cousin was at White Bracton ; that means
there had been some prearrangement ; he did not
know the name of the pub at White Bracton, therefore the prearrangement, such as it was, was very
incomplete.   Nigel sent a code, to be used in case
of emergency—why hadn't that code been arranged
already ?   It means, surely, that when Nigel wrote
there was already some hitch in the plan ; things
weren't quite working out to time, and therefore
it would be prudent to have a cipher.'

' Yes, I suppose that's sound, as far as it goes.'

' But it's not nearly all.   The alias, H. Anderton,
must obviously have been arranged beforehand.
If Derek ever went to the pub at White Bracton—
that's to say, if he ever went to the right pub—he
must have looked about for letters addressed to
H. Anderton.   And if he had found one, he would
have lost no time in taking it down from the rack.
You wouldn't want to take any risks in such a
correspondence.'

' Yes, confound it all, I wondered why the letter
was unclaimed, but I didn't see how important it
was.   You mean Nigel doesn't know where Derek
is ? '

' Didn't know, anyhow.   And, what's still odder,
he thought he *did* know.   Surely it's fair to say
that there must have been a disarrangement of

their plans ? And, if so, the clues we picked up round the island and so on may still have a meaning.'

' But this morning's message looks as if they'd got in touch again.'

' Not a bit of it. If it was really Derek who wrote that post card, it shows that he hasn't kept informed of his cousin's movements in the least. If he had, he would have known, in the first place, that Nigel has gone down from Oxford ; and in the second place he would know that Nigel's movements have been suspicious, and that his old digs would be watched by the police. Therefore he wouldn't have sent him an incriminating message at that address. (I say incriminating, because there is always a chance of any cipher being read.) No, if Derek wrote that post card, it was a hopeless shot in the dark. But, of course, Derek didn't write that post card.'

' You mean that he can't know the cipher, because he never got the letter addressed to him at White Bracton ? But that letter may have been verbally confirmed since.'

' Not a bit of it. The two cousins haven't met, or Derek would know that Nigel isn't in Oxford any longer.'

' That's true. But he might have written the post card, knowing that it would fall into the hands of the police, precisely because he wanted it to fall into the hands of the police. After all, up till now Derek Burtell has had a good motive for stopping in the background. But since Aunt Alma's death he's got a remarkably good motive for reappearing.'

' But does he know what was in the will ? If

not, it would be risky to reappear. Besides, why not simply reappear, instead of setting puzzles to the police ? Besides, at the risk of being rude, I must say I think he'd have set a much easier puzzle to the police while he was about it. I am personally rather proud of myself for having solved it at all.'

' Still, he might have guessed that we should have the White Bracton letter in our hands by now. . . . I don't know ; I suppose you're right about Derek. What you mean is that Nigel sent that post card from Paddington to himself ? '

' Exactly. And we're still completely without evidence whether Derek is alive or dead. I doubt if Derek knew, or knows, that the White Bracton letter was ever written. But Nigel knows that it was written, and Nigel might quite reasonably guess, mightn't he, that with all the hue and cry there's been, the White Bracton letter would have been found. Don't you think so, Mr. Quirk ? '

' Why, certainly I'm of that opinion. Seems to me it was very odd the idea of making inquiries at White Bracton never occurred to anybody till I got my little brain-wave.'

' But what's Nigel's game ? ' objected Leyland. ' He wanted his cipher to fall into the hands of the police, to make them think—what ? That Derek was alive ? '

' Of course. Assuming that Nigel has lost track of Derek, it's the simplest way he could find of convincing the police that Derek isn't dead—or at any rate that he wasn't dead when Aunt Alma died, and her will took effect. After that, Derek

can die as much as he wants to. The point is that
he mustn't be allowed to predecease Aunt Alma,
and so rob himself of the legacy. Do *you* find any
difficulty in that explanation, Mr. Quirk ? '

' Why, no ; I can't say that I do.'

' Then you must be very differently built from
me. I find one enormous difficulty in that explanation. How did Nigil know *for certain* that Mrs.
Coolman had left her money to Derek, and therefore that it was necessary for Derek to reappear ?
If he didn't know for certain, you see, he could
hardly have acted so promptly. From the point
of view of the original legacy, it was still imperative
that Derek should stay dead.'

' Surely it was worth the risk,' suggested Angela.
' Because Derek didn't need to be dead until September the 16th. It wouldn't do much harm for him
to come to life in the meantime, as long as he was
killed again.'

' It would hardly do for him to develop a habit
of alternate decease and resuscitation. Such a
habit would awake suspicions among the most
guileless of lawyers.'

' I see one thing clearly,' broke in Leyland.
' Whatever way you look at it, there's no reason
to believe that Nigel knows more than we do about
what's happened to his cousin. If the post card
was his work, he was obviously trying a shot in
the dark. And therefore it's still important to find
the man in the punt before we find Nigel Burtell.'

' In a sense,' Bredon admitted. ' And yet if we
could lay our hands on Nigel, he might have something to tell us.'

' I suppose it's something ', said Leyland, ' to know that he's loose in London. He may have been seen there by people who knew him.'

' If he's really living there. But the post card, you must remember, was handed in at Paddington. In order to post a letter at Paddington, you don't need to be living in London. It's quite as simple to be living anywhere on the Great Western. You just take a train up to London and then take the next train back.'

' I've just one quarrel to pick with your analysis, Mr. Bredon,' suggested the American, who for some minutes appeared to have been plunged in thought. ' You allow that young Nigel wanted his post card to fall into the hands of the police. Well, if that's so, why didn't he send it to the address of Derek Burtell's flat in London ? It would reach quicker, for one thing ; and for another thing he could be quite certain, instead of just guessing, that it would fall into the hands of the police.'

' I know. But to put the London address on the post card would suggest collusion. Putting himself in Derek's place, the most natural assumption would be that the Oxford address was permanently likely to answer.'

' Well,' said Angela, ' one way and another we seem to be about as far on as we were before.'

' I know,' agreed her husband. ' Don't you think it's time you told us all you know about the business, Mr. Burtell ? '

CHAPTER XVIII

IN UNDISGUISE

FOR perhaps a quarter of a minute the whole company stared at one another. Then the family weakness of the Burtells saved the situation, and Nigel fainted.

It was when he had been carried up to his room, and Angela had imperiously assumed all responsibility for him, that Bredon and Leyland were free to discuss the situation. 'How long have you known?' asked Leyland. 'Did you recognize him from the start?'

'Not exactly. There was something reminiscent about him, though. The staff of the Gudgeon ought by rights to have recognized him, but they didn't, you see. It's quite easy to suspect a person of being in disguise; not nearly so easy to suspect him of being in undisguise.'

'How do you mean—in undisguise?'

'Why, that Nigel Burtell, the undergraduate, went about permanently disguised. He was round-shouldered, for example, but a singularly expensive tailor managed to turn him out a straight man. It was at Millington Bridge, wasn't it, that the landlady remembered him as a gentleman who held himself very straight? Anyhow, that was the impression he contrived to make everywhere; or

rather, his tailor contrived to make it for him.
Mr. Quirk was the real Nigel, as his friends never
saw him. The real Nigel, too, had his face disfigured
by a yellow blotch—you've been seeing it on Mr.
Quirk all this last week. As an undergraduate,
he got rid of the defect by making up ; he was a
pretty good actor, you know, and his make-up
imposed upon the world at large. . . . Though I
imagine some of his friends wouldn't have minded
much if they had known about it ; it would only
have been a single affectation added to the rest.
Of course, if that had been his natural complexion,
it would have been tanned a deep brick-red after
ten days on the river, and Mr. Quirk couldn't have
happened. But I think his hair made more difference than anything ; he used to wear it very long
and brushed straight back—rather shiny hair it
was ; and when he had it cropped quite close (that
was at a small shop in Swindon) it showed up his
slight baldness and made him look absolutely
different. Another thing everybody remembered
was his voice, a slow, affected, disgustingly superior
drawl. That was quite unreal, too ; he found no
difficulty in dropping it when need arose, and
talking like an American instead.'

' He's certainly a good actor. I can't think how
he managed to keep up the American part so well.'

' You mean his pronunciation of English ? No,
that was comparatively simple ; his mother, as you
know, married an American, and his home was in
the States, as far as he had one. What impresses
me more is the way he managed to keep up the
American attitude towards life—that curious fresh-

ness and simplicity they have; that was foreign
to his nature, if you like. That habit of always
talking as if everything was quite different on the
other side of the Atlantic—I shouldn't be surprised
to hear an American say that the earth goes round
the sun *on the other side*. He did that to perfection.
Yet, in a sense, that simplicity was itself only a
shedding of his own beastly affectedness. I don't
think he had any positive disguise, if you see what
I mean, except, of course, the horn spectacles;
and they don't go far.'

'But you say you didn't recognize him straight
away from the start? Didn't even feel suspicious
about him?'

'No; why should I? I did take just a look to
make sure he wasn't Derek; but that was obvious;
there's no trace of drugs on him. I didn't think
of his being Nigel because, when he introduced
himself here, Nigel wasn't yet missing. If you'd
come in at two o'clock, telling me that Nigel had
disappeared, and then Mr. Quirk had rolled up at
four, I should have spotted the thing at once. As
it was, he got the start of you; he was already
established here before you came. The human mind
doesn't solve problems until they have been set.'

'He took big risks in coming here.'

'Ah, but he had no notion I was here, you see.
I was out when he arrived, and it was too late to
draw back when Angela introduced us. As I say,
I had a slight thrill of recognition, but I bottled it
up—I always do. Of course, somebody coming out
from Oxford might have recognized him, but it
wasn't likely; Oxford's all down by now. And as

for the staff of the hotel, they never notice that kind of thing. Business, to them, is an endless succession of strange faces; consequently no one face calls for remark.'

'What gave you the notion that something was wrong?'

'Why, I believe the first thing was when he told Angela it was lucky I was such a good photographer. What did he know about it? It puzzled me. Then, you remember, there was that business of the note-case.'

'Which note-case? The one at the island or the one the scouts found?'

'The one the scouts found. Of course, it was nonsense supposing that Derek Burtell carried two purses. That meant that one or the other was a fraud, a blind. It seemed natural to suppose that it was the one with the visiting-card in it. The visiting-card had so obviously been *put* there. Now, the curious thing was that those scouts had been diving in that precise spot from Monday till Saturday, but it wasn't till Saturday they came across the note-case. Was it possible, I asked myself, that the note-case had been dropped in calmly overnight? If so, who had dropped it? Then I remembered that Mr. Quirk had been anxious to know the precise spot where the canoe was found, and that he had gone out for a walk there the evening before. I wanted to know more about Mr. Quirk.'

'Thank God that riddle's solved. It was driving me crazy.'

'I still didn't feel certain that Mr. Quirk was Nigel. I toyed with the idea that he was some

American friend whom Nigel had put on to watch me. I'd only seen Nigel for quite a short time, you must remember, and in a rather dark room. But my suspicions were aroused, and I thought it would be a good thing to watch Mr. Quirk pretty closely, and give him his head. Though I never dared to credit him with the audacity which he proceeded to show.'

'You mean all that business about Millington Bridge—the one cousin sleeping in the two rooms? Yes, it was pretty bold. Why did he give us such a big slice of the truth?'

'Oh, I've no doubt as to his primary object. He wanted us to take him into his confidence, so that he could keep a watch on what we were doing. And in order to do that, he felt he must put up some sensational bit of detective work, to make us value his help. But I'm not quite so sure about his giving us a slice of the truth.'

'Surely you don't believe that both cousins slept at Millington Bridge that night?'

'Well, we've no positive evidence about it except the finger-marks on the decanters. And those, of course, Nigel himself had just made, while we were looking at the window-frames.'

'Good Lord! My opinion of Mr. Quirk as a detective is going down; but I am beginning to think highly of him as a criminal.'

'It was a bad mistake he made, though. Of course, I never believed that those marks had been on the decanter the best part of a week. Grease! Why, he would have had to use plaster of Paris. I wonder that took you in, Leyland.'

' It all depends on whether you're expecting a thing like that or not. I was perfectly taken in by Mr. Quirk, and I never dreamt that he could have made the finger-marks.'

' Anyhow, as I say, he made a mistake. Because, as you know, I had got the print of Nigel Burtell's finger and thumb, and that told me exactly who Mr. Quirk was. All Saturday and Sunday, while you were away, I kept a keen eye on his movements. What worried me was the man's audacity in coming to the very inn where I was staying. Then I found the book he'd been reading, Warren's *Ten Thousand a Year*. If you've ever been old-fashioned enough to read that story, you will remember that the solicitors in it are Messrs. Quirk, Gammon, and Snap. That showed me where he'd taken the name from. And that showed me that he'd come to the Gudgeon quite carelessly, without even going to the trouble of inventing an alias before his arrival. In a word, he didn't know I was at the Gudgeon at all—he had simply come there to watch proceedings. He wasn't expecting the hotel people to ask him his name.'

' Yes, that's pretty smart work. But why didn't you let on to me, if you don't mind my asking ? '

' Well, on the Saturday and Sunday you weren't there, anyhow. And I'm afraid I must confess that I thought you might want to arrest him straight away, and spoil the little game I was playing with him. Have you ever noticed what happens if you catch sight of a rabbit before it catches sight of you, even at close quarters ? If you stand absolutely still, the rabbit goes on feeding quite happily, and you can watch it for a long time. I enjoy doing that ; I enjoyed doing the same thing with Mr. Quirk. I loved watching the skill with which Nigel Burtell posed as Mr. Quirk, and remembering the equal skill with which Mr. Quirk used to pose as Nigel Burtell. As long as you and I made no move, he wouldn't run away ; he was too vain for that. But the next day, yesterday, I confess that I did take liberties with you. I let Mr. Quirk go up to London.'

' To London ? '

' Yes, by the three-twelve, and back by the four forty-five. That's what he did when he went over to Oxford. I had misgivings about the whole thing ; it seemed as if he might be doing a bolt. But somehow I felt convinced that he wouldn't bolt *now*, because his game wasn't fully played yet. He now had to create evidence, you see, that Derek didn't die before Aunt Alma. So I risked letting him go away and manufacture his evidence. You'd have looked a pretty good fool if he had got away, because he was travelling on your train.'

' Confound you, I wish you wouldn't take these risks.'

' Loyalty to employers, you see. You want to find a murderer. I want to find out whether there's a corpse. For that purpose, it was worth while giving Nigel his head. If I hadn't, we should never have known anything about White Bracton.'

' What *do* we know about White Bracton ? '

' Why, that on Monday night Nigel addressed a letter to Derek at the inn there. In fact, we know for certain that Nigel, on Monday night, still believed his cousin to be alive, and believed he knew his address. That shows there was some hanky-panky about Nigel's actions, and also about Derek's intentions. When Angela has finished soothing the fevered brow, I hope to find out what.'

'It will be queer to hear Mr. Quirk not talking American.'

'It will be queer to think of him as not being an American. What an excellent disguise it was, after all! If we meet one of our own fellow-countrymen, a stranger, at an inn or in a railway-carriage, it is our instinct to want to know everything about him—what part of the country he comes from, what is his business, and so on. But an American we take for granted. We don't want to hear what part of his country he comes from, because we know that we couldn't place it on the map within a thousand miles. We are terrified of hearing all about his business. He is so ready to impart information that we never ask him questions.'

'Bredon, we're beating about the bush. What each of us really wants to ask the other is whether he thinks Nigel Burtell is a murderer—or at least, a murderer's accomplice. You say Nigel didn't know where Derek was on Monday night, or he wouldn't have written a letter to him at White Bracton. But you see as clearly as I do that it might all be part of his alibi ; that he may have deliberately written that letter, and then deliberately led us on to find it, in the hopes of persuading us that he was entirely ignorant of his cousin's death. Nigel Burtell is going to tell us his story—at least, if he doesn't want to we shall find means to make him. But what we both want to know is whether the story he means to tell us is a true one.'

'Personally, I'm waiting to see what it is before I start wondering whether it's true. But I'll tell you this much. I believe the late Mr. Quirk was right when he said that it's no good trying to prove Nigel was the murderer's accomplice until we can find the murderer. Unless we do that, Nigel will always be able to profess ignorance of what happened. His alibi, you see, remains good. A canoe with a hole that size in it *can't* have drifted downstream in the given time; therefore it was propelled downstream; Nigel didn't do that, because he was on the nine-fourteen train; therefore somebody else did it; either Derek Burtell, still alive, or else a third person. And that third person must be found before we can definitely prove how Derek died, or indeed (for that matter) whether Derek is dead.'

'I never quite see why you lay so much stress on the question of the boat's drifting. Surely even without that the alibi would be good—look at the time it must have taken, even if Derek was already dead, to photograph his corpse and lug it up on to the island.'

'I'm not so sure. It was quick work, of course, but the train, you found, wasn't actually dead on time. I'll tell you what, when we've heard Nigel Burtell's story, we might do worse than spend part of to-morrow trying to reconstruct the thing. We'll go up to Shipcote Lock, and you can act as the dummy corpse while I see how long it takes to do the trick.'

'I was thinking of going and asking for an interview with Mr. Farris.'

'No need. *He* can't afford to bolt, anyhow. Hullo, Angela, how's the patient?'

CHAPTER XIX

THE STORY NIGEL TOLD

NIGEL'S trouble proved to be something more serious than a common fainting-fit. It was a heart attack, which demanded a visit from the doctor, and its inevitable sequel—the prescription of 'a few days in bed'. Leyland was delighted at this turn of affairs. He had an intense horror of making unnecessary arrests, of putting suspects in prison and letting them out again with apologies. Nothing was so repellent to his professional pride. Yet it would have been difficult to avoid taking out a warrant against Nigel, so clever had been his manœuvres, so widely had his description been circulated. In bed, and with his clothes removed under some hospital pretext, Nigel was as good as arrested ; the invalid is, for all practical purposes, a jail-bird. It was not, however, till the morning after his seizure that he was allowed to give any account of himself.

'I think I ought to warn you, Mr. Burtell,' Leyland began, 'that, though no arrest has been made, I mean to make notes of your story, and shall be prepared to produce them in case of emergency.'

'Yes, rather,' said the sick man. 'I'm hanged if I know whether I'm a criminal or not, you see. The situation has got so complicated. I think I should find it easiest if you just let me tell the story my own way, and don't interrupt me till afterwards.

' You know, of course, that Derek and I weren't on very good terms. There was a woman—but I expect you've heard all about that. Anyhow, I was rather surprised at getting a visit from him the other day, suggesting that I should go out with him in a canoe up the river. He explained why; Aunt Alma, he said, was beginning to sit up and take notice of the fact that she had great-nephews, and was wishing that we could hit it off better. If I was willing, he would come down to Oxford and meet me ; I would have a boat ready, and we would go up to Cricklade, making the best of a bad job, and tell Aunt Alma about it afterwards. I agreed, only I was doubtful about being able to finish the journey before my Viva. He pointed out that I could go ashore anywhere I liked, if we were pressed for time. Actually, I had made a mistake about my Viva, and expected it a day earlier than it came.

' It was a queer journey, one way and another, but there's no need to describe it in detail. For a good deal of the time, Derek wasn't worth talking to ; he'd brought some of his drug with him, the silly ass, and he took it at intervals. Once he let me try some, and it pretty well laid me out— beastly, I thought it. But, what was much more important, in the course of the journey he explained to me a plan he'd got for saving his financial position, with or without Aunt Alma. He was sick of London, he said, and the fellows he met in London ; he wanted to emigrate somewhere, and start

afresh. Only he'd no intention of starting penniless ;
and that's what he'd have to do if things went on
as they were. But why shouldn't he, instead of
emigrating in the ordinary way, simply manage to
disappear ? If he did that, his death would be
presumed after a time, and the beastly Insurance
Company would have to pay up ; the fifty thousand
would remain safely in the family.

' Only, as he explained to me with some candour,
a confederate was necessary to the plan, and that
confederate had got to be myself. In three years'
time the fifty thousand would come to me, and I
could borrow in the meanwhile on the strength of
it. He suggested, then, that he should disappear,
and I should automatically become my grandfather's
heir ; we were to go halves in all the profits that
resulted. He didn't (he was kind enough to explain)
trust me a yard. But this agreement, once made,
I should necessarily have to keep ; if I tried to
play him false, he could simply reappear and, with
some loss of dignity, expose me. He intimated
that this was my only chance of seeing the colour
of the legacy ; he was quite determined not to die
before he was twenty-five, and so leave the field
open to me ; sooner than that, he would turn
teetotaller.

' I had no moral scruples about the suggestion,
but I hesitated a little at the idea of breaking the
law in order to enrich a fellow like Derek. But
it appealed to my pocket, and it appealed to my
sense of adventure. We struck the bargain, and
then he began to talk to me about the details.
This canoe trip, he said, was providential ; it was

quite easy to disappear when you went out on the river, and the police would drag it for a fortnight, and then say you were dead. I said I thought most bodies of people drowned in the Thames were recovered, but he assured me there would be no difficulty so far as that was concerned. And I must say he had worked out the plan very ingeniously. That was the extraordinary thing, because Derek, you know, was always a bit of a chump. I think it was that dope he used to take which had given him the idea ; while its effect lasted, it really made Derek quite lively, and his brain worked like a two-year-old.

'The great trouble about disappearing, he said, was that you couldn't actually hide in a haystack ; you must still go about and meet people, but of course under an alias. And the difficulty of an alias was that it began just where your old self left off—Derek Burtell disappeared, if you see what I mean, and immediately Mr. X came into existence. A clever detective would spot that ; would connect the facts and put two and two together. To avoid that difficulty, you must make your alias overlap with your real self. Mr. X must come into existence at least a day before Derek Burtell disappeared. You see the idea ? And he had a sound way of working the scheme. When we reached our last stage, at Millington Bridge, I was to go up to the inn twice in succession, pretending to be two different people ; I was to sleep in two beds, wash in two basins, get through two breakfasts, and pay two bills. So that everybody would take it for granted we had both slept at Millington Bridge.

Meanwhile, he would totter off to White Bracton,
a mile or two away, and establish himself there as
a Mr. H. Anderton, a commercial traveller, or something of that sort. (He wasn't sure, he said,
whether we shouldn't finish up on a Sunday, and
if we did, of course it wouldn't look well to be a
commercial.) The point of the plan was that Mr.
Anderton would come into existence on (say)
Sunday night, and Derek Burtell wouldn't disappear
till Monday. Who would be likely to connect the
two, when everybody assumed that Derek Burtell
spent the night at Millington Bridge, and we could
prove that Mr. Anderton spent it at White Bracton?

' All that we carried out. I left him at Millington
Bridge, and did the two-headed man trick, while
he sloped off. Next morning he met me a little
way down below the bridge, and asked me if it
had all gone off all right. White Bracton, he said,
was a pretty putrid hole, but he got a shake-down
at the inn ; still, he felt awfully sleepy. So we
went on down to Shipcote Lock ; it was still quite
early in the morning, and there was nobody about
much, though we passed one man in a punt.'

' Excuse me one moment,' Bredon interrupted,
' but did you really take a photograph of Burgess,
the lock-keeper ? '

' Of course I did. You showed it me, didn't you ?
The last one that came out on that spool ; the other
two were fogged.'

' Did you never expose the last two, then ? '

' I didn't, but Derek may have. You see, while
we were in the lock, just when I was going off to
the station, Derek shouted up that I might as well

leave him the camera, and then he could finish up the spool if he saw anything worth taking. So I gave it him.'

' You're contradicting, aren't you, what you told me at Oxford—that you must have dropped the films near the station ? '

' Yes. I thought it best to say that, because I couldn't imagine how the films got there, and I thought it might lead to awkward inquiries.'

' One more question before you go on. Did you *throw* the camera down, or did you go down the steps and hand it to your cousin ? '

' Went down and handed it to him. Derek couldn't catch for nuts. Then he pushed off from the bottom of the steps, and I crossed the weir bridge and took the path for the station. We had agreed that I must have a perfect alibi, so that I should know nothing about his disappearance. I got the exact time from the lock-keeper. I looked round to see somebody on the way to the station, so that he could swear to me. But there was no-body ; and so—it was a suggestion Derek had made —I cut through the hedge on my left, and went through a sort of farm place that was quite out of my way, really—there were certain to be people about there, Derek said. I only saw one old lady in a top window, but I took off my hat to her, so that she'd remember my passing through.

' I had dawdled purposely, so as to be able to catch the train at the last moment ; that was another of Derek's ideas. If I travelled without a ticket, he said, I could own up to the man at the barrier in Oxford station, and he'd have to sell me a ticket, so he'd remember about it afterwards, and cover my alibi. That worked out all right. Then, of course, my Viva was going to cover the next stage of the proceedings. That didn't come off, but I took a taxi out here, and asked for a drink so that I could have an argument about the time with the barmaid. That covered the other end of my alibi, you see.

' Then I had to sit down and wait—we hadn't intended, of course, that I should have so long to wait—that was due to the mistake about the Viva. The arrangement was that at about half-past one I should be somewhere near the disused boat-house ; the canoe, we calculated, ought to be somewhere near there by then. I left Derek to arrange that as he thought best ; he was to give the impression, as best he could, that he'd fallen into the river with a heart-attack, that the canoe had been swamped, and so on.

' Well, I did the agitated part all right, and took a man from here with me so as to have a witness when I found the canoe. It came up to time splendidly, and the man got it in to shore, then started diving to see if he could find Derek any-where. While he was doing that, I found a beastly hole in the bottom of the canoe, as I was trying to right it. That annoyed me, because I assumed that Derek had done it as the simplest way of swamping the boat, forgetting, the silly chump, that people would ask questions about it after-wards. That was the first thing that went wrong about the plan.

' But the next thing was much worse. We had

agreed that he was to send a letter to me as soon
as he got home to White Bracton—that would be
about ten o'clock in the morning, and it ought to
arrive the same night. I was to write to him from
my digs just to confirm the fact that everything
had gone off all right. Afterwards, there was to
be no correspondence, for fear my letters should be
watched. Now, when I got home that night, there
was no letter waiting for me. So I thought out a
cipher, and wrote it off to " H. Anderton ", thinking
that it might be easier for him to send messages
that way, through the papers if necessary. But
next morning there was still no letter from White
Bracton. I began to get alarmed, and yet I could
do nothing without attracting suspicion. And so
it went on from one day to the next ; no message
from Derek, and no prescriptions about what I
should do.

' You don't know, probably, what the end of
term's like at Oxford—the end of one's last term,
I mean. There's a sickening feeling of being at
a loose end that makes you want to go away and
die somewhere. All that ridiculous aesthetic business looks so empty and pointless when you've got
to go down ; it felt like being in a theatre when
you've lost your hat at the end of a play, and
they're all turning down the lights. Its effect on
me was that I wanted to cut adrift from the whole
business and start again on a fresh tack ; I suppose
it was a kind of conversion. . . . If Derek was
going out to the Colonies, why shouldn't I ? And
then in a flash the thought occurred to me : If
Derek was going to disappear, why shouldn't I ?

' I didn't know then that my own movements had aroused any suspicion. I wanted to keep near the scene of action, but staying in Oxford, with all that mockery of a past behind me, was too much. Why shouldn't I fade off into the surrounding country somewhere, and become a fresh person for a bit ? There was no need to disguise myself ; I had only to drop a disguise. It might be safer, perhaps, to pose as an American ; I've lived so much in the States that the impersonation was hardly any effort to me. I thought of this pub, which had seemed rather comfortable ; I was sure they wouldn't recognize me with my hair cut short and all the rest of it. I determined to do it. Fortunately I'd lots of cash in hand, because I'd been meaning to travel on the Continent, and hadn't yet booked my passage. I would let my luggage go up to London without me, and disappear into the blue by the next train, a few minutes later. It all seemed to work without a hitch. At the last moment I got the impression that somebody was watching me ; so I was very careful to skip off while he wasn't looking.

' The train journey was a simple one—I expect you've worked it out for yourselves. Change platforms at Swindon, then double back by a slow train to Faringdon, and you're within a 'bus ride from here. On my way I called at White Bracton, and was really appalled to find my letter to " H. Anderton " still in the rack. Then for the first time I realized that something had gone very wrong indeed. I hung about for nearly an hour, waiting till the passage should be empty and I could get hold of the letter, but they never gave me a chance ; so I got tired of it and came on here.

' I had hoped to find the inn empty ; and it was annoying when a strange lady came up and talked to me. But I remembered that I was an American, and it was therefore my duty to introduce myself by name ; I picked it at random from a book I'd been looking at. Then I found I'd put my foot in it, because suddenly you walked in, and I had to be presented to you. But you seemed to have no suspicion at all. You must be a far better actor than I am, because until yesterday evening I hadn't the faintest idea that you suspected who I was. I got reckless, and determined to see the thing through. Among other things, I thought I'd help to establish Derek's death. I had a card which Derek had left on me ; I had a fiver of his, which he'd given me when we were settling up our hotel bills ; I put them into a note-case and planted them out in the river for the scouts to find. Then I thought it would be a good idea to worm myself into your confidence, so I planned out that Millington Bridge affair, with the marks on the decanters. You seemed to be drinking it all in.

' Aunt Alma's death was what altered the look of things. When you told me about the will, I realized what a silly position I'd put myself in. Here was all Aunt Alma's money going to that ass Farris, unless Derek could be produced, and I hadn't the faintest idea where Derek was ! So I remembered the letter at White Bracton, and I thought I'd try the cipher stunt. I posted the card to myself at Paddington. I could have cried with delight when the visit to White Bracton worked out so well. And then . . . well, there I was, and here I am. Can I be prosecuted for a conspiracy to defraud ? I suppose I can ; but it isn't worth while unless you can find Derek alive ; and if you do, why there's all Aunt Alma's money to pay off our liabilities with. On the whole, I'm feeling more comfortable than I've felt for a week.'

'M'm !' said Leyland, ' you've been conspiring to defeat the ends of justice all right, by your own account, but I'm hanged if I know whether it's actionable. May I just ask whether you've given us a complete list of your movements ? Or whether we have to thank you for any more of the little conundrums we've been trying to solve in these last ten days ? '

' No, I think not. . . . Oh yes, of course, there was one thing I did, but not very important. When I found the canoe, you know, and saw that it had a hole dug in the bottom of it, it worried me a good deal ; because Derek's disappearance was meant to suggest accidental death. But this neat little hole in the bottom of the boat suggested murder or suicide or a game of some sort. Nobody could think *that* was an accident. Then it occurred to me that it might be taken for an accident if only the edges of the hole weren't so confoundedly regular. Well, there was this chap who was with me, you know, plunging about in the water like any old porpoise. So I got hold of a sharp piece of stone, and worried round the edges of the hole at the bottom, in the hope that it would look as if the canoe had run aground and got smashed up that way.'

'Did you now?' said Bredon, his eyes burning. 'And did you by any chance happen to make the hole at all larger while you were about it?'

'Oh yes, lots. It was quite a little hole to start with.'

Bredon got up and walked about the room with his hands in his coat pockets, whistling.

CHAPTER XX

A RECONSTRUCTION

'NO,' said Bredon as he and Leyland paddled up, it seemed for the fiftieth time, to Shipcote Lock. 'I don't find Nigel Burtell's story incredible in the least. I was never at a University, but I can quite understand how a creature of poses like that might experience a sudden revulsion just at the end of his time there. In a small world it must be difficult for a self-conscious person *not* to pose—not to wonder what people are thinking of him and whether people are thinking of him ; not to impose upon them a false personality if his true personality is not worth imposing. And to leave all that behind must engender a desire to return to the simple emotions. But then, unfortunately, murder is one of the simple emotions ; and I shouldn't be really surprised to hear that Nigel had returned to that. He's so confoundedly plausible, you see ; I wouldn't put it beyond him to give us a perfectly genuine analysis of his emotions, and then conceal from us the central fact. And it remains certain that he's blown his own alibi to bits. If there was only a hole about the size of a pin's head in the bottom of that canoe, the wind and the stream would carry it no end of a distance before it filled up. And, dash it all, that's all there

was.   Why shouldn't the murder have been done
before the canoe left the iron bridge ?   And if it
was, why shouldn't it have been Nigel that did it ? '

' I know, I know.   But then, you've always been
building such a lot on that argument.   To me, the
whole thing has been a question of the total time
involved.'

' Well, we're going to find out all about that now.'

' Yes ;   and yet I'm not sure that all this recon-
struction business is really a fair test.   You see,
you go about the business in cold blood, all gingered
up beforehand and quite certain what you're going
to do next.   Interruptions and sudden after-
thoughts don't put you off your stroke.   When
you undress by the bank, and dress again afterwards,
your stud won't lose itself in the grass, one sleeve
of your shirt won't pull itself inside out, because
you won't really be in a hurry, only pretending to
be in a hurry.   To catch a train and do a murder
while you're about it in twenty minutes is all right
on paper, but when a man comes to do it he's bound
to lose his head.   Look at those two photographs,
for example.   I dare say you're right in thinking
that the one of the footsteps was only due to an
unintentional exposure of the film.   But the one
of the body in the canoe is an admirable snapshot.
Well, you take photographs, don't you ?   Think
what a confounded lot of sprawling and squinting
and shifting one's feet about there is, before one
gets the beastly thing right.   Could a man do all
that, when he was just catching a train, and it was
a matter of life and death to him ?   That's my
trouble.'

' It's difficult, I grant you. I suppose there isn't any other conceivable way in which that photograph could have been taken ? No. . . . Wait a moment, though. . . . I say, Leyland, you haven't got that print I gave you in your pocket by any chance, have you ? '

' Of course I have. We want to get the whole setting of the thing exactly right. It's in my coat pocket, up there in the bows, if you think you can reach it without upsetting the canoe. Go gently, now.'

Bredon retrieved the print, and looked at it intently for a good half-minute. Then he passed it back over his shoulder to Leyland, with the question : ' Do you notice anything funny about the shadows in that picture ? '

' You mean. . . . Good Lord, what fools we've been ! They go from left to right ! '

' With the picture facing North . . . and the time supposed to be nine in the morning. No, it won't do, will it ? I wonder we didn't think of that before. We know they came back late in the afternoon to cart the body away, and of course it was then that they put it into the canoe and photographed it.'

' That's all very well, but what about the fifth film, the one that shows the footsteps ? That was surely taken in the morning, because it shows the footsteps still wet. We know the footsteps were there in the morning—Burgess swears to them.'

' Oh, the footsteps were photographed in the morning right enough. Otherwise the steps would cast a shadow—they face East, you see. But then,

I've always believed that film was an accidental exposure. If Nigel (say) was carrying the camera when he walked up the steps, and his foot slipped at the top, the exposure would be over and done with in no time.'

' Yes, if it *was* accidental. But, now I come to think of it, why shouldn't they have taken a photograph of the footprints in the evening? All they had to do, don't you see, was to fake the footsteps on the left-hand side of the bridge, instead of the right. Then a photograph taken in the late afternoon would look as if it had been taken in the early morning.'

' Good for you, Leyland! Only I'm hanged if I see what they could have wanted to do it for. The thing still works out all wrong, you know. Why did these murderers want to leave traces about which made it quite certain that the man had been murdered? What impression did they want to create, which you and I are too stupid to see? Confound it all, they've overshot themselves rather badly there. It seems to me just meaningless.'

' Anyhow, we've cleared up one point. When you give your little exhibition this morning there's no need to take a camera with you. All you've got to do on your way to the train is to lift the body out of the canoe the quickest way you can and lug it up on to the clay bank. By the way, what are you going to do about a dummy body? I'm hanged if I'm going to understudy the corpse in that act.'

' We'll have to raise something from Burgess. A roll of carpet will do. Hullo! here's the good old island. You get out and take your photographs

while I paddle up to the lock and covet Mrs. Burgess'
best piece of drugget.'

Very carefully and methodically, Leyland took
six photographs of the trail through the bracken,
and two close-ups of the clay bank with the button-
impress. By the time he had finished, Bredon had
returned with a substantial roll of oil-cloth, which
he deposited on the left-hand bank of the island.
A few minutes later they had taken possession of
the lock. Mr. Burgess, wondering but obedient,
was told to go on gardening, keeping a look-out
to make sure that all their operations were beyond
his range of vision. The lower gates of the lock
were opened, and Bredon, standing at the bottom
of the steps, gave a long, straight shove to the
canoe, which carried Leyland, stop-watch in hand,
briskly downstream. Bredon walked at a moderate
pace towards the weir bridge. The moment he
had crossed it, finding himself hidden from Mr.
Burgess' observation, he ran at full speed some
forty yards along the bank, then sat down and
undressed to his bathing-suit. He lowered himself
without noise into the weir-stream, swam it, and
pushed his way recklessly through the undergrowth
at the southernmost end of the island. On the
lock-stream, Leyland was now floating very slowly ;
it would clearly take him some time to reach the
iron bridge at that rate. Bredon ran to the bridge,
walked backwards up the steps, swam up to the
canoe, brought it to shore, boarded it, and paddled
at full speed past the bridge. Here he landed, and
lifted Leyland, none too gently, on shore ; then
devoted himself to dragging the roll of oil-cloth up

to the middle of the island. Leyland, when he had tethered the canoe, walked back to the lock, and set out for the station on Mr. Burgess' bicycle, along the field path. He had only waited a moment or two when a rousing chorus of barks from Spinnaker Farm announced that Bredon, his work done, his clothes resumed, was hurrying up.

'Sorry, sir,' said Leyland gravely, as the panting figure appeared round the corner; 'the nine-fourteen's just away. All the same, you did a pretty good time. Twenty-five minutes, I make it. You know, he might conceivably have caught that train, if it was four or five minutes late. Did you have any checks?'

'Yes; got one of my sleeves inside out. That's the power of suggestion, confound you. And there was a beast of a barbed wire gate I had to climb over at the farm, which looked as if it ought to have been unlocked. Confound it all, I never realized what a hard time we let Nigel in for when we made him scramble through bracken with bare shins. He may have done it all, but he was a perfect fool if he did.'

'Where you lost time,' said Leyland, 'was in clambering up those steps. I calculated that you might have saved three minutes if you'd swum out to the canoe higher up and started paddling at once. What the deuce did the man do it for, considering the waste of time? Burgess can hardly be lying about those footprints.'

'I believe I'm just beginning to understand that. Look at it this way—the sixth photograph, we now know, wasn't taken till the evening. Hitherto we

imagined that the footprints were left on the bridge
when Nigel (or somebody) went up to take the
photograph of Derek in the canoe. But the footsteps were there in the morning, and the photograph
wasn't taken till the evening. Then why were the
footprints there at all? You saw me walking up
those steps backwards, and I must have looked a
fool as I did it; certainly I felt a fool. It was, as
you say, sheer waste of time. Which makes me
suspect that the footprints were left there on
purpose, in order to create a certain impression.'

'That's all very well, but it was a mere fluke that
Burgess went along and saw them. If he hadn't
happened to go just then, they'd have made no
impression on anyone, because nobody would have
seen them.'

'Precisely. And, don't you see, that's why it
was necessary to photograph them. The marks were
made in order that they might be photographed.
And the photograph was left about on purpose.
Now, what impression was it that the murderer
was trying to make?'

'God knows.'

'So do I. The silly part about these footsteps
from the first is that they only went up one set of
stairs, instead of two, and that they only went
one way, instead of coming and going. That suggested to us either that somebody in the canoe had
pulled himself up by his arms on to the bridge and
walked off it, or else that somebody had walked
up the steps, backwards, and then jumped from
the bridge into the stream. Either notion is pretty
good nonsense, and therefore neither notion is the

impression which this rather acute criminal intended to convey.'

' Pity he didn't take more trouble to make his impressions foolproof.'

' Don't you see why ? He thought that old Burgess would go on rootling in his garden ; how was it to be expected that he would suddenly start hen-hunting in the wooded part of the island ? Those footprints were not meant to be seen by Mr. Burgess, or by any human eye.'

' Then why on earth——'

' *They* weren't meant to be seen, but the photograph was meant to be seen. Now, suppose Burgess had never observed or reported the footprints, and yet we had discovered the photograph, what should we suppose about the footprints ? '

' I see what you mean. We should suppose that they went right across the bridge, from one side to the other, and along both sets of stairs. . . . Yes, I see. They were meant to look like the footprints of a man walking across, barefoot, from the Western bank of the river to the island ? '

' Talk sense. If the man was walking that way, and took the photograph as he did it, the film wouldn't register any footprints, because the footprints wouldn't have happened yet. You must make your footprints first and photograph them afterwards. No, the film was meant to look as if it represented the tracks of a man walking backwards, from the island to the Western bank. In fact, to suggest that the murderer was somebody who went off afterwards in the direction of Byworth.'

' In other words, that he did not go off by river,
nor in the direction of Spinnaker Farm and the
station.'

' Exactly. Which recalls to us the interesting
fact that there was one person who certainly did
go off in the direction of the station, and that was
Nigel.'

' Hullo ! You are coming down on that side,
then ? '

' I didn't say so. But I'm not exactly taking
my eye off Nigel just yet, that's all.'

' Meanwhile, have you got a match ? '

' Just used my last. There's an automatic
machine on the other platform, though. We'll go
across and talk to it, and then get back.'

As they stood on the down platform there was
a rumble and a whistle from near by, and a desultory
porter showed signs of interest. A train puffed in
from the Oxford direction, with the self-importance
of one who is conscious that he is a rare visitor. A
single passenger got out, a tall, well-built young
man in a brown aquascutum which half concealed
and half revealed the fact that he wore shorts underneath it. Confronted with the desultory porter,
he began an exhaustive search of his pockets, and
was rewarded at last by the discovery of his ticket ;
but not before a pink, perforated slip had fluttered
to the ground unregarded. Unregarded, I mean,
by the principals in the action ; Leyland and Bredon
exchanged an immediate glance, and the stranger's
back was hardly turned before they pounced upon it.

' This is too good to be true,' said Leyland as
they turned it over. ' It's quite, quite certainly

the one the man in the punt took at Eaton. F.N.2, as I live—the beastly number would have been found written on my heart if we hadn't come across this. Quick, what do we do ? '

' I'm going back to the canoe and upstream to meet him. · He can't be coming back to pick up the punt. Look, he's gone off along the road— towards Millington Bridge.'

' I'll follow, I think, and if he goes downstream you can take me on board when we meet. Here, take the bike. By Gad, this is the end of a perfect day.'

CHAPTER XXI

A WALK IN THE DARK

BREDON made no great pace up the river; he was exhausted by his twenty-five minutes of variety performance at the lock, and there was, besides, no need for haste. If the unknown took his punt downstream at all—Leyland, in any other contingency, would be able to keep close on his tracks—he must needs reach Millington Bridge before he could get a lodging for the night or a high road to bring him back into touch with civilization. And it would be easy work for Bredon to reach Millington first, in his lighter craft. Actually when the bridge stood up before him, dark-outlined against a cream and silver horizon of late sunset, he saw a figure leaning over the parapet towards him, and was hailed in Leyland's voice: 'Tie up the canoe at the raft, and join me up here. I'm on the look-out.'

Millington Bridge is not among those one-way-traffic concerns in which our thrifty forefathers delighted; there is room to pass a lorry on it; but, by a kind of false analogy, it has a sharp angle over each of its jutting piers in which the pedestrian may take refuge from the dangers and the mud-splashings of the road. It is easy to lean over the parapet at these points, not nearly so easy to stop doing it ; the leisurely flow of the stream beneath laughs at the scruples which would forbid you to spend another five minutes in doing nothing . . . another ten minutes . . . another quarter of an hour, so as to make it a round number by the clock. To Leyland, and to Bredon, who now joined him, no such scruples even presented themselves. The stranger, it appeared, was taking a quite easy course down the river ; and Leyland had had no difficulty in outwalking him. In a few more minutes he was due ; meanwhile, there was nothing to be done but watch the stream below them and talk over their immediate plans.

It was one of those evenings when the clouds that have ushered out the setting sun find relief (you would say) after the formalities of that majestic exit by chasing one another and playing leap-frog across the clear expanse of sky. The sky itself had passed from fiery gold to a silver gilt that faded into silver ; and now the massed cloudscape that had hung, in islands and capes and continents, with bays and lagoons of fire between them, across the Western horizon, broke up into grotesque shapes which breasted the sky southwards—a lizard, a plane-tree upside-down, a watering-can, an old man waving a tankard. They moved along in procession, like the droll pantomime targets of the shooting-range at a country fair, cooling off as they did so from crimson to deep purple, from purple to slate-blue. The river, in the fading light, had lost something of its companionableness, but had taken on an austerer charm ; the patches of light on it were less dazzling but more solemn,

the shadows had less of contrast but more of depth.
A silence had fallen on nature which made you
instinctively talk in a low voice, as if the fairies
were abroad. The willow-thicket that nestled
under the extreme right arch of the bridge, below
which they were standing, stirred and whispered
with the first presage of a breeze.

'He can't be long now,' said Leyland. 'When
he comes round the corner we can walk away slowly
towards the canoe—he'll hardly recognize us. What
I'm afraid of is that he may want to stop the night
here ; in that case I shall have to stop here, and
you, if you don't mind, ought to go back and hold
Nigel's hand for a bit. Do you mind making a
land journey of it ? I'd rather keep the canoe.'

'Not a bit. Good evening for a walk. But I
bet he doesn't stop here. He's still time to get
through Shipcote Lock, and it's all the better for
him if he can do it in the half-light.'

'D'you mean he suspects that he's being trailed ? '

'At least he must know that he's walking into
danger.'

'I dare say you're right. Hang it all, why doesn't
he come ? If he goes straight on, we must follow
at a safe distance in the canoe.'

'What about the lock ? It'll give him a good
lead if Burgess has to fill up and let out again before
we can get through.'

'I've thought of that. You and I are going to
drag over the weir. That puts us ahead, of course ;
at the end of the weir stream, where it joins the lock-
stream, we'll go across on to the Byworth bank,
and lie up in those bushes till he comes past. We

can leave the canoe moored to the bank; he won't
find anything suspicious about it. We still follow,
and then, of course, we can't exactly tell what
he'll do.'

' No. I take it, though, that he has no reason
for knowing that Inspector Leyland of the C.I.D.
has his headquarters at the Gudgeon Inn, Eaton
Bridge.'

' None that I know of. Perhaps fortunately for us.
Confound it all, what on earth is he waiting for ? '

They stood there perhaps five minutes longer,
and then, beyond the furthest fringe of the willows
to their left, a punt-pole, rising and dropping
rhythmically, betrayed the stranger's approach.
The watchers turned, with a single motion, and
walked slowly to the end of the bridge; before
the flashing pole was out of sight downstream they
too had embarked, and were paddling noiselessly
in its wake.

It was the simplest piece of shadowing-work
conceivable. They had only to hug the shore and
keep a good look-out at the turns; for the rest,
they were content to follow the conspicuous white
flash ahead of them, while they were concealed by
every tuft of rushes, every stretch of overhanging
bank. At any moment, with their superior mobility,
they could have made a spurt and overhauled the
fugitive. They had no wish and no need to over-
haul him; it was enough to shepherd him along in
the direction of Eaton Bridge; there, surely, or
close by, he would be bound to spend the night
—it would be too late for him to demand the opening
of another lock. Was a hunt ever so effortless and

so noiseless ? They felt almost disappointed that
the course was not longer, so easy was the game,
so safe the quarry. The shadows fell thicker as
they went, the sky's colour died from silver to dark
blue ; lights came out in the rare farmsteads, and
the cattle in the fields showed only as indistinct
blotches of grey.

The negotiation of the lock at Shipcote needed
more care. They had to wait till the stranger was
well inside the lock, and even until the water itself
had begun to subside, before they could reach the
weir unobserved. But fortunately Mr. Burgess
was no hustler, especially in his mood of evening
repose ; meanwhile, the dragging of the canoe over
short grass and thistles was an easy task, and a
spurt down the weir-stream felt almost a relief
after their dawdling progress. Long before the
punt had come in sight they had reached the end
of the island, crossed the reunited stream, moored
the canoe, and contrived to lie up in a willow-patch
only a few yards away from it. They waited a
little in silence, and then heard the dull ripple before
the punt's bows, the intermittent scrape of the
pole against its side.

The stranger, however, when he came in sight
of the moored canoe, did not seem so incurious
about it as Leyland had anticipated. He stood
for a moment or two with his pole poised, clearly
irresolute, perhaps even (in some mysterious way)
alarmed. He looked round him furtively ; then,
with a quick outward thrust, brought his punt
close in to the mooring-place. Leyland and Bredon
were both puzzled and disconcerted by the gesture.

To betray their presence would be inopportune, and, to tell the truth, somewhat ridiculous : meanwhile, it hardly seemed probable that the stranger, whatever interest he took in the boat's presence, would be at the pains of towing it off with him. But they had forgotten one possibility. With a quick motion, still looking nervously around him, the man caught up the two paddles that lay idle in the canoe, deposited them in his own boat, and with one vigorous shove started out again downstream.

A canoe without paddles is almost as helpless as a dismasted ship. You may improvise substitute instruments, but they will not carry you far or fast. What had been only a breath at Millington Bridge had now developed into a stiff breeze, and there was no hope, even, of crossing the river and making use of a practicable tow-path. To go back to Shipcote Lock in search of a paddle would waste precious time ; the loan of Mr. Burgess' bicycle would have been a more happy solution, but Bredon had unfortunately punctured it in riding back along the field path from the station. All these considerations occurred to the minds of the marooned couple, and were rapidly discussed in terms which it would be an affectation to print. Bredon suggested that he might try swimming to the opposite bank with the canoe in tow ; but the wind had set in from the East, and they agreed that the attempt would be time-taking, if not actually hopeless. In fact, there was nothing for it but to follow along their own bank, trusting to luck that they would be able to make a forced march through the fields.

It was a hope which flattered them with fair
prospects, and then plunged them into embarrass-
ments. At first only the resistance of the standing
hay about their trouser-legs threatened them with
discomfort. But soon the hay gave place to bracken,
rougher in its impact and more clinging in its
embraces ; in the gathering darkness, they stumbled
into holes and hidden runlets, or squelched painfully through patches of bog. Then came barbed-
wire fences, and willow-fringed brooks with a
treacherous carpet of reeds ; hedges that delayed
you in a search for a stile, painful barriers of bur-
dock and thistle. All journeys seem long in the
dark ; the familiar distance between Shipcote and
Eaton Bridge had lengthened itself out into a
nightmare. Their feet were wet and slippery from
the bogs they had blundered into, pricked by a
hundred thorns and hayseeds ; a mass of uncomfortable details, ridiculous in themselves, insignifi-
cant if you had had to face them in the daylight
and at your leisure, made a martyrdom of their
benighted journey. Fatigue and nerve-strain con-
jured up disquieting pictures which lodged obstinately in the imagination—the stranger leaving his
punt at Eaton Bridge and motoring back to Oxford ;
the stranger pulling over the rollers at the next lock
unobserved ; the stranger slinking into the Gudgeon
and holding nefarious confabulations with Nigel,
his presumed accomplice. When they reached the
disused boat-house, they mistook its outline for
the Gudgeon ; when they reached the Gudgeon,
they were already wondering why the day had not
begun to break.

All this time, naturally, they caught no glimpse of the punt. They did not even pass any belated river-goers who might have had news of its progress. They came back to the Gudgeon angry, defeated, with no clear idea in their minds except the sheer necessity of sitting down and having a meal.

'You poor dears!' cried Angela as they came in. 'Supper's on the table, and has been for some time. I've felt dreadfully like the deserted wife in the comic papers, sitting up for hubby with the poker. I told them to light a fire, by the way. Come right inside.'

No, nobody had passed in a punt that she knew of. No, it was not closing time yet; in fact, there were still a few people about in the bar. 'I may say that I bought a whole bottle of whisky, in case you should be too late. They looked at me with considerable amazement. Nigel's asleep upstairs; the doctor says he can get up a bit to-morrow. Don't attempt to tell me what you've been doing till you've had your supper.' They were, indeed, hardly fit for the strain of conversation, and Angela almost immediately seized upon the excuse of 'tucking up the baby' to leave them in the enjoyment of a bachelor *tête-à-tête*. It was only as he looked down at the bottom of his second pint that Leyland asked, 'Well, and what next? I shall curse myself all my life for not remembering to take the paddles out of that canoe.'

'Confound it all, though, how on earth could we expect him to know that he was being shadowed, and that the canoe had got ahead of him? That's

what I can't get over. If he's any sense, realizing
that he was being followed and not wanting to be
caught, he'll have left the punt somewhere close to
the bridge, and legged it for Oxford by road. Probably he was in time to catch the late 'bus, which
would mean getting to Oxford at a respectable
hour. If you feel up to it, of course, we might
take the car to Oxford and see if we can track him
through the 'bus people. It's almost incredible
that he should have had the effrontery to go on by
river.'

A door opened somewhere in the passage, and
for a moment they heard, from the bar, the voices
of agriculturalists raised in high debate—heard,
from the kitchen, the inevitable drone of wireless.
The door shut again, and there were uncertain steps
in the passage, as of a man hesitating which way
he should turn. Then Angela was heard asking,
'Did you want anybody?' and an unknown voice
replied, 'I was wondering if I could see Inspector
Leyland. I'm sorry to bother him at such a time
of night, but it's really rather important. My
name's Farris (would you tell him?), Edward
Farris.'

It was not likely that the bearer of such a name
would be kept waiting. Angela looked in, raised
her eyebrows, and held the door open for the new-
comer. Four eyes, still blinking after a long trudge
in the darkness, turned towards it, and saw, unmistakable on the threshold, the figure of the stranger
in the punt.

CHAPTER XXII

ANOTHER STORY

MR. EDWARD FARRIS, for all his vigorous physique, somewhat recalled in his speech and manner that legendary person who was said to be ' descended from a long line of maiden aunts'. His voice was carefully modulated, his pronunciation meticulously exact ; he marshalled his thoughts, without apparent effort, under headings A, B and C ; he brushed cigarette-ash off his trousers with irritating particularity. In a word, you might have supposed from first impressions that Mrs. Coolman had advertised for a lady's companion and had got one.

' My name must, I think, be familiar to you,' he began, ' assuming, what I suppose I am right in assuming, that your presence here is connected with the recent doings of the Burtell family. Their aunt, Mrs. Coolman, had been very good to me ; I was, to all intents and purposes, her adopted child ; I had the melancholy privilege of being the last person she saw on this side of the grave. Thank you, yes, soda-water. Right up, please.

' I ought perhaps to explain that the Burtell cousins were not personally known to me, except in their extreme youth. Partly because they saw very little of their aunt, partly because I felt that they must regard me as something of an intruder in the family. I knew them, however, by reputation, and I could not but feel regret when, at the very end of her life, Mrs. Coolman began to take a fresh interest in them. However, it was not for me to interfere. When she asked me what character they bore, I did not like to particularize ; but I said it was unfortunate they were on such bad terms with each other. This, of course, was common knowledge.

' Mrs. Coolman was of a somewhat masterful disposition ; she liked to influence other people's lives. She immediately determined that this reproach must be removed from the family. I wrote at her dictation—for her eyesight was failing somewhat—a letter to her nephew Derek, less than a month ago, urging him to effect a reconciliation. He replied not long afterwards, in terms of what I could not help regarding as somewhat insincere affection. Nigel and he, he wrote, had decided to bury the past ; they were on terms of frequent communication ; and indeed, even as he wrote, he was off for a tour up the river with his cousin in a canoe. The tour had been recommended for his health ; but he had no doubt it would prove to be also a pleasure trip, with old Nigel in his company.

' I am afraid that my manner on this occasion must have betrayed a certain incredulity. Mrs. Coolman, with the excitability of those who have the misfortune to suffer from heart trouble, took it amiss ; she asked me whether I really supposed that Derek was telling a lie ? Did I suggest that

she should demand to see the lock tickets? I
confess that I was a little put out on my own side.
I reminded her that a lock ticket does not specify
the number of persons present in the boat. " Very
well, then," she said (I cannot vouch for her exact
words), " you shall go and see for yourself. You
will hire a punt at Oxford in a few days' time and
go up to meet them. If you do not meet them,
or if you find on inquiry that they have not been
seen together, you shall come back and tell me."
I supposed at first that she was speaking in irony,
but discovered later on that she meant what she
said. To tell the truth, I think she had doubts
about her nephews' sincerity, and wished to make
sure of it on her own account ; meanwhile, she
screened this anxiety by a pretence that she only
did it to satisfy my scepticism. I trust that I am
making myself clear.

' Before I left, I found that this unfortunate
incident had made a great impression on her. She
told me that it was her intention to make a fresh
will, in which she would leave the bulk of her
property to her elder nephew. She implied, what
I had guessed but did not know for certain, that up
till then I had been her principal heir. You will
readily believe that I set out from Wallingford in
a distressed state of mind. Moreover, I felt that
my mission was uncomfortably ridiculous. What
an unenviable reputation I should earn, if by any
unforeseen chance the two Burtells should hear of
my presence on the river ! I determined to take
every precaution. I hired the punt under an
assumed name, that of Mr. Luke Wallace, to be

exact ; and, to prevent gossip, I took my own stores with me, resolving that I would not stay at an inn till I was well past the track of the two cousins. I have grave reason to fear that my precautions were insufficient, and that one of them, at least, has taken my interference in a very vindictive spirit.

' Apart from this uneasiness, my tour was a pleasant one. I enjoy living rough, and being alone with nature. It was not till I had passed Shipcote Lock,—in fact, it was just above Shipcote Lock, that I passed the canoe with the two cousins in it. I suppose it can only have been a matter of a few hours before Derek's regrettable disappearance.'

' Excuse me, Mr. Farris,' broke in Leyland, ' you must see for yourself that your evidence may be very valuable. Did you pass anybody else on the way, either before or after the lock ? I need not explain to you that there have been suspicions of foul play.'

' Let me see ; I passed an encampment of boy scouts lower down the river. After that, I do not think that I noticed anybody until I saw the lock-keeper. Then, immediately afterwards, I saw the two Burtells, and after that nobody, I think, until Millington Bridge.'

' That, I suppose, would be about half an hour later ? '

' Oh no, it would be an hour or two later. I had luncheon there. Rather more than two hours if anything. You see, it was a very hot morning, and I'd made an early start ; and then, I had a book with me I was rather interested in ; and so I just sat there in the punt reading, close above the lock.'

'M'm !' said Leyland ; 'it's a pity you didn't select a spot just below the lock ; it would have saved us all a lot of trouble. And then I suppose you turned back home, as you'd finished your errand ? '

'Why, no ; I wanted to make quite certain, you see, while I was about it, that the two cousins had really been together. I asked at Millington Bridge, but the account the maid gave me there didn't seem to suggest that they had been together much. So I went on to an inn rather higher up, the Blue Cow. I wanted to find out if anything was remembered about the Burtells there. Besides, I had arranged to go up that far, and my letters were to be forwarded there by one of the servants at Wallingford—under the assumed name, of course. It was lucky that I had made these provisions, because as it turned out it was at the Blue Cow that I found with my letters a telegram, summoning me back to poor Mrs. Coolman's death-bed. Well, of course, I couldn't wait. I punted across the river, stowed away the boat in the first suitable place I could find, and then walked across country to Shipcote station, where I fortunately got a train.

' I'm afraid you are all thinking my explanation very long-winded, but I want you to realize the whole circumstances, for fear you should regard me as fanciful. Before Mrs. Coolman died, on the Wednesday, to be exact, she made a fresh will. She explained its provisions to me herself. She had left me a livelihood, but she had bequeathed the bulk of her property to her elder great-nephew. " Unless ", she added, " I outlive him, and that does not seem likely to happen now. The lawyer made me put your name in too, in case Derek should be unable to succeed." You may imagine my feelings when she told me this ; it was all but certain that Derek was dead, yet we had strict orders from the doctor not to allude to the subject in her presence.

' After her death, I was naturally detained by business matters. But I had not forgotten the punt, and it seemed to me that to continue my interrupted journey by taking it back to Oxford would be a way of recuperating from the strain of the last few days. I took train this afternoon, via Oxford, to Shipcote, and went back to the place where I had left my punt.

' I expect you will think that my nerves have been playing me false, but I could not get out of my mind the picture of young Nigel. I had, I still have, a strong suspicion that he made away with his cousin in order to succeed as his heir. And now it occurred to me that in all probability only one life stood between Nigel and a fresh inheritance, and that life was my own. I do not know the law in these matters, but I suppose that his claims would be the next to be considered. And if Nigel had in any way heard of Mrs. Coolman's final dispositions, would he stick at committing another crime ? It was only, you understand, a vague idea at the back of my mind. But, on the way from Shipcote Station to the river, I had an uncomfortable suspicion that I was being followed. More than once, looking back, I thought that there was somebody tracking my footsteps, and anxious not to let me see that he was doing so. Even when I had started downstream in the punt, I could not shake off the suspicion. I quite clearly saw some one on the bank behind me, and when we were just in sight of Millington Bridge he passed ahead of me, keeping well inland. I am certain that, as he passed, he looked at me with no ordinary curiosity.

'I determined, perhaps foolishly, to repay him in his own kind. I put the punt in to shore, landed, and went very carefully along the bank, hiding as far as possible behind the willows. When I reached the bridge, I saw him leaning over it, as if he were looking out for me. Very carefully I crossed the road, and concealed myself under the extreme arch of the bridge, which runs partly over dry ground. In a moment or two I heard him in conversation with a companion, and what they said assured me that my worst fears were realized. They were on my track ; they were in close touch with Nigel, and they had the intention of heading me off somewhere below Shipcote Lock. But two encouraging points emerged from their conversation. One was that they intended to go ashore at the end of the lock-stream—why, I do not know—and leave their canoe moored. The other was that Inspector Leyland of the C.I.D., whom they appeared to mention with some awe, was staying at the Gudgeon Inn, Eaton Bridge.'

Bredon was compelled to go to the window and clean out his pipe ; he was not certain of his own

gravity. Leyland, to his admiration, sat perfectly
unmoved.

'Well,' continued Farris, 'I hadn't the courage
to break my journey at Millington Bridge. I went
on down to Shipcote, and when I found their canoe
moored, I—I stole the paddles.' He chuckled a
little at the memory of his own cleverness. 'Since
then I've seen nothing of the canoe. But they
may have followed me by land; and I thought the
best thing I could do was to report the matter at
once to the police. I have a room booked here
for the night.'

'I see,' said Leyland. 'Oh Lord, tell him,
Bredon.' And they told him.

. . . . .

'Now that', said Bredon next morning, 'is as
straightforward a tale as I've ever heard told. You
can still go on suspecting him if you like; I do
myself, rather. But I'm just going over to Oxford
to apply one more test to Master Nigel's perfor-
mances. Coming?'

'Afraid not. Too many darned suspects about
in this pub; I mean to keep an eye on them.'

So it was Bredon alone who went over to Oxford,
Bredon alone, though armed with a note from Leyland, who went into Mr. Wickstead's well-known
boot-shop, and demanded whether Mr. Nigel Burtell
was a customer; whether, if so, they had any
record of his size. He was assured, in horror-
stricken accents, that of course Mr. Burtell dealt
there; Mr. Burtell was one of the best-dressed
young gentlemen in Oxford; of course they kept his
measure on record. They brought out a portentous

volume, in which every client had a page devoted to himself, a complete chiropodic *dossier*. There was not a corn, it seemed, in any of the more exclusive Colleges which was not on record here. True, there was no absolute facsimile of the rising generation's footsteps; but there was an outlined figure, pencilled from the life, which gave the exact conformation, and whatever facts it did not divulge were chronicled in the margin. A vast book, alphabetically arranged, from which your name never disappeared until you had paid off your bill to Messrs. Wickstead, or given them any other indication that you intended to take your custom elsewhere.

Bredon turned the pages languidly, dawdling over one name after another as if he were afraid of not finding what he wanted when it came to the point. He noticed his own surname, and wondered whether he had some unsuspected relative in residence. At last he reached 'Burtell', and, mastering his excitement, began to plough through the highly documented record. 'Something about a hammer-toe here, I see,' he remarked.

'A hammer-toe? Oh dear me, no, sir; Mr. Burtell's toes are perfectly straight; you must be reading the wrong side of the page. Allow me, sir —there's "Shape of the toe"; nothing about hammer-toes there, you see.'

'Yes, I see,' said Bredon. 'Yes, confound it all, I see.'

CHAPTER XXIII

BREDON PLAYS PATIENCE AGAIN

'WOULD you be shocked', asked Nigel, 'if you thought I'd done it?'

He was sitting up, for the first time, in a costume as nearly approaching full dress as Leyland would permit. Angela sat opposite him, knitting vaguely. Her attitude throughout his stay in bed had been rather embarrassed, and he was evidently determined to establish more normal relations.

'I'm too old to be caught that way,' she said. 'You want me to say or imply that I don't think you did it. You'd better ask me whether I'd be shocked if I *knew* you'd done it. Because, after all, it makes a lot of difference if you can give a person the benefit of the doubt. As it is, I'm only provisionally shocked, if you understand what I mean.'

'But the idea of talking to a murderer does shock you?'

'Of course it does. If I read in the paper that a total stranger has broken his neck I'm not shocked —not really. But if my hair-dresser broke his neck I should be shocked—why, I don't know.'

'But that's a different kind of shock.'

'I'm not so sure. I suppose very good people

when they come in personal contact with really wicked people, do really disapprove of them morally. But an ordinary humdrum person, like me, doesn't really feel disapproval, only a sort of surprise. You have to readjust your values, to realize that the man you had tea with yesterday was the man who robbed the bank; and it's that feeling of surprise at the suddenness of the thing, to my mind, that means being shocked.'

'Perhaps you're right. But, look here, would you be shocked if I told you this—that I would cheerfully have murdered my cousin at any time, if I could have made quite sure of not being hanged for it?'

'Go steady. Don't say anything you don't want to say. Remember that I chatter to my husband continually, and I may pass on any remark you make.'

'Oh, that doesn't matter. Your husband, I'm quite sure, thinks me capable of any crime, morally. So does Leyland; he'd put me in jug to-morrow if he could see any way of explaining how I'd done it. So it doesn't matter what they think about my character. Only I'd rather like to know what *you* think about me.'

'I've told you; I'm provisionally shocked. I shouldn't be shocked, though, merely by your saying that you *would* do your cousin in for twopence, because I shouldn't believe you meant what you said.'

'But I do say it, and I do mean it. I don't think a person like Derek has any right to exist, and I don't see that it would have been wrong for me to put him out of the way. Selfish, of course—I should only have been doing it to gratify my own feelings and my own pocket. But not wrong, because he'd no right to exist. A fellow like that doesn't really qualify by any standard ; the parsons couldn't approve of him, the State gets no earthly good out of him ; and as for the aesthetic point of view, he simply doesn't count. He neither enjoys any of the higher pleasures nor helps anybody else to enjoy them. He's no function. That's my point.'

' Oh, but that's just what seems to me absolute nonsense. Either everybody's life ought to be respected or nobody's. It's absurd to suppose that because you can appreciate Scriabin and Derek couldn't, the man who murdered Derek was doing something worse than if he'd killed you.'

' That's putting it rather personally. I'm not quite sure that I've any right to exist either. I've made a pretty good fool of myself, and I shall make a worse fool of myself if I come in for any money as the result of all this—you see if I don't.'

Nigel, like most people who fancy themselves as rogues, rather liked to have good women talking to him for his good. It enhanced your sense of importance, to have people trying to reform you, as long as they talked sympathetically and looked nice. But Angela was adroit at refusing such openings ; her common sense was admirably poised. ' Yes,' she admitted, ' I should think you'd make a ghastly mess of it. I can imagine you doing a frightful lot of harm. But I haven't put strychnine in your Bovril for all that, and I'm not going to.

By the way, it's nearly time I gave you some—
Bovril, I mean.'

' Yes, but that would be for sentimental reasons,
wouldn't it ? I mean, you'd probably hate killing
a mouse. But you don't mind mice being killed.
So why should you mind Derek being killed ? Or
me, for that matter ? '

' I didn't say I would,' Angela reminded him.
' I only said I'd sooner not know the person who
did it, because I don't think he'd be a nice person
to know.'

' Then I can't be a nice person to know. Because
I'm the kind of person who would have killed Derek,
if I'd had the opportunity, and if somebody else
hadn't (apparently) got in before me.'

' Oh, I don't mind knowing people who *think* they
would have murdered Derek. Because, as I say,
I don't believe you are the kind of person who
would have. Unless, of course, you did.'

' Isn't that a tiny bit inconsistent ? '

' Not at all. Actions speak louder than words.
Tell me you did it, and I'll believe you. Tell me
you would have done it, and I won't believe you
because I don't think you know yourself. Of
course, it's different when one's excited ; but when
it comes to cold-blooded murder, why, I believe
we're all a little less unscrupulous than we think
we are.'

' All the same, where would have been the harm
in murdering Derek ? He's for it, anyhow ; you
can't go on drinking and doping like that without
doing yourself in. What's the good of his being
alive ? He's only keeping me out of fifty thousand.'

'With which, as you say, you'd only make a beast of yourself. No, it's all nonsense worrying about the consequences of actions. The only thing is to stick to the rules of the game ; and murder isn't sticking to the rules ; it's an unfair solution, like cheating at patience.'

'Well, it's only speeding up the end. You'd hardly argue, would you, that Derek was worth keeping alive ? '

'Everybody's worth keeping alive—or rather, very few people are worth it, but everybody's got to be kept alive if it can be managed. Look at you the other day—we all thought you were a murderer, with nothing in front of you but the gallows. And yet we rallied round with hot-bottles and restoratives, and treated you as if you were the Shah of Persia. No use to anybody, particularly, but we had to do it, because one has to stick to the rules. Once try to make exceptions, and we shall all get into no end of a mess.'

'Blessed if I'd do it.'

'You would, though. If you were waiting behind a bush to murder a man, and he fell into the river on the way, you'd jump in and rescue him.'

'You try me. If it was Derek, I'd let him sink and heave a brick after him.'

'No, you wouldn't. You mustn't keep on contradicting, or I shall put you to bed and tell you not to agitate yourself. Now, I'm going to make your Bovril, if I can get at the bottle. I left it next door, and my husband's in there playing patience ; so it's quite possible I shall get shot out head first.'

And indeed, she found her husband in no accommodating mood. ' I want a 'bus time-table,' he said, retrieving a three of spades from the waste-paper basket.

' Why not ring for one ? ' suggested Angela, with an assumption of *hauteur*.

' I've been wanting to for a long time, but I can't get at that dashed bell without disturbing the cards. Do be a sport and ask for one.'

' All right. Chuck over the Bovril, though.' And she did contrive to secure a dog's-eared sheet from downstairs, which he thumbed this way and that abstractedly, while she watched him from the doorway. ' Good ! ' he announced at last. ' Things begin to clear up a bit. Tell the third chauffeur to have the Rolls round this afternoon, because we've got to make a little expedition to Witney.'

' We've lots of blankets at home, you know.'

' Oh, go and feed Bovril to the patient. I'm busy.'

Bredon appeared at luncheon with symptoms of suppressed excitement which Angela recognized and welcomed. He was vivacious, and, in the presence of Mr. Farris, he talked about everything rather than the Burtell mystery. ' Anything fresh this morning ? ' he asked, when he got Leyland alone.

' A little. Only a little, and dashed puzzling at that. You remember Nigel told us that before all this happened he had been on the point of going off to the Continent. Well, that suggested to me that he'd probably already got a passport, and it didn't seem to me very safe to leave a passport in the keeping of such a slippery young customer. So I asked him about it, and he said he'd left it in his digs—told me exactly where I could find it. Apparently there were some few of his personal possessions that he'd left behind, to be picked up later. Well, I went over and searched, and there wasn't a confounded trace of the passport.'

'You think he was just lying?'

'We could find out, of course, from the passport office. But I don't think he was lying, because though I didn't find the passport itself, I found the odd copies of his passport photographs, one of them authenticated by his College chaplain. It's a mystery to me why the law always wants clergymen to do these things, because of all professions I think the parsons are the most careless about the way they give testimonials. However, there they were; and indeed, here they are—have a look at them if you like. I don't call it a very good portrait, and it's rather blurred at that; but these passport people will take anything.'

'Yes, it's a dashed bad likeness, somehow. You can see the family chin all right, though. By the way, here's another point—who took that photograph? Because you were hunting all over the place for a portrait of Nigel, and couldn't get one; I think you said you circularized the Oxford and London photographers pretty thoroughly.'

'Oh, apparently it's an amateur one. Actually it was done by Derek, before they started out on the river tour. At least, so Nigel says.'

'But it can't have been immediately before.'

'No, it would be about a week before, when they were arranging the trip together. Hullo, what's wrong with you?'

' Only that I think I've picked up an extra link.
In fact, I'm pretty sure I have. Look here, Leyland,
are you coming over to Witney this afternoon ? '

' Not unless I'm wanted specially.'

' No, I don't think you'd be much use. Hullo,
here's Angela with the car. Look here, I may have
rather important things to tell you this evening, so
try to be on hand about tea-time.'

' Rather. Bring all your friends. We're becoming quite a party here, aren't we ? '

' No, I shan't bring anybody. But if I'm right
—and I feel quite certain I'm right this time—I
shall have news for you which will set you tele-
graphing all over the place.'

' Another pub-crawl ? ' suggested Angela, as the
car turned the corner into the main road.

' Exactly. But there can't be many pubs in
Witney—decent ones, I mean.'

' Whose name do we ask for this time ? '

' No name, particularly. Just to find out if
anybody came there for the night on Sunday, the
Sunday before last.'

Their search was rewarded at the first and most
obvious hotel. For a wonder, the hotel register had
been kept, and it was not surprising to find that
only one guest had arrived on the Sunday. Angela,
looking over her husband's shoulder, read the
words ' L. Wallace, 41 Digby Road, Coventry '.

' Luke Wallace ! ' she cried, ' why, that's dear
old Farris ! Miles, this is bright of you. But why's
he gone and changed his address ? He was in
Cricklewood last time. Miles, I'm hanged if I see
how you expected to find this.'

' Oh, give a man time ! Is it possible you don't see that I *wasn't* expecting it ? I don't want Luke Wallace here one little bit. He spoils the whole show. Farris ! What on earth was he doing here ? And why on earth did he want a fresh address ? I think I'm going mad.'

' So shall I, unless you tell me what it is you're after. Do you know, I quite enjoy seeing you puzzled, when you yourself are deliberately keeping me on the rack like this.'

' The rack, the rack ! Luke Wallace on the letter-rack ! That's it, that does it all. Now, go and ask that young creature in the cage what she can remember about Mr. L. Wallace.'

But neither the lady in the cage nor the hotel porter could remember much about Mr. Wallace. He had attracted attention by arriving on a Sunday, by arriving late at night, and by leaving early the following morning. He had no heavy luggage with him, but talked of having left some at Oxford. He had inquired about the trains to Oxford, and had taken the earliest on Monday morning. Nothing more was known.

At the Gudgeon, they found Leyland writing up his diary at a table by the window, while Mr. Farris, in an uncomfortable rush-bottomed chair, was reading the local directory. ' Well,' said Bredon cheerfully, ' it's up to you now. Angela's going upstairs to ask Nigel a few questions ; when I know the answer to those, I shall be able to leave the whole business in your hands.'

' What exactly do you want me to do ? ' asked Leyland.

'Why, get on to the Continental police, and ask them to obtain all the information they can about the movements of a traveller who crossed the Channel about ten days ago, giving the name of Mr. Luke Wallace.'

Leyland gave one anguished glance in the direction of Mr. Farris, imagining that Bredon had not noticed him. Farris himself sprang to his feet with a look of utter bewilderment. 'The Channel? The Continent? But I assure you I haven't left England since Christmas! Really, Mr. Bredon——'

'It's all right; nothing to do with you. Except that, apparently, somebody's been borrowing your alias. That can hardly be described as impersonation, though of course it's open to you to regard it as a breach of copyright. But I shouldn't use that alias any more, if I were you, because the gentleman who borrowed it will, before long, be much in the mouths of the police.'

'That's all very well,' objected Leyland, 'but surely the fellow will have had the sense to take a fresh alias when he got across to the other side. Why stick to the old name, when he can always invent a new one?'

'He might do that, of course. But he's been at such pains to identify himself, for a particular object, as Mr. Luke Wallace, that I have a strong suspicion he will stick to the name. You see, he thinks that the identification will put us off the scent.'

'And the real name?'

'Is, of course, Derek Burtell.'

CHAPTER XXIV

BACKED BOTH WAYS

ANGELA came in before anybody had time to add further comment. 'France, Belgium,' she said. 'A good way up the river, near Ditcham Martin, just after breakfast. Yes, each took three of the other—Derek's suggestion.'

'That settles it,' said Bredon. 'Leyland, I really think you might return Nigel his trousers. All the same, we won't ask him downstairs just now, because I may be taking his name in vain a bit.'

'Derek Burtell!' said Leyland in a stupefied way. 'How long have you been on his track?'

'Only since yesterday. I thought it all out this morning. But, of course, we ought to have recognized it was either he or somebody like him who was responsible for all this mystery-making.'

'Somebody like him? How, like him?'

'Somebody who took drugs. Don't you see, this whole business has puzzled us from the first because there were signs of extraordinary cunning at work, and yet it didn't figure out right. It didn't give us a wrong impression, as it was obviously meant to · it simply gave us no impression at all. It was fantastic, like a dream. And that was because it was a dream, really—an opium dream, only carried out in real life.

' Derek, as we know, was a quite unimaginative person. But Derek was taking the stuff in large quantities ; and whatever else is certain about the effects of drug-taking, it's certain that it turns people into champion liars. Derek, in an ordinary way, was too stupid to lie, or at least to lie cleverly. But the drug let him out. They say every man has one good story in him ; and Derek has produced one story, not by writing it but by acting it. I don't think it would ever have formed itself properly in his imagination if it hadn't come to him in those moments of exaltation when the drug-taker sees clearly and imagines without effort. Like Kubla Khan, you know. Only this time there was no gentleman from Porlock to interfere, and the dream was realized. The outline was a framework of splendid deception ; the details were untidily managed, because Derek hadn't got the drug in him when he arranged them.

' Derek Burtell hated his cousin. We know that, and we know why. But his hatred took something like a moral form ; he at any rate believed that his cousin was as good as a murderer, because he was responsible for that woman's death. He didn't want to kill Nigel : he wanted Nigel to be executed by the laws of his country. Since Nigel couldn't be punished for the murder he had done, he should be punished for a murder he hadn't done. He should be punished for murdering Derek, and Derek would disappear in circumstances which would make everybody think he was murdered.'

'One moment, Miles,' said Angela. 'Did Derek mean to give up his fifty thousand altogether? Because if Nigel had been hanged, the legacy would never have been available.'

'My impression is that he was backing himself both ways. If Nigel were hanged, well and good; he would sooner have his vengeance than any amount of legacies. But if Nigel escaped suspicion, the other plan would hold: Nigel would come in for the legacy, Derek would get into communication with him, and they would split the proceeds. Derek took his cousin fully into his confidence up to a point. Beyond that point he kept him in the dark. And I suppose he never dreamed that Nigel would have the face to tell that story he told us yesterday morning, or that he would be believed if he did. It would be supposed that Nigel was just inventing the tale of the bargain, to save his own skin. I believe you did think that, Leyland.'

'I'm still waiting to be told why I'm not to think so.'

'Because of Mr. Luke Wallace's visit to Witney. We shall come to that. What I want you to take on trust for the moment is that everything Nigel has told us about his movements on that Sunday and that Monday is strictly true. The things he didn't tell us were things he didn't know.

'Derek's difficulty was this—he didn't want to commit suicide; not so much because he cared about his life, as because he didn't want his cousin to get the legacy. He had, therefore, to create the impression that he was dead, with Nigel's complicity; he had also, without Nigel's complicity, to create the impression that he had been murdered. What steps he took to create the impression that he was dead, Nigel has already told us. They weren't very clever ones; they were, I take it, the invention of Derek in his normal state. To disappear and leave a canoe floating about on a river, to lie low until your death is presumed, to start again in the Colonies under a fresh name—all that is a sufficiently clumsy idea, and a hundred accidents might have upset the plan. But the steps he took to create the impression that he had been murdered were, at least in their outline, very ingenious; I give them full marks for ingenuity. They were Derek Burtell's Kubla Khan. Tell me, Leyland, why have you and I assumed up till now that it was a murder?'

'Because it seemed certain that some human being had been with Derek after the moment when Burgess lost sight of him at the lock.'

'Exactly. And what is our evidence that Derek Burtell was not alone during all that time?'

'The photograph; or rather the two photographs. No, a man can take a snapshot of his own footprints. But he can't take a photograph of his own body lying stretched full-length in a canoe. Don't tell me he did it by some arrangement of strings, because I won't believe it.'

'No, that's what's been at the back of our minds all the time, imposing on us the idea of murder, or at least foul play. But what if the figure in the canoe was not really Derek's, but somebody else's? The hat, remember, was drawn over the face.'

'But the chin was Derek's.'

'It was a Burtell chin. But are you sure it was Derek's, and not Nigel's?'

'But, hang it all, that doesn't make things any clearer. He couldn't photograph Nigel if Nigel wasn't there. And if Nigel was there, Derek wasn't alone.'

'Yes, I ought to explain, I suppose, that the photograph of Nigel was taken by Derek much higher up the river, near a place called Ditcham Martin. There is a light bridge over the river there, very much like the one at Shipcote Lock; it's a common type, you know, except for the cement steps. Derek persuaded his cousin to take some of the drug, just to try it; you remember Nigel told us that it "laid him out". It did lay him out, on the floor of the canoe. Derek got on shore, let the canoe drift, and hopped up on to the bridge with the camera. The next film to be exposed was Number Three; Derek didn't expose that, nor Number Four, nor Number Five. He turned the spool on to Number Six, and with Number Six he took a snapshot of his cousin as he floated under the bridge. Then he turned the spool back again to Number Three; not difficult to do, though of course he must have had to get a darkened room to do it in.'

'And this happened, I suppose, in the evening? That's why the shadows went from left to right instead of right to left.'

'No, that's the funny thing. Derek was careful to take his photograph at the right time of day, soon after breakfast. But he'd forgotten that on that particular bend the river is flowing South, or nearly South ; you can see it on the map here. So that was that.   Long before the cousins reached Millington Bridge, the sixth film contained damning evidence of Derek's murder—at least, Derek thought so.

' Now we can take the story in its historical order. At the Blue Cow, a little above Millington Bridge, Derek suggested to Nigel that idea that they should sleep in separate places.   Derek himself would put up at White Bracton, a mile or so from Millington Bridge, while Nigel came to the hotel at Millington Bridge twice over, and so created the impression that they both slept there.   Thus, at White Bracton, the useful Mr. Anderton would come into existence ; he was to be Derek's future alias.   Only, without telling his cousin, Derek altered the plan.   He caught a late 'bus, and went all the way on to Witney.   Nor, at Witney, did he give the name of H. Anderton.   He gave the first name that came into his head—his imagination, you see, had broken down ;   and that was the name " Luke Wallace ", which he had seen on a packet of letters in the letter-rack at the Blue Cow.   Observe that Derek had now got a new name and a new address, of which Nigel could suspect nothing.

' By 'bus, or perhaps by an early train, he reached Millington Bridge in good time on Monday morning. He pretended that he had slept at White Bracton, but not very well ;   he pretended, therefore, that he was sleepy, and appeared to doze off on the floor of the canoe.   In fact, he was pretending to be already a corpse.   You, Mr. Farris, could not have

sworn in a court of law, could you, that both passengers in the canoe were alive ? '

' Quite certainly not. To 'tell the truth, it gave
me a slight shock when I saw Derek lying so motionless. But then I remembered that he was said to
be addicted to drugs, and thought that explained
it.'

' I see. Nor did Burgess at the lock see Derek
move, or hear him speak. He did speak to Nigel
from the canoe ; but by that time the water had
sunk low, and the lock walls prevented any sound
reaching Burgess' ears. In a court of law, Burgess
would have had to depose that he had heard Nigel
speaking to Derek, but not Derek speaking to
Nigel. When inquiries came to be made, nobody
would be able to swear to having seen Derek alive
on the Monday. If those inquiries were very
carefully made, it would also be seen that there
was no real evidence of Derek's having slept at
Millington Bridge. The trick by which Nigel pretended to be two people would have been discovered,
and it would have looked black against Nigel. It
would have looked as if he had been ingeniously
concealing his cousin's death.'

' Do you know,' said Angela, ' I believe I prefer
Nigel to Derek.'

' Well, it was Derek doped ; so perhaps we
oughtn't to be too hard on him. At the lock,
Nigel acted precisely as he told us the other day ;
and, on Derek's suggestion throughout, he acted
precisely like a man who is interested in establishing
an alibi. He went out of his way by Spinnaker
Farm ; he asked questions about the time, and so

on. Meanwhile, Derek had given the canoe one
shove to get it out of the lock, and lay doggo until
he heard Burgess walk away. Now was his time
to finish his preparations.

'Film Number Five on the spool had not been
exposed. Something must be done with it, and it
was an opportunity for doing something ingenious.
Nigel was quite truthful when he told me that his
cousin was fond of trick photography. He took,
on Number Five, what appeared to be an accidental
exposure, but was really a deliberate snapshot of
his own footprints on the bridge—footprints which
he had deliberately made, in order to suggest that
somebody had been standing on the bridge with
bare feet to photograph the corpse. What precise
inference he meant us to draw from the footprints
I don't know. He certainly didn't expect that
Burgess would come along and see the footprints
themselves. But there was one thing he had to
be careful about. Derek Burtell had hammer-
toes ; Nigel hadn't. And, oddly enough, it was
in looking to see whether Nigel had that I found
out about Derek. Their foot-statistics were close
together at Wickstead's, on opposite sides of the
same page. That was when I really cottoned on
to its being Derek who worked the whole plant.
So Derek only left the marks of his heels and insteps.

'He paddled down a short way, and then left,
on the bank, those traces which you and I, Leyland,
investigated so credulously. He wormed himself
along on his back through the bracken, careful to
make dragging marks with his boots. He lay flat
on the clay bank, taking good care that one button

should leave its impress. He paddled round the end of the island into the weir-stream, driving his canoe hard into the bank so as to make a mark. He made a single track, walking, between the weir-stream and the clay bank. He crossed the weir-stream, and left the film lying about for some-body to find. I forgot to say that he had already dropped his note-case in the lock-stream, so as to look as if it had fallen out when his corpse was lugged ashore. In fact, I think he meant to create the exact impression which the various clues did create, Leyland, on you and me.'

' Yes. I'm going to meet Mr. Derek Burtell, if I have to search every doss-house on the Continent of Europe.'

' Then he paddled across the main stream to the Byworth bank. Before he turned the canoe adrift he managed, probably with one of those composite pen-knives, to dig a tiny hole in the bottom of the canoe. That, of course, was perfectly inconsistent with his main plan ; in the given circumstances, the supposed murderer would have been a fool to do anything of the kind. What he calculated on, I suppose, was that the hole in the canoe would immediately produce in everybody's mind the impression of foul play—as indeed it would have, if Nigel hadn't doctored the hole when he found it. Derek himself went off in the Byworth direction, leaving the impression that he had been murdered by Nigel at Millington Bridge or above it, ferried down next morning to Shipcote, photographed from the bridge and lugged ashore at the island, retrieved somehow and smuggled away later in the day. It was a fantastic impression; but then, as I say, this wasn't a deep plot laid by a cunning schemer; it was an opium-dream.

'I dare say he had actually left some luggage at Oxford, but that won't help us, for we don't know under what name it was left. In any case he must have taken train at Oxford, I suspect for Southampton. That meant crawling across country by Didcot and Newbury, instead of risking the possibility of a recognition in London. And there, I suppose, he would take ship to Havre.'

'And his passport?' asked Leyland. 'You mean that he——'

'Yes, he'd provided himself with a passport, rather ingeniously. When he went up to make plans with Nigel, Nigel was just getting a passport, and he wanted an amateur photograph of himself. He asked Derek to do it, and Derek, foreseeing his own need of a passport, took three photographs of Nigel, and got Nigel to take three of himself, in exactly the same pose, *on the same plates*. (Nigel, of course, didn't realize this.) It was only one chance in a thousand, but one of the films did come out, as you can see, a perfect composite photograph. The photograph was sufficiently like Nigel to deceive the College chaplain. It was sufficiently like Derek to deceive the passport authorities at Havre. It was with that passport, then, that he got away. Of course, this was long before any hue and cry had been made over either cousin. What he's done since I don't know, but as the passport is visa'd for France and Belgium, I suppose he's in one or the other. Perhaps, if you circulate the news about

Mrs. Coolman's will, Derek will reappear of his own accord. If not, I suggest a complete inquiry into the whereabouts of Mr. Wallace. I don't suppose he will have been using another alias all the time, because he obviously meant to trade on the previous history of Mr. L. Wallace. If anybody suspects that L. Wallace is Derek Burtell, they will be silenced, he thinks, when they learn that L. Wallace stayed at Witney on the Sunday night when Derek Burtell was safely tucked up at Millington Bridge. Remember, though, he's been brought up in France ; so he may by now be posing as a native.'

' We'll find him all right,' said Leyland grimly. ' If I can get leave, I'll go after him myself.'

' Go steady with your revolver, then. The Company won't like it a bit if he's a corpse by the third of September.'

CHAPTER XXV

A POSTSCRIPT

September 6th.

DEAR MRS. BREDON,

'It was very kind of you to write and ask after me, and I hope it wasn't mere curiosity that prompted you to do it, as you suggest. I've been here, of course, in this rather delightful Belgian country town, ever since the police got news that Derek was here—the result, somebody told me, of a wireless broadcast. Anyhow, it seemed only decent to come out and see that he was being looked after. Though that, indeed, was quite unnecessary, because the nuns have made him comfortable all the time, as far as he could be made confortable.

'To answer your question—yes, I think your husband was exactly right in every particular. One or two explanations have been forthcoming, e.g. why Derek left me so little time to commit my imaginary murder in. It turns out that I was to blame for this, because I took so much longer getting away from Millington Bridge than I was expected to. As he had worked the thing out, we ought to have arrived at Shipcote with a clear half-hour or more for me to catch the train in. As it was, I started out late from the inn ; and

Derek, though he was annoyed by the delay,
couldn't offer to help me with the paddling, because
it was part of his plan to appear very tired and
sleepy. If we had been more punctual, my " alibi "
would have been singularly imperfect. But then
if we'd been more punctual Derek would have
passed Farris in the lock stream, and that would
have complicated things all round.

' The footprints on the bridge had, after all, a
certain *raison d'être*. Derek meant it to be supposed that I meant it to be supposed that the
murderer had come from Byworth, and had made
off in the Byworth direction ; that he walked backwards as a piece of obvious bluff which the police
would see through. (Only a dope-fiend, I imagine,
could have worked out that idea of triple bluff, and
expected the police to follow two-thirds of the
calculation.) You were expected to think that the
films dropped from my pocket on the Shipcote
bank by accident.

' There's nothing more, I think, for me to clear
up except Derek's movements after he left the
river. He did, of course, go via Southampton and
Havre, and he travelled straight on to Paris. There
he took refuge in a class of society where no questions are asked and shaving is optional. He started
growing a moustache and beard, and was listening
eagerly for news of my arrest. But when that
didn't happen, and the papers still refused to
recognize his death, he left Paris and came here,
dropping the name of Wallace as he did so. He
had started taking drugs again, and soon after he
got here he fainted in the street. He was brought

to this hospital, where the nuns had never heard
the name of Burtell ; and he was too sick to read
the newspapers at the time when Aunt Alma died.
In fact, he knew nothing more of what was going
on here until the police tracked him down.

'There's one other circumstance about Derek
which may not interest you, but interested me
profoundly. He was engaged to some French girl,
who proceeded to turn up at his bedside as soon
as she heard of his whereabouts, and I'm blessed
if they didn't get married. Which was all very
proper and romantic ; but it had the awkward
consequence that D. drew up a will in favour of
his wife, which he calmly asked me to witness ! So
Aunt Alma's legacy will not come into my branch
of the family.

'However, what I wanted to tell you about was
my first interview with Derek. It was almost
immediately after I got here ; he insisted on seeing
me alone ; and, though I dreaded the interview,
I had to go through with it. He was frightfully
broken down, poor chap, whimpering all the time
and very nearly crying. He grovelled quite dreadfully about his attempt to let me in for a murder
charge ; said that he'd been made silly by drugs,
and wasn't really responsible for his actions. He
said he didn't think he'd really have let me swing
—which I didn't believe. And I had to sit there
like a fool, saying " Oh, shut up ; don't mention
it ", and that sort of thing ; and all the time I
could see that he was leading up to something—I
couldn't make out what.

'At last it came. They had cut him off, of

course, from his drug, and he was simply dying to get some. There was some, apparently, hidden away in his luggage, and he hadn't dared to ask the doctor for it, or any of the nuns. He wanted me to fetch it and give it him. I said, of course, that he was far better without it ; that he'd only kill himself if he took more. He said he didn't mind ; he was for it anyhow ; what difference could a week or two make ? I was still arguing about it when the nurse came in and turned me out ; said I mustn't tire him by talking to him any longer. I went straight to Derek's luggage, and found the dope just where he'd told me. I put it into my pocket, and went out for a little walk by myself.

' What Derek said was perfectly true, and I knew it better than he did. The doctor had told me that the poor chap hadn't an earthly chance. He wasn't a bit interested in life, and I honestly think he'd sooner have poisoned himself with a last dose or two than flickered out gradually. A streak of good-fellowship in my nature kept on urging me to let him have the stuff. At the same time, I knew that it would kill him off—the doctor had warned me of that ; and as there was still three weeks or so to run before he turned twenty-five, that would mean that grandpapa's fifty thousand came into my pocket, where it was needed, instead of being handed over to a beastly Insurance Company, which wouldn't even say thank you for it.

' I leant over a bridge across the river ; and all the time my mind was back at the Gudgeon, with the open window and the sun streaming in, and the motors buzzing over Eaton Bridge, and that fool

peacock on the lawn. I remembered exactly how
you said that if I were waiting to murder a man and
he fell into the river, I should find myself jumping in
to rescue him. I remember what you said about
sticking to the rules of the game, because it was
the only thing to do. And I remembered how I'd
protested, and sworn that I'd do nothing of the
kind ; and how old-fashioned I thought you. Well,
here I was, in very much the required position.
Here was a man I'd always hated, and I couldn't
summon up any respect for him even on his death-
bed. He'd been spreading himself, only a fortnight
or so before, in an attempt to get me hanged on a
false charge of murder. It wasn't a question of
killing him ; it was only a question of providing
him, at his own earnest demand, with a kind of
drug which had come to be necessary to his happi-
ness, but which, quite incidentally, would kill him
if he took it. It was a kind of Philip Sidney touch ;
and my reward for it would be fifty thousand down
—fifty thousand which poor old grandpapa never
meant to go out of the family.

' And the awful thing was that I found you were
right. It wasn't that your wishes in the matter
had any influence with me ; you hadn't expressed
a wish, you'd only made a prophecy. And all my
conscious reaction on that was an intense desire
to prove you wrong ; to be able to write and tell
you that you were wrong. And yet I couldn't do
it ; some curious inhibition stood in my way. It
can hardly have been a moral scruple, for I don't
remember having any these last four or five years.
It wasn't the fear of being found out, because

Derek was in such a dicky state anyhow that
nobody would have been surprised at his pegging
out any time. It was just an absurd something.
There was nothing for it but to stick to the rules
—leave it to chance whether Derek lived till his
birthday or not. My hand (not my mind, not my
will) dropped the packet very deliberately into the
river.

' Next day this French girl turned up, and that
seemed to brace Derek a bit ; the doctor admitted
that it was a slight rally, but said there was still
no hope. The days dragged on, and by the night
of September the second I found myself in a curious
state of equilibrium. I wasn't wanting Derek to
die, or wanting him to live. I wasn't even personally interested, so it seemed to me, in the question
whether he lived or died. I was simply a detached
spectator, with only a spectator's excitement about
the game Fate was playing with Derek and with
me. I went to bed with an effort, and when I
got up I found there was a priest buzzing round,
which made me think for a moment that it was all
over. But it wasn't ; Derek died about ten o'clock
on his birthday morning, looking ridiculously happy.

' Well, I hadn't cheated ; and if that was virtue
in me, the virtue will jolly well have to be its own
reward. My step-father has raised a job for me
out in the States, a job which means " starting at
the bottom ", in the discouraging modern phrase.
So I am going to turn into Mr. Quirk after all.
The European creases of my mind will all be flat-
tened out in that world of engaging simplicity ;
and if we ever meet again (which is improbable)

you will find me explaining to you that two and two makes four on the other side.

'Don't for the Lord's sake condole with me, or congratulate me. The thing had got to happen; it has happened; and I'm glad I didn't interfere.

'Yours kindly,

'NIGEL BURTELL'

A CATALOGUE OF
SELECTED DOVER BOOKS
IN ALL FIELDS OF INTEREST

A CATALOGUE OF SELECTED DOVER
BOOKS IN ALL FIELDS OF INTEREST

CELESTIAL OBJECTS FOR COMMON TELESCOPES, T. W. Webb. The most used book in amateur astronomy: inestimable aid for locating and identifying nearly 4,000 celestial objects. Edited, updated by Margaret W. Mayall. 77 illustrations. Total of 645pp. 5⅜ x 8½.
20917-2, 20918-0 Pa., Two-vol. set $10.00

HISTORICAL STUDIES IN THE LANGUAGE OF CHEMISTRY, M. P. Crosland. The important part language has played in the development of chemistry from the symbolism of alchemy to the adoption of systematic nomenclature in 1892. ". . . wholeheartedly recommended,"—Science. 15 illustrations. 416pp. of text. 5⅝ x 8¼.   63702-6 Pa. $7.50

BURNHAM'S CELESTIAL HANDBOOK, Robert Burnham, Jr. Thorough, readable guide to the stars beyond our solar system. Exhaustive treatment, fully illustrated. Breakdown is alphabetical by constellation: Andromeda to Cetus in Vol. 1; Chamaeleon to Orion in Vol. 2; and Pavo to Vulpecula in Vol. 3. Hundreds of illustrations. Total of about 2000pp. 6⅛ x 9¼.
23567-X, 23568-8, 23673-0 Pa., Three-vol. set $32.85

THEORY OF WING SECTIONS: INCLUDING A SUMMARY OF AIR-FOIL DATA, Ira H. Abbott and A. E. von Doenhoff. Concise compilation of subatomic aerodynamic characteristics of modern NASA wing sections, plus description of theory. 350pp. of tables. 693pp. 5⅜ x 8½.
60586-8 Pa. $9.95

DE RE METALLICA, Georgius Agricola. Translated by Herbert C. Hoover and Lou H. Hoover. The famous Hoover translation of greatest treatise on technological chemistry, engineering, geology, mining of early modern times (1556). All 289 original woodcuts. 638pp. 6¾ x 11.
60006-8 Clothbd. $19.95

THE ORIGIN OF CONTINENTS AND OCEANS, Alfred Wegener. One of the most influential, most controversial books in science, the classic statement for continental drift. Full 1966 translation of Wegener's final (1929) version. 64 illustrations. 246pp. 5⅜ x 8½.(EBE)61708-4 Pa. $5.00

THE PRINCIPLES OF PSYCHOLOGY, William James. Famous long course complete, unabridged. Stream of thought, time perception, memory, experimental methods; great work decades ahead of its time. Still valid, useful; read in many classes. 94 figures. Total of 1391pp. 5⅜ x 8½.
20381-6, 20382-4 Pa., Two-vol. set $17.90

YUCATAN BEFORE AND AFTER THE CONQUEST, Diego de Landa. First English translation of basic book in Maya studies, the only significant account of Yucatan written in the early post-Conquest era. Translated by distinguished Maya scholar William Gates. Appendices, introduction, 4 maps and over 120 illustrations added by translator. 162pp. 5⅜ x 8½.
23622-6 Pa. $3.00

THE MALAY ARCHIPELAGO, Alfred R. Wallace. Spirited travel account by one of founders of modern biology. Touches on zoology, botany, ethnography, geography, and geology. 62 illustrations, maps. 515pp. 5⅜ x 8½.
20187-2 Pa. $6.95

THE DISCOVERY OF THE TOMB OF TUTANKHAMEN, Howard Carter, A. C. Mace. Accompany Carter in the thrill of discovery, as ruined passage suddenly reveals unique, untouched, fabulously rich tomb. Fascinating account, with 106 illustrations. New introduction by J. M. White. Total of 382pp. 5⅜ x 8½. (Available in U.S. only)   23500-9 Pa. $5.50

THE WORLD'S GREATEST SPEECHES, edited by Lewis Copeland and Lawrence W. Lamm. Vast collection of 278 speeches from Greeks up to present. Powerful and effective models; unique look at history. Revised to 1970. Indices. 842pp. 5⅜ x 8½.   20468-5 Pa. $9.95

THE 100 GREATEST ADVERTISEMENTS, Julian Watkins. The priceless ingredient; His master's voice; 99 44/100% pure; over 100 others. How they were written, their impact, etc. Remarkable record. 130 illustrations. 233pp. 7⅞ x 10 3/5.   20540-1 Pa. $6.95

CRUICKSHANK PRINTS FOR HAND COLORING, George Cruickshank. 18 illustrations, one side of a page, on fine-quality paper suitable for watercolors. Caricatures of people in society (c. 1820) full of trenchant wit. Very large format. 32pp. 11 x 16.   23684-6 Pa. $6.00

THIRTY-TWO COLOR POSTCARDS OF TWENTIETH-CENTURY AMERICAN ART, Whitney Museum of American Art. Reproduced in full color in postcard form are 31 art works and one shot of the museum. Calder, Hopper, Rauschenberg, others. Detachable. 16pp. 8¼ x 11.
23629-3 Pa. $3.50

MUSIC OF THE SPHERES: THE MATERIAL UNIVERSE FROM ATOM TO QUASAR SIMPLY EXPLAINED, Guy Murchie. Planets, stars, geology, atoms, radiation, relativity, quantum theory, light, antimatter, similar topics. 319 figures. 664pp. 5⅜ x 8½.
21809-0, 21810-4 Pa., Two-vol. set $11.00

EINSTEIN'S THEORY OF RELATIVITY, Max Born. Finest semi-technical account; covers Einstein, Lorentz, Minkowski, and others, with much detail, much explanation of ideas and math not readily available elsewhere on this level. For student, non-specialist. 376pp. 5⅜ x 8½.
60769-0 Pa. $5.00

CATALOGUE OF DOVER BOOKS

THE SENSE OF BEAUTY, George Santayana. Masterfully written discussion of nature of beauty, materials of beauty, form, expression; art, literature, social sciences all involved. 168pp. 5⅜ x 8½.   20238-0 Pa. $3.50

ON THE IMPROVEMENT OF THE UNDERSTANDING, Benedict Spinoza. Also contains *Ethics, Correspondence*, all in excellent R. Elwes translation. Basic works on entry to philosophy, pantheism, exchange of ideas with great contemporaries. 402pp. 5⅜ x 8½.   20250-X Pa. $5.95

THE TRAGIC SENSE OF LIFE, Miguel de Unamuno. Acknowledged masterpiece of existential literature, one of most important books of 20th century. Introduction by Madariaga. 367pp. 5⅜ x 8½.
20257-7 Pa. $6.00

THE GUIDE FOR THE PERPLEXED, Moses Maimonides. Great classic of medieval Judaism attempts to reconcile revealed religion (Pentateuch, commentaries) with Aristotelian philosophy. Important historically, still relevant in problems. Unabridged Friedlander translation. Total of 473pp. 5⅜ x 8½.   20351-4 Pa. $6.95

THE I CHING (THE BOOK OF CHANGES), translated by James Legge. Complete translation of basic text plus appendices by Confucius, and Chinese commentary of most penetrating divination manual ever prepared. Indispensable to study of early Oriental civilizations, to modern inquiring reader. 448pp. 5⅜ x 8½.   21062-6 Pa. $6.00

THE EGYPTIAN BOOK OF THE DEAD, E. A. Wallis Budge. Complete reproduction of Ani's papyrus, finest ever found. Full hieroglyphic text, interlinear transliteration, word for word translation, smooth translation. Basic work, for Egyptology, for modern study of psychic matters. Total of 533pp. 6½ x 9¼. (USCO)   21866-X Pa. $8.50

THE GODS OF THE EGYPTIANS, E. A. Wallis Budge. Never excelled for richness, fullness: all gods, goddesses, demons, mythical figures of Ancient Egypt; their legends, rites, incarnations, variations, powers, etc. Many hieroglyphic texts cited. Over 225 illustrations, plus 6 color plates. Total of 988pp. 6⅛ x 9¼. (EBE)
22055-9, 22056-7 Pa., Two-vol. set $20.00

THE STANDARD BOOK OF QUILT MAKING AND COLLECTING, Marguerite Ickis. Full information, full-sized patterns for making 46 traditional quilts, also 150 other patterns. Quilted cloths, lame, satin quilts, etc. 483 illustrations. 273pp. 6⅞ x 9⅝.   20582-7 Pa. $5.95

CORAL GARDENS AND THEIR MAGIC, Bronsilaw Malinowski. Classic study of the methods of tilling the soil and of agricultural rites in the Trobriand Islands of Melanesia. Author is one of the most important figures in the field of modern social anthropology. 143 illustrations. Indexes. Total of 911pp. of text. 5⅝ x 8¼. (Available in U.S. only)
23597-1 Pa. $12.95

THE PHILOSOPHY OF HISTORY, Georg W. Hegel. Great classic of Western thought develops concept that history is not chance but a rational process, the evolution of freedom. 457pp. 5⅜ x 8½. 20112-0 Pa. $6.00

LANGUAGE, TRUTH AND LOGIC, Alfred J. Ayer. Famous, clear introduction to Vienna, Cambridge schools of Logical Positivism. Role of philosophy, elimination of metaphysics, nature of analysis, etc. 160pp. 5⅜ x 8½. (USCO) 20010-8 Pa. $2.50

A PREFACE TO LOGIC, Morris R. Cohen. Great City College teacher in renowned, easily followed exposition of formal logic, probability, values, logic and world order and similar topics; no previous background needed. 209pp. 5⅜ x 8½. 23517-3 Pa. $4.95

REASON AND NATURE, Morris R. Cohen. Brilliant analysis of reason and its multitudinous ramifications by charismatic teacher. Interdisciplinary, synthesizing work widely praised when it first appeared in 1931. Second (1953) edition. Indexes. 496pp. 5⅜ x 8½. 23633-1 Pa. $7.50

AN ESSAY CONCERNING HUMAN UNDERSTANDING, John Locke. The only complete edition of enormously important classic, with authoritative editorial material by A. C. Fraser. Total of 1176pp. 5⅜ x 8½. 20530-4, 20531-2 Pa., Two-vol. set $16.00

HANDBOOK OF MATHEMATICAL FUNCTIONS WITH FORMULAS, GRAPHS, AND MATHEMATICAL TABLES, edited by Milton Abramowitz and Irene A. Stegun. Vast compendium: 29 sets of tables, some to as high as 20 places. 1,046pp. 8 x 10½. 61272-4 Pa. $17.95

MATHEMATICS FOR THE PHYSICAL SCIENCES, Herbert S. Wilf. Highly acclaimed work offers clear presentations of vector spaces and matrices, orthogonal functions, roots of polynomial equations, conformal mapping, calculus of variations, etc. Knowledge of theory of functions of real and complex variables is assumed. Exercises and solutions. Index. 284pp. 5⅝ x 8¼. 63635-6 Pa. $5.00

THE PRINCIPLE OF RELATIVITY, Albert Einstein et al. Eleven most important original papers on special and general theories. Seven by Einstein, two by Lorentz, one each by Minkowski and Weyl. All translated, unabridged. 216pp. 5⅜ x 8½. 60081-5 Pa. $3.50

THERMODYNAMICS, Enrico Fermi. A classic of modern science. Clear, organized treatment of systems, first and second laws, entropy, thermodynamic potentials, gaseous reactions, dilute solutions, entropy constant. No math beyond calculus required. Problems. 160pp. 5⅜ x 8½. 60361-X Pa. $4.00

ELEMENTARY MECHANICS OF FLUIDS, Hunter Rouse. Classic undergraduate text widely considered to be far better than many later books. Ranges from fluid velocity and acceleration to role of compressibility in fluid motion. Numerous examples, questions, problems. 224 illustrations. 376pp. 5⅝ x 8¼. 63699-2 Pa. $7.00

THE AMERICAN SENATOR, Anthony Trollope. Little known, long unavailable Trollope novel on a grand scale. Here are humorous comment on American vs. English culture, and stunning portrayal of a heroine/villainess. Superb evocation of Victorian village life. 561pp. 5⅜ x 8½.
23801-6 Pa. $7.95

WAS IT MURDER? James Hilton. The author of *Lost Horizon* and *Goodbye, Mr. Chips* wrote one detective novel (under a pen-name) which was quickly forgotten and virtually lost, even at the height of Hilton's fame. This edition brings it back—a finely crafted public school puzzle resplendent with Hilton's stylish atmosphere. A thoroughly English thriller by the creator of Shangri-la. 252pp. 5⅜ x 8. (Available in U.S. only)
23774-5 Pa. $3.00

CENTRAL PARK: A PHOTOGRAPHIC GUIDE, Victor Laredo and Henry Hope Reed. 121 superb photographs show dramatic views of Central Park: Bethesda Fountain, Cleopatra's Needle, Sheep Meadow, the Blockhouse, plus people engaged in many park activities: ice skating, bike riding, etc. Captions by former Curator of Central Park, Henry Hope Reed, provide historical view, changes, etc. Also photos of N.Y. landmarks on park's periphery. 96pp. 8½ x 11. 23750-8 Pa. $4.50

NANTUCKET IN THE NINETEENTH CENTURY, Clay Lancaster. 180 rare photographs, stereographs, maps, drawings and floor plans recreate unique American island society. Authentic scenes of shipwreck, lighthouses, streets, homes are arranged in geographic sequence to provide walking-tour guide to old Nantucket existing today. Introduction, captions. 160pp. 8⅞ x 11¾. 23747-8 Pa. $7.95

STONE AND MAN: A PHOTOGRAPHIC EXPLORATION, Andreas Feininger. 106 photographs by *Life* photographer Feininger portray man's deep passion for stone through the ages. Stonehenge-like megaliths, fortified towns, sculpted marble and crumbling tenements show textures, beauties, fascination. 128pp. 9¼ x 10¾. 23756-7 Pa. $5.95

CIRCLES, A MATHEMATICAL VIEW, D. Pedoe. Fundamental aspects of college geometry, non-Euclidean geometry, and other branches of mathematics: representing circle by point. Poincare model, isoperimetric property, etc. Stimulating recreational reading. 66 figures. 96pp. 5⅝ x 8¼.
63698-4 Pa. $3.50

THE DISCOVERY OF NEPTUNE, Morton Grosser. Dramatic scientific history of the investigations leading up to the actual discovery of the eighth planet of our solar system. Lucid, well-researched book by well-known historian of science. 172pp. 5⅜ x 8½. 23726-5 Pa. $3.50

THE DEVIL'S DICTIONARY. Ambrose Bierce. Barbed, bitter, brilliant witticisms in the form of a dictionary. Best, most ferocious satire America has produced. 145pp. 5⅜ x 8½. 20487-1 Pa. $2.50

HISTORY OF BACTERIOLOGY, William Bulloch. The only comprehensive history of bacteriology from the beginnings through the 19th century. Special emphasis is given to biography-Leeuwenhoek, etc. Brief accounts of 350 bacteriologists form a separate section. No clearer, fuller study, suitable to scientists and general readers, has yet been written. 52 illustrations. 448pp. 5⅝ x 8¼. 23761-3 Pa. $6.50

THE COMPLETE NONSENSE OF EDWARD LEAR, Edward Lear. All nonsense limericks, zany alphabets, Owl and Pussycat, songs, nonsense botany, etc., illustrated by Lear. Total of 321pp. 5⅜ x 8½. (Available in U.S. only) 20167-8 Pa. $4.50

INGENIOUS MATHEMATICAL PROBLEMS AND METHODS, Louis A. Graham. Sophisticated material from Graham *Dial*, applied and pure; stresses solution methods. Logic, number theory, networks, inversions, etc. 237pp. 5⅜ x 8½. 20545-2 Pa. $4.50

BEST MATHEMATICAL PUZZLES OF SAM LOYD, edited by Martin Gardner. Bizarre, original, whimsical puzzles by America's greatest puzzler. From fabulously rare *Cyclopedia*, including famous 14-15 puzzles, the Horse of a Different Color, 115 more. Elementary math. 150 illustrations. 167pp. 5⅜ x 8½. 20498-7 Pa. $3.50

THE BASIS OF COMBINATION IN CHESS, J. du Mont. Easy-to-follow, instructive book on elements of combination play, with chapters on each piece and every powerful combination team—two knights, bishop and knight, rook and bishop, etc. 250 diagrams. 218pp. 5⅜ x 8½. (Available in U.S. only) 23644-7 Pa. $4.50

MODERN CHESS STRATEGY, Ludek Pachman. The use of the queen, the active king, exchanges, pawn play, the center, weak squares, etc. Section on rook alone worth price of the book. Stress on the moderns. Often considered the most important book on strategy. 314pp. 5⅜ x 8½. 20290-9 Pa. $5.00

LASKER'S MANUAL OF CHESS, Dr. Emanuel Lasker. Great world champion offers very thorough coverage of all aspects of chess. Combinations, position play, openings, end game, aesthetics of chess, philosophy of struggle, much more. Filled with analyzed games. 390pp. 5⅜ x 8½. 20640-8 Pa. $5.95

500 MASTER GAMES OF CHESS, S. Tartakower, J. du Mont. Vast collection of great chess games from 1798-1938, with much material nowhere else readily available. Fully annotated, arranged by opening for easier study. 664pp. 5⅜ x 8½. 23208-5 Pa. $8.50

A GUIDE TO CHESS ENDINGS, Dr. Max Euwe, David Hooper. One of the finest modern works on chess endings. Thorough analysis of the most frequently encountered endings by former world champion. 331 examples, each with diagram. 248pp. 5⅜ x 8½. 23332-4 Pa. $3.95

THE COMPLETE BOOK OF DOLL MAKING AND COLLECTING, Catherine Christopher. Instructions, patterns for dozens of dolls, from rag doll on up to elaborate, historically accurate figures. Mould faces, sew clothing, make doll houses, etc. Also collecting information. Many illustrations. 288pp. 6 x 9. 22066-4 Pa. $4.95

THE DAGUERREOTYPE IN AMERICA, Beaumont Newhall. Wonderful portraits, 1850's townscapes, landscapes; full text plus 104 photographs. The basic book. Enlarged 1976 edition. 272pp. 8¼ x 11¼. 23322-7 Pa. $7.95

CRAFTSMAN HOMES, Gustav Stickley. 296 architectural drawings, floor plans, and photographs illustrate 40 different kinds of "Mission-style" homes from *The Craftsman* (1901-16), voice of American style of simplicity and organic harmony. Thorough coverage of Craftsman idea in text and picture, now collector's item. 224pp. 8⅛ x 11. 23791-5 Pa. $6.50

PEWTER-WORKING: INSTRUCTIONS AND PROJECTS, Burl N. Osborn. & Gordon O. Wilber. Introduction to pewter-working for amateur craftsman. History and characteristics of pewter; tools, materials, step-by-step instructions. Photos, line drawings, diagrams. Total of 160pp. 7⅞ x 10¾. 23786-9 Pa. $3.50

THE GREAT CHICAGO FIRE, edited by David Lowe. 10 dramatic, eye-witness accounts of the 1871 disaster, including one of the aftermath and rebuilding, plus 70 contemporary photographs and illustrations of the ruins—courthouse, Palmer House, Great Central Depot, etc. Introduction by David Lowe. 87pp. 8¼ x 11. 23771-0 Pa. $4.00

SILHOUETTES: A PICTORIAL ARCHIVE OF VARIED ILLUSTRATIONS, edited by Carol Belanger Grafton. Over 600 silhouettes from the 18th to 20th centuries include profiles and full figures of men and women, children, birds and animals, groups and scenes, nature, ships, an alphabet. Dozens of uses for commercial artists and craftspeople. 144pp. 8⅜ x 11¼. 23781-8 Pa. $4.50

ANIMALS: 1,419 COPYRIGHT-FREE ILLUSTRATIONS OF MAMMALS, BIRDS, FISH, INSECTS, ETC., edited by Jim Harter. Clear wood engravings present, in extremely lifelike poses, over 1,000 species of animals. One of the most extensive copyright-free pictorial sourcebooks of its kind. Captions. Index. 284pp. 9 x 12. 23766-4 Pa. $8.95

INDIAN DESIGNS FROM ANCIENT ECUADOR, Frederick W. Shaffer. 282 original designs by pre-Columbian Indians of Ecuador (500-1500 A.D.). Designs include people, mammals, birds, reptiles, fish, plants, heads, geometric designs. Use as is or alter for advertising, textiles, leathercraft, etc. Introduction. 95pp. 8¾ x 11¼. 23764-8 Pa. $4.50

SZIGETI ON THE VIOLIN, Joseph Szigeti. Genial, loosely structured tour by premier violinist, featuring a pleasant mixture of reminiscenes, insights into great music and musicians, innumerable tips for practicing violinists. 385 musical passages. 256pp. 5⅝ x 8¼. 23763-X Pa. $4.00

TONE POEMS, SERIES II: TILL EULENSPIEGELS LUSTIGE STREICHE, ALSO SPRACH ZARATHUSTRA, AND EIN HELDEN-LEBEN, Richard Strauss. Three important orchestral works, including very popular *Till Eulenspiegel's Marry Pranks*, reproduced in full score from original editions. Study score. 315pp. 9⅜ x 12¼. (Available in U.S. only) 23755-9 Pa. $8.95

TONE POEMS, SERIES I: DON JUAN, TOD UND VERKLARUNG AND DON QUIXOTE, Richard Strauss. Three of the most often performed and recorded works in entire orchestral repertoire, reproduced in full score from original editions. Study score. 286pp. 9⅜ x 12¼. (Available in U.S. only) 23754-0 Pa. $8.95

11 LATE STRING QUARTETS, Franz Joseph Haydn. The form which Haydn defined and "brought to perfection." (*Grove's*). 11 string quartets in complete score, his last and his best. The first in a projected series of the complete Haydn string quartets. Reliable modern Eulenberg edition, otherwise difficult to obtain. 320pp. 8⅜ x 11¼. (Available in U.S. only) 23753-2 Pa. $8.95

FOURTH, FIFTH AND SIXTH SYMPHONIES IN FULL SCORE, Peter Ilyitch Tchaikovsky. Complete orchestral scores of Symphony No. 4 in F Minor, Op. 36; Symphony No. 5 in E Minor, Op. 64; Symphony No. 6 in B Minor, "Pathetique," Op. 74. Bretikopf & Hartel eds. Study score. 480pp. 9⅜ x 12¼. 23861-X Pa. $10.95

THE MARRIAGE OF FIGARO: COMPLETE SCORE, Wolfgang A. Mozart. Finest comic opera ever written. Full score, not to be confused with piano renderings. Peters edition. Study score. 448pp. 9⅜ x 12¼. (Available in U.S. only) 23751-6 Pa. $12.95

"IMAGE" ON THE ART AND EVOLUTION OF THE FILM, edited by Marshall Deutelbaum. Pioneering book brings together for first time 38 groundbreaking articles on early silent films from *Image* and 263 illustrations newly shot from rare prints in the collection of the International Museum of Photography. A landmark work. Index. 256pp. 8¼ x 11. 23777-X Pa. $8.95

AROUND-THE-WORLD COOKY BOOK, Lois Lintner Sumption and Marguerite Lintner Ashbrook. 373 cooky and frosting recipes from 28 countries (America, Austria, China, Russia, Italy, etc.) include Viennese kisses, rice wafers, London strips, lady fingers, hony, sugar spice, maple cookies, etc. Clear instructions. All tested. 38 drawings. 182pp. 5⅜ x 8. 23802-4 Pa. $2.75

THE ART NOUVEAU STYLE, edited by Roberta Waddell. 579 rare photographs, not available elsewhere, of works in jewelry, metalwork, glass, ceramics, textiles, architecture and furniture by 175 artists—Mucha, Seguy, Lalique, Tiffany, Gaudin, Hohlwein, Saarinen, and many others. 288pp. 8⅜ x 11¼. 23515-7 Pa. $8.95

THE CURVES OF LIFE, Theodore A. Cook. Examination of shells, leaves, horns, human body, art, etc., in *"the* classic reference on how the golden ratio applies to spirals and helices in nature . . . . "—Martin Gardner. 426 illustrations. Total of 512pp. 5⅜ x 8½.   23701-X Pa. **$6.95**

AN ILLUSTRATED FLORA OF THE NORTHERN UNITED STATES AND CANADA, Nathaniel L. Britton, Addison Brown. Encyclopedic work covers 4666 species, ferns on up. Everything. Full botanical information, illustration for each. This earlier edition is preferred by many to more recent revisions. 1913 edition. Over 4000 illustrations, total of 2087pp. 6⅛ x 9¼.   22642-5, 22643-3, 22644-1 Pa., Three-vol. set **$28.50**

MANUAL OF THE GRASSES OF THE UNITED STATES, A. S. Hitchcock, U.S. Dept. of Agriculture. The basic study of American grasses, both indigenous and escapes, cultivated and wild. Over 1400 species. Full descriptions, information. Over 1100 maps, illustrations. Total of 1051pp. 5⅜ x 8½.   22717-0, 22718-9 Pa., Two-vol. set **$17.00**

THE CACTACEAE,, Nathaniel L. Britton, John N. Rose. Exhaustive, definitive. Every cactus in the world. Full botanical descriptions. Thorough statement of nomenclatures, habitat, detailed finding keys. The one book needed by every cactus enthusiast. Over 1275 illustrations. Total of 1080pp. 8 x 10¼.   21191-6, 21192-4 Clothbd., Two-vol. set **$50.00**

AMERICAN MEDICINAL PLANTS, Charles F. Millspaugh. Full descriptions, 180 plants covered: history; physical description; methods of preparation with all chemical constituents extracted; all claimed curative or adverse effects. 180 full-page plates. Classification table. 804pp. 6½ x 9¼.
23034-1 Pa. **$13.95**

A MODERN HERBAL, Margaret Grieve. Much the fullest, most exact, most useful compilation of herbal material. Gigantic alphabetical encyclopedia, from aconite to zedoary, gives botanical information, medical properties, folklore, economic uses, and much else. Indispensable to serious reader. 161 illustrations. 888pp. 6½ x 9¼. (Available in U.S. only)
22798-7, 22799-5 Pa., Two-vol. set **$15.00**

THE HERBAL or GENERAL HISTORY OF PLANTS, John Gerard. The 1633 edition revised and enlarged by Thomas Johnson. Containing almost 2850 plant descriptions and 2705 superb illustrations, Gerard's *Herbal* is a monumental work, the book all modern English herbals are derived from, the one herbal every serious enthusiast should have in its entirety. Original editions are worth perhaps $750. 1678pp. 8½ x 12¼.
23147-X Clothbd. **$75.00**

MANUAL OF THE TREES OF NORTH AMERICA, Charles S. Sargent. The basic survey of every native tree and tree-like shrub, 717 species in all. Extremely full descriptions, information on habitat, growth, locales, economics, etc. Necessary to every serious tree lover. Over 100 finding keys. 783 illustrations. Total of 986pp. 5⅜ x 8½.
20277-1, 20278-X Pa., Two-vol. set **$12.00**

GREAT NEWS PHOTOS AND THE STORIES BEHIND THEM, John Faber. Dramatic volume of 140 great news photos, 1855 through 1976, and revealing stories behind them, with both historical and technical information. Hindenburg disaster, shooting of Oswald, nomination of Jimmy Carter, etc. 160pp. 8¼ x 11.   23667-6 Pa. $6.00

CRUICKSHANK'S PHOTOGRAPHS OF BIRDS OF AMERICA, Allan D. Cruickshank. Great ornithologist, photographer presents 177 closeups, groupings, panoramas, flightings, etc., of about 150 different birds. Expanded *Wings in the Wilderness*. Introduction by Helen G. Cruickshank. 191pp. 8¼ x 11.   23497-5 Pa. $7.95

AMERICAN WILDLIFE AND PLANTS, A. C. Martin, et al. Describes food habits of more than 1000 species of mammals, birds, fish. Special treatment of important food plants. Over 300 illustrations. 500pp. 5⅜ x 8½.
20793-5 Pa. $6.50

THE PEOPLE CALLED SHAKERS, Edward D. Andrews. Lifetime of research, definitive study of Shakers: origins, beliefs, practices, dances, social organization, furniture and crafts, impact on 19th-century USA, present heritage. Indispensable to student of American history, collector. 33 illustrations. 351pp. 5⅜ x 8½.   21081-2 Pa. $4.50

OLD NEW YORK IN EARLY PHOTOGRAPHS, Mary Black. New York City as it was in 1853-1901, through 196 wonderful photographs from N.-Y. Historical Society. Great Blizzard, Lincoln's funeral procession, great buildings. 228pp. 9 x 12.   22907-6 Pa. $8.95

MR. LINCOLN'S CAMERA MAN: MATHEW BRADY, Roy Meredith. Over 300 Brady photos reproduced directly from original negatives, photos. Jackson, Webster, Grant, Lee, Carnegie, Barnum; Lincoln; Battle Smoke, Death of Rebel Sniper, Atlanta Just After Capture. Lively commentary. 368pp. 8⅜ x 11¼.   23021-X Pa. $11.95

TRAVELS OF WILLIAM BARTRAM, William Bartram. From 1773-8, Bartram explored Northern Florida, Georgia, Carolinas, and reported on wild life, plants, Indians, early settlers. Basic account for period, entertaining reading. Edited by Mark Van Doren. 13 illustrations. 141pp. 5⅜ x 8½.   20013-2 Pa. $6.00

THE GENTLEMAN AND CABINET MAKER'S DIRECTOR, Thomas Chippendale. Full reprint, 1762 style book, most influential of all time; chairs, tables, sofas, mirrors, cabinets, etc. 200 plates, plus 24 photographs of surviving pieces. 249pp. 9⅞ x 12¾.   21601-2 Pa. $8.95

AMERICAN CARRIAGES, SLEIGHS, SULKIES AND CARTS, edited by Don H. Berkebile. 168 Victorian illustrations from catalogues, trade journals, fully captioned. Useful for artists. Author is Assoc. Curator, Div. of Transportation of Smithsonian Institution. 168pp. 8½ x 9½.
23328-6 Pa. $5.00

SECOND PIATIGORSKY CUP, edited by Isaac Kashdan. One of the greatest tournament books ever produced in the English language. All 90 games of the 1966 tournament, annotated by players, most annotated by both players. Features Petrosian, Spassky, Fischer, Larsen, six others. 228pp. 5⅜ x 8½. 23572-6 Pa. $3.50

ENCYCLOPEDIA OF CARD TRICKS, revised and edited by Jean Hugard. How to perform over 600 card tricks, devised by the world's greatest magicians: impromptus, spelling tricks, key cards, using special packs, much, much more. Additional chapter on card technique. 66 illustrations. 402pp. 5⅜ x 8½. (Available in U.S. only) 21252-1 Pa. **$5.95**

MAGIC: STAGE ILLUSIONS, SPECIAL EFFECTS AND TRICK PHO-TOGRAPHY, Albert A. Hopkins, Henry R. Evans. One of the great classics; fullest, most authorative explanation of vanishing lady, levitations, scores of other great stage effects. Also small magic, automata, stunts. 446 illustrations. 556pp. 5⅜ x 8½. 23344-8 Pa. $6.95

THE SECRETS OF HOUDINI, J. C. Cannell. Classic study of Houdini's incredible magic, exposing closely-kept professional secrets and revealing, in general terms, the whole art of stage magic. 67 illustrations. 279pp. 5⅜ x 8½. 22913-0 Pa. $4.00

HOFFMANN'S MODERN MAGIC, Professor Hoffmann. One of the best, and best-known, magicians' manuals of the past century. Hundreds of tricks from card tricks and simple sleight of hand to elaborate illusions involving construction of complicated machinery. 332 illustrations. 563pp. 5⅜ x 8½. 23623-4 Pa. $6.95

THOMAS NAST'S CHRISTMAS DRAWINGS, Thomas Nast. Almost all Christmas drawings by creator of image of Santa Claus as we know it, and one of America's foremost illustrators and political cartoonists. 66 illustrations. 3 illustrations in color on covers. 96pp. 8⅜ x 11¼.
23660-9 Pa. $3.50

FRENCH COUNTRY COOKING FOR AMERICANS, Louis Diat. 500 easy-to-make, authentic provincial recipes compiled by former head chef at New York's Fitz-Carlton Hotel: onion soup, lamb stew, potato pie, more. 309pp. 5⅜ x 8½. 23665-X Pa. $3.95

SAUCES, FRENCH AND FAMOUS, Louis Diat. Complete book gives over 200 specific recipes: bechamel, Bordelaise, hollandaise, Cumberland, apricot, etc. Author was one of this century's finest chefs, originator of vichyssoise and many other dishes. Index. 156pp. 5⅜ x 8.
23663-3 Pa. $2.75

TOLL HOUSE TRIED AND TRUE RECIPES, Ruth Graves Wakefield. Authentic recipes from the famous Mass. restaurant: popovers, veal and ham loaf, Toll House baked beans, chocolate cake crumb pudding, much more. Many helpful hints. Nearly 700 recipes. Index. 376pp. 5⅜ x 8½.
23560-2 Pa. $4.95

ILLUSTRATED GUIDE TO SHAKER FURNITURE, Robert Meader. Director, Shaker Museum, Old Chatham, presents up-to-date coverage of all furniture and appurtenances, with much on local styles not available elsewhere. 235 photos. 146pp. 9 x 12.   22819-3 Pa. $6.95

COOKING WITH BEER, Carole Fahy. Beer has as superb an effect on food as wine, and at fraction of cost. Over 250 recipes for appetizers, soups, main dishes, desserts, breads, etc. Index. 144pp. 5⅜ x 8½. (Available in U.S. only)   23661-7 Pa. $3.00

STEWS AND RAGOUTS, Kay Shaw Nelson. This international cookbook offers wide range of 108 recipes perfect for everyday, special occasions, meals-in-themselves, main dishes. Economical, nutritious, easy-to-prepare: goulash, Irish stew, boeuf bourguignon, etc. Index. 134pp. 5⅜ x 8½.   23662-5 Pa. $3.95

DELICIOUS MAIN COURSE DISHES, Marian Tracy. Main courses are the most important part of any meal. These 200 nutritious, economical recipes from around the world make every meal a delight. "I . . . have found it so useful in my own household,"—*N.Y. Times.* Index. 219pp. 5⅜ x 8½.   23664-1 Pa. $3.95

FIVE ACRES AND INDEPENDENCE, Maurice G. Kains. Great back-to-the-land classic explains basics of self-sufficient farming: economics, plants, crops, animals, orchards, soils, land selection, host of other necessary things. Do not confuse with skimpy faddist literature; Kains was one of America's greatest agriculturalists. 95 illustrations. 397pp. 5⅜ x 8½.   20974-1 Pa. $4.95

A PRACTICAL GUIDE FOR THE BEGINNING FARMER, Herbert Jacobs. Basic, extremely useful first book for anyone thinking about moving to the country and starting a farm. Simpler than Kains, with greater emphasis on country living in general. 246pp. 5⅜ x 8½.   23675-7 Pa. $3.95

PAPERMAKING, Dard Hunter. Definitive book on the subject by the foremost authority in the field. Chapters dealing with every aspect of history of craft in every part of the world. Over 320 illustrations. 2nd, revised and enlarged (1947) edition. 672pp. 5⅜ x 8½.   23619-6 Pa. $8.95

THE ART DECO STYLE, edited by Theodore Menten. Furniture, jewelry, metalwork, ceramics, fabrics, lighting fixtures, interior decors, exteriors, graphics from pure French sources. Best sampling around. Over 400 photographs. 183pp. 8⅜ x 11¼.   22824-X Pa. $6.95

ACKERMANN'S COSTUME PLATES, Rudolph Ackermann. Selection of 96 plates from the *Repository of Arts,* best published source of costume for English fashion during the early 19th century. 12 plates also in color. Captions, glossary and introduction by editor Stella Blum. Total of 120pp. 8⅜ x 11¼.   23690-0 Pa. $5.00

CATALOGUE OF DOVER BOOKS

THE ANATOMY OF THE HORSE, George Stubbs. Often considered the great masterpiece of animal anatomy. Full reproduction of 1766 edition, plus prospectus; original text and modernized text. 36 plates. Introduction by Eleanor Garvey. 121pp. 11 x 14¾.   23402-9 Pa. $8.95

BRIDGMAN'S LIFE DRAWING, George B. Bridgman. More than 500 illustrative drawings and text teach you to abstract the body into its major masses, use light and shade, proportion; as well as specific areas of anatomy, of which Bridgman is master. 192pp. 6½ x 9¼. (Available in U.S. only)
                    22710-3 Pa. $4.50

ART NOUVEAU DESIGNS IN COLOR, Alphonse Mucha, Maurice Verneuil, Georges Auriol. Full-color reproduction of *Combinaisons ornementales* (c. 1900) by Art Nouveau masters. Floral, animal, geometric, interlacings, swashes—borders, frames, spots—all incredibly beautiful. 60 plates, hundreds of designs. 9⅜ x 8-1/16.   22885-1 Pa. $4.50

FULL-COLOR FLORAL DESIGNS IN THE ART NOUVEAU STYLE, E. A. Seguy. 166 motifs, on 40 plates, from *Les fleurs et leurs applications decoratives* (1902): borders, circular designs, repeats, allovers, "spots." All in authentic Art Nouveau colors. 48pp. 9⅜ x 12¼.
                    23439-8 Pa. $6.00

A DIDEROT PICTORIAL ENCYCLOPEDIA OF TRADES AND IN-DUSTRY, edited by Charles C. Gillispie. 485 most interesting plates from the great French Encyclopedia of the 18th century show hundreds of working figures, artifacts, process, land and cityscapes; glassmaking, paper-making, metal extraction, construction, weaving, making furniture, clothing, wigs, dozens. of other activities. Plates fully explained. 920pp. 9 x 12.
                    22284-5, 22285-3 Clothbd., Two-vol. set $50.00

HANDBOOK OF EARLY ADVERTISING ART, Clarence P. Hornung. Largest collection of copyright-free early and antique advertising art ever compiled. Over 6,000 illustrations, from Franklin's time to the 1890's for special effects, novelty. Valuable source, almost inexhaustible.
Pictorial Volume. Agriculture, the zodiac, animals, autos, birds, Christmas, fire engines, flowers, trees, musical instruments, ships, games and sports, much more. Arranged by subject matter and use. 237 plates. 288pp. 9 x 12.
                    20122-8 Clothbd. $15.00

Typographical Volume. Roman and Gothic faces ranging from 10 point to 300 point, "Barnum," German and Old English faces, script, logotypes, scrolls and flourishes, 1115 ornamental initials, 67 complete alphabets, more. 310 plates. 320pp. 9 x 12.   20123-6 Clothbd. $15.00

CALLIGRAPHY (CALLIGRAPHIA LATINA), J. G. Schwandner. High point of 18th-century ornamental calligraphy. Very ornate initials, scrolls, borders, cherubs, birds, lettered examples. 172pp. 9 x 13.
                    20475-8 Pa. $7.95

GEOMETRY, RELATIVITY AND THE FOURTH DIMENSION, Rudolf Rucker. Exposition of fourth dimension, means of visualization, concepts of relativity as Flatland characters continue adventures. Popular, easily followed yet accurate, profound. 141 illustrations. 133pp. 5⅜ x 8½.
23400-2 Pa. $2.75

THE ORIGIN OF LIFE, A. I. Oparin. Modern classic in biochemistry, the first rigorous examination of possible evolution of life from nitrocarbon compounds. Non-technical, easily followed. Total of 295pp. 5⅜ x 8½.
60213-3 Pa. $5.95

PLANETS, STARS AND GALAXIES, A. E. Fanning. Comprehensive introductory survey: the sun, solar system, stars, galaxies, universe, cosmology; quasars, radio stars, etc. 24pp. of photographs. 189pp. 5⅜ x 8½. (Available in U.S. only)
21680-2 Pa. $3.75

THE THIRTEEN BOOKS OF EUCLID'S ELEMENTS, translated with introduction and commentary by Sir Thomas L. Heath. Definitive edition. Textual and linguistic. notes, mathematical analysis, 2500 years of critical commentary. Do not confuse with abridged school editions. Total of 1414pp. 5⅜ x 8½. 60088-2, 60089-0, 60090-4 Pa., Three-vol. set $19.50

Prices subject to change without notice.

Available at your book dealer or write for free catalogue to Dept. GI, Dover Publications, Inc., 31 East 2nd St. Mineola., N.Y. 11501. Dover publishes more than 175 books each year on science, elementary and advanced mathematics, biology, music, art, literary history, social sciences and other areas.